CAST OF CHARACTERS

Tim Dawson-Gower. A happy-go-lucky Oxford undergraduate who's altogether a very decent young chap.

Nigel Dawson-Gower. Tim's older brother, a dashing ex-commando who fought with the French Resistance during the war and is now bored with peacetime. Tim worships him.

The Hon. Francis Clandon. Tim's roommate and co-owner of his car.

Madame and Monsieur Defay. Tim's hospitable hosts in the village of Pontchâtelet in the Loire Valley.

Jeannette Defay. Their beautiful daughter, who Tim has a crush on.

Zézette Brunet, née Denise Despuys. *Une femme galant*, or a woman of easy virtue, she was once the mistress of a notorious war criminal.

Jean Despuys. A young Frenchman attending classes at Oxford, who's altogether charming but essentially untruthful.

Mathieu Sansom. A fellow of St. Denis's College and a friend of Jean Despuys. He dislikes bloodhounds.

Dr. Burdock. The absentminded Praefect of Pentecost College.

Richard Ringwood. An Oxford-educated Scotland Yard inspector.

The Bloodhound. Ringwood's superior officer, who's never quite trusted him.

Inspector Colman. A conscientious young Oxford detective.

Yves Kéhidou. The *Commissaire de Police* at Pontchâtelet, a capable Breton who is Ringwood's genial host while he's in France.

Sylvie Kéhidou. His wife, a saucer-eyed blonde..

Toussaint Painlevé. An *agent de ville*, or police inspector, in the village of Pontchâtelet.

Jeannot. A true hero of the Resistance, now terribly scarred from having withstood the most intense torture during the German Occupation.

Titi. A small-time smuggler who also fought bravely in the Resistance.

Auguste Bruco. A forger and confidence man, now specializing in rich widows, but also a distinguished veteran of the Resistance.

Maxime Fleuret. Also known as Blancbec, a despised and infamous traitor to his country. Zézette was his mistress during the Occupation.

Plus assorted deans, secretaries, dons, tutors, landladies, relatives, police officers, friends, neighbors, children, and of course:

Ranter. Richard's beloved bloodhound, who, like her master, always gets her man.

D1608117

Books by Katharine Farrer

The Inspector Ringwood Trilogy

The Missing Link (1952)
The Cretan Counterfeit (1954)
Gownsman's Gallows (1957)

At Odds with Morning (1960)

Being & Having by Gabriel Marcel (1949)
(Translator)

Gownsman's Gallows

By Katharine Farrer

Introduction by
Tom & Enid Schantz

The President once asked him,
"Did you ever hear of
Gownsman's Gallows?"—"No,
Mr. President!"—"What, sir, do
you tell me, sir, that you never
heard of Gownsman's Gallows?
Why, I tell you, sir, that I have
seen two undergraduates
hanged on Gownsman's Gal-
lows in Holywell—hanged, sir,
for highway robbery."

*The President of Magdalen in
1853, recorded by Augustus
Hare in 'The Years with Mother'
(Allen & Unwin)*

The Rue Morgue Press
Lyons / Boulder

À LA FAMILLE LAFOY
AUX MAURINÈRES
'*O mes doux Pénates d'argile!*'
Jean-François Ducis

Gownsman's Gallows
Copyright © 1957
New material
Copyright © 2005 The Rue Morgue Press
ISBN: 0-915230-83-6

FIRST AMERICAN EDITION

Reprinted with the permission of
The Trustees of K.D. Farrer Estate

The Rue Morgue Press
P.O. Box 4119
Boulder, CO 80306
800-699-6214
www.ruemorguepress.com

Printed by
Johnson Printing

PRINTED IN THE UNITED STATES OF AMERICA

Meet Katharine Farrer

Editor's Note: The following introduction is somewhat revised from the version that first appeared in The Missing Link. *Katharine's nephew, Nick Newton, has provided some additional background information, plus there are comments about the use of French in* Gownsman's Gallows.

Since, as a critic once remarked, all dons read detective stories, it's not surprising that many mystery novels have been set in the English university town of Oxford. From Dorothy L. Sayers to Colin Dexter, fictional detectives, amateur and professional, have prowled its streets, its pubs, and even the halls of its many colleges. Academics have often been featured as detectives, most notably in the works of Edmund Crispin featuring Gervase Fen. While they might well have enjoyed many of these books, only a handful of Oxford dons actually wrote detective novels set at their colleges. J.C. Masterman, a fellow of Christ College, is a prime example of a don who excelled, however briefly, at the form. His *An Oxford Tragedy* (1933) not only provides an accurate portrayal of Oxford but also is an entertaining and well-constructed classical detective novel. But where Masterman's novel is at its best when he sticks to college life, Katharine Farrer, the wife of an Oxford don, moves with assured ease from the college halls to the private homes of that ancient city, especially in her marvelously titled first novel, *The Missing Link*, which involves the kidnapping of a don's baby.

While it might have seemed natural to make her detective a don, given her background, Farrer chose to use a professional policeman as her protagonist. In many respects, the Oxford-educated Richard Ringwood resembles other gentleman coppers in the genre, including Michael Innes' Inspector John Appleby and Ngaio Marsh's Roderick Alleyn, though his casual disregard for such legal amenities as search warrants might cause either of those gentlemen to frown. Ringwood was, in many ways, inspired by Katharine's husband, Austin Farrer, who was described by Rowan Williams, the Archbishop of Canterbury, as "possibly the greatest Anglican mind of the twentieth century." Ringwood is 33 years old when *The Missing Link*, the first book in the trilogy, opens, newly engaged to Clare Liddicote, a 22-year-old recent Oxford graduate who is staying on at the university for another semester to enjoy learning for its own sake. Their courtship mirrors that of the Farrers, who married in 1937 after a four-year-long engagement when Austin was 33, already well-established in his profession, and Katharine 26. But while there are some other minor superficial similarities, it is in their attitude and outlook on life and to each other that Richard and Clare most resemble the Farrers.

Chief among these attitudes is the sense that their marriage is to be a partnership. Richard may be older and more experienced than Clare, but he respects her intellect and her abilities, even to the point of soliciting her help in carrying out his current investigation. He is more interested in gaining her approval than the appreciation of either his fellows or superiors. He is never happier than when he can discuss a point in a case or in a book or in a play with Clare. They are the two halves that make a whole. As Clare remarks, after Richard quotes from *The Wind in the Willows*, "Have you noticed how we have all the same favorite books?"

All evidence points to the fact that Austin and Katharine Farrer shared a similar relationship, even though he enjoyed a far more celebrated public life. His work as a theologian is so revered, even today, that in 2004, on the centenary of his birth, major celebratory workshops on his teachings and writings were held in Oxford and Baton Rouge, Louisiana. He was Chaplain and a Fellow of Trinity College, Oxford, from 1935 until 1960, and Warden of Keble College, Oxford, from 1960 to his death in 1968. Most of his scholarly writings on theology remain in print. But he was more than a scholar. His fellows also described him as perhaps the finest pulpit preacher of his era, a minister who knew how to reach his congregation, primarily students at his college.

It was probably only natural that Katharine was attracted to a theologian, since her own father, F.H.J. Newton, was a noted minister. She was born in 1911 in Wiltshire but brought up along with Arthur, her eight-year-younger brother, in two successive parsonages in Herfordshire. She attended St. Helen's School in Northwood, and at 18 went up to St. Anne's, Oxford, where she read Classical Mods and Greats. While still a student, she published her first short stories under a pseudonym. Education was an important aspect of her family life. On her father's side, she was related to Miss Frances Mary Buss, a pioneer in higher education for women in England in the nineteenth century. Miss Buss, as she was known, opened the North London Collegiate School for Girls in 1850 at the age of 23 and later worked with Emily Davies in opening exams for women at Cambridge in 1865. Katharine also taught, following her graduation in 1933, as a classics teacher first at Bexhill, then at Gerrards Cross. Already engaged to Austin, she also instructed scripture classes. On her mother's side, she was related to the Des Anges family who were involved in the Port Royal movement in France during the reign of Louis XIV. The movement was started by Cornelius Jansen, who taught that people are saved by God's grace, not by their own will power, a theological position that fits in quite well with the teachings of Katharine's husband.

At Oxford, the Farrers naturally gravitated to like-minded intellectual Christians. Austin—and presumably Katharine—belonged to the Inklings, a group of scholars dedicated to the destruction of scientific materialism, whose other members included founder J.R.R. Tolkien, author of *The Lord of the Rings* trilogy, Charles Williams, the metaphysical poet and novelist, Dorothy L. Sayers, the creator of the Lord Peter mystery series, and C.S. Lewis, the Christian apologist who wrote science fiction and children's fantasy literature. Lewis, in particular, held the Farrers in high esteem, dedicating one of his books jointly to them. Austin ministered to Lewis and both he and Katharine took care of him while he was dying. The gravesite of the Farrers (Katharine died four years after Austin in 1972) is one of the stops on the C.S. Lewis walking tour of Oxford. Although there are plenty of inside jokes about Oxford life and personalities in *The Missing Link*, C.S. Lewis isn't mentioned. However, one of the other Inklings is referred to when Clare admonishes Richard to stop talking like a character in a Charles Williams novel. Like many good faculty wives, Katharine was fond of entertaining and was an enterprising cook. An invitation to the Farrers for dinner meant good food as well as lively conversation.

Other elements in *The Missing Link* reflect aspects of the Farrers' life together. Living in a place like Oxford, they were exposed to all kinds of ideas on the rearing of children. Katharine certainly shows where her own sympathies lie. One of the highlights of the novel is the contrasting theories on how to raise a baby, the loving attentive one displayed by one don and his wife and the thoroughly modern creed of benign neglect practiced by the, as Jacques Barzun so accurately describes them, "terrifyingly intellectual" Links, an approach that today might well earn them a visit from Social Services. But there are even more personal touches from the Farrers' home life. The affectionate portrait of Dr. Field's developmentally disabled—"deficient," as her employer describes her—serving girl no doubt is drawn from their experiences in dealing with their own daughter, Caroline, who was born in 1939. Katharine was a small woman with what her nephew described as "an almost sparrow-like countenance." Her small size made for a difficult delivery. Caroline was born developmentally disabled and her need for special education required that she attended a residential institution. Both K (as her friends called her) and Austin were devastated by the need for Caroline to leave home but that pain was moderated by the girl's progress at school. Today Caroline is in her mid-60s and still lives in Oxford at a beautiful convent where for many years she worked in the Church Embroidery Room. Although she is now retired, she continues to work there as a volunteer.

When Katharine returned to work, her own scholarly endeavors complemented those of her husband's. In 1949, she translated Gabriel Marcel's major 1935 work, *Etre et Avoir,* into English as *Being & Having: An Existentialist Diary*. It's worth noting here that Franco-American scholar Jacques Barzun was very critical of Farrer's French in her third and last Ringwood novel, *Gownsman's Gallows*, published in 1957, maintaining it wasn't altogether "correct." Of course, translating French into English requires different skills from doing the opposite, the chief requirement being a full understanding of what the author you are translating actually means to convey to his audience. In this case, Farrer obviously knew her Christian existentialism. That's why fellow mystery writer Anthony Boucher's translations of Georges Simenon's Inspector Maigret novels are so much better than those done by ordinary translators, however good their French might be.

Having said that, much of the French used in the original edition of *Gownsman's Gallows* has been translated into English in the present edition by Sallie and Victor Verrette. A great deal of Farrer's French seems to have been employed for show, and it makes no sense to us to have one sentence of dialog in French and the other five in English when it has been made clear that the characters are speaking French all of the time. Besides, it shouldn't be necessary to know another language to enjoy an English detective novel, Dorothy Sayers not withstanding. (She even had long passages in Latin.) However, it's possible that Farrer chose to put some of the more vulgar phrases in French so as not to offend English readers of the 1950s. Apparently it's acceptable to be racy as long as you do it in French. We've left just enough French to give the book a bit of Gallic flavor but not enough to irritate the average reader. One bit of French that remains (you'll have to look for it yourself) contains a clue that would give too much away if translated, but rest assured that it's not necessary to solve the mystery. Farrer also obviously enjoyed writing verse in French. She was fond of poetry in all its guises but was especially taken by the Romantics.

Farrer's only mainstream novel, *At Odds With Morning* (1960), reflects her interest in theology, featuring, as it does, a satire of a self-appointed saint. But even her three Ringwood novels, *The Missing Link* (1952), *The Cretan Counterfeit* (1954) and *Gownsman's Gallows* (1957), occasionally hint at the theology she shared with her husband. A policeman's lot is a pretty thankless one, as Clare comes to find out. The reward is not in being praised by those you help but in just doing your job—and doing it well—because that's how people ought to live their lives. Being good and being good at what you do should be reward enough. A good Christian doesn't get into heaven by doing good deeds. He or she gets into heaven because God is good. But for all her interest in theology, God isn't mentioned much in *The Missing Link*, although there are obviously touches of the supernatural, especially in the prophecies made by the old gypsy woman. A literalist might say if you believe in God and if God is good, why doesn't He just tell Ringwood outright where the baby is hidden. The answer to that question lies in one of Austin Farrer's writings when he comments that when Jesus was confronted by a bent nail in his days as a carpenter, he didn't resort to invoking the spirit of the Holy Ghost to straighten it. He got out a hammer and anvil.

Unfortunately, the Farrers weren't always able to solve their own personal problems as easily. Katharine suffered from frequent bouts of pneumonia and bronchitis throughout her life, exacerbated by a heaving smoking habit. Plagued by insomnia as well, she became addicted to alcohol and barbiturates in the late 1950s, bringing an end to a promising career as a writer. Her various illnesses required her to become increasingly dependent on Austin, who, in turn, suffered from the stress and often found himself greatly tired. After his death, the highly strung Katharine moved into a smaller apartment far from the traffic noises (Oxford's narrow streets weren't planned with the automobile in mind) that had so bothered her during the earlier years of her marriage. She continued to entertain there and to work on readying the three volumes of Austin's sermons for publication but did not live to see them published. She died at home on March 26, 1972 following a fall.

The best of Katharine and Austin's life together is to be found in her books, especially in her often sparkling and witty dialog, no doubt inspired by the conversations at hundreds of Oxford dinners where the couple entertained the best and the brightest of their generation. As important as religion was in their lives, you don't need to know theology to appreciate her mystery novels. Always the good hostess, Katharine well knew that the first role of the mystery writer is to entertain. *The Missing Link*, whose clever title you will come to appreciate more fully once you finish the book, is a sly, witty book that meanders its way, often comically, to one of the more exiting—and terrifying—climaxes to be found in any traditional mystery. *The Cretan Counterfeit* is an often wryly amusing look at archaeology and the extent that some people will go to earn a reputation. Her third and final Ringwood book, *Gownsman's Gallows*, is set in two of the places she loved best, Oxford and France, and is as much an adventure novel as it is a clever detective story.

Tom & Enid Schantz
Lyons, Colorado
October 2004
Revised July 2005

CHAPTER 1

No outsider would believe that a dead body could have lain undiscovered for long in Priory Road. For it is not a country lane, but an Oxford residential street lined on both sides with houses all the way down to the river, and hardly five minutes' walk away from the High.

Nevertheless, Priory Road at night is a lonely place. It leads nowhere, for it runs down a slope, to end in a wooden bridge over a dank and narrow stretch of the river Cherwell; on the far side there is nothing but empty fields, often flooded and therefore never built upon, fields so unvisited that even here, so near the city's heart, you may hear a fox barking at night or see a heron flap across to fish in the early morning. The silence is almost rural, but the loneliness has a quality of its own.

If you cry for help in the country and no help comes, it is because nobody has heard your cry. But if you lack succor in Priory Road, it is because nobody will attend. All the residents, from the dons at the top of the road to the landladies and college servants at the bottom, mind their own business and shut up house early. Only last winter an old lady who had lived there for years broke her leg on her way to the pillar box at the corner. She took two hours crawling home along the ice-covered pavement. She did call, as loudly as her age and weakness would permit, but the windows remained shut, and the people behind them deaf, townsfolk busy on their own affairs and with ears self-trained to listen only to sounds within the household.

It is uncanny, this loneliness neither urban nor rural, but the road itself is a little sinister too. A historian once told me that the University gibbet stood there till the eighteenth century, and knowing the place I was not surprised. The churchyard is bad to pass at night, with its black yew trees sweeping the ground and its looming, leaning gravestones that seem just yawning aside to give up their dead, as in those macabre paintings of the General Resurrection. Quite near the churchyard, there is a close double row of elm trees, whose trunks, thick, knobbed, and hollow, assume a great variety of facial expressions once the light has gone. You walk past them resolutely, telling yourself that they are only trees, after all; and then suddenly an owl hidden in one of them will make a noise like a young child being strangled—not that you have ever heard one, but you know instinctively that the simile is accurate. Yes, a bad place at night, especially under those trees. And that was where the dead body was lying, with its head on the road and its feet by an elm bole.

No doubt most pedestrians preferred to use the other side of the street, where there is pavement. There is no pavement under the elm trees, and it is dark, as well as being—well, *bad*. Somebody walking home might, as easily as not, have missed seeing the body. As for cars, residents driving home late would naturally keep on the left, that is, the other side of the street,, whereas in the unlikely event of a car coming the other way, up from the river—well, it would be going fairly fast so as not to change gear for the slope. The road is wide and uncongested.

So there the dead body lay, unnoticed in a streetful of houses. A hedgehog, snuffling his way up from the fields in search of food, paused to investigate, but not for long. There were better pickings round the dustbins.

* * *

The unlikely event occurred. Just before midnight a car did drive under the elm trees, coming up the slope from the river. At least its part-owner, Tim Dawson-Gower, an undergraduate in his second year at Pentecost, called it a car. His brother Nigel, who was eight years older and expecting a new Jaguar, referred to it as "Tim's barouche." Tim took the insult meekly.

For he admired his dashing, ex-commando brother more than

anyone, and was very grateful to him for coming down this week-end. This evening, on the river, he had poured out his hopes and fears, while Nigel sat in the slow-moving punt, smoking endless cigarettes and snapping his fingers. Tim suddenly realized that Nigel was bored and that the college gates shut in ten minutes. He said so, and Nigel brightened a little and began suggesting ways his brother could climb in.

"No, honestly, not this term, Nigel. The dean's gunning for me and Francis already. We've simply got to toe the line and pass this exam. If I'm sent down I shall never get a decent job. I do hope the Camel will start all right. I've got to turn her, too."

"Quicker to pull the fence down. Look, the posts are loose already."

"No, *please*, Nigel."

The finger-snapping began again as Tim ran ahead to light the headlamps, which burned oil. People might laugh, but it *did* save the battery. He used a lot of matches before the yellow beams flared along the bright brass radiator and the high square body which Tim himself had painted a rich crimson. He opened the bonnet, and asked Nigel to work the throttle while he cranked her up. She started at the fourth spasm.

"I'd better just turn her before we shut the bonnet. It seems to catch on the steering rod sometimes. Aren't you getting down?"

Nigel, from his unsafe perch on the front wing, surrounded by smoke, merely remarked that the exhaust pipe, a brazen serpent running along the side of the car, had two new holes in it; he seemed disinclined to get down. So Tim mounted, by the brass foot plate, to the driving-seat, leaned his arm over the side to take off the outside handbrake, and began turning the car. It took six runs before he had the long nose pointing to the road. Then Nigel stepped down, closed the bonnet, and climbed up beside his brother.

"You—you don't mind me driving, Nigel? The steering, you see…"

"O.K." Nigel lighted another cigarette. "Your funeral. Look, there's a hedgehog."

But Tim, negotiating the bridge, had no time to look. Not that there was anything *wrong* with the Camel's steering. She just had this idiosyncrasy of pulling to the left if you braked or accelerated too suddenly; managed properly, she was as steady as a rock. Over the bridge, Tim accelerated for the rise, keeping the car straight by pulling the wheel hard over to the right, and she took the slope in top, with all six cylinders working like a military band. They were doing over thirty past the churchyard, and when they reached the elm trees, Tim braked, but did not steer quite hard enough to the right and so passed closer under the elm trees than he had intended. There was a soft jar and a bump, and Tim leaned out hastily to pull the handbrake. Nigel looked over the brass rail on his side, and then, with the cigarette still in his mouth and his glossy eyelashes lowered, said,

"Your funeral! Well, there's many a true word spoken in jest, as they say. He looks dead enough. Got a torch? Well, matches, then. I've run out."

* * *

Nigel clambered down but Tim was too horrified to move. At his brother's direction he backed the car away. When he saw the thing lying there in the road, he trod on the accelerator instead of the footbrake and hit the curb on the opposite side. Then he took a grip on himself, and drove gently across so that the car stood between the body and the road and hid it from view.

He could half-see the body now, lying face down with the head pointing out towards the middle of the road—a horribly misshapen head. Nigel turned it over and struck a match. That one glimpse of the face was appalling.

"Revolting tie he's got on," said Nigel in an ordinary voice. "D'you know any college or club with those colors?"

"N-no." Tim had got out but he could not bring himself to look. "Oh Nigel! What's that noise?"

Nigel gripped his arm with fingers that felt electric. "Shut up! Wait!"

It was an old man putting out milk bottles on the step of the house behind the elm trees. Each bottle made a separate clink on the stone. The man cleared his throat as if about to speak, and Tim held his breath, but the only sound that followed was the slam of the front door, and then darkness and silence.

"If you can't stop chattering your teeth, Tim, for God's sake hang your mouth open," whispered Nigel angrily. "What's the flap in aid of, anyhow? Can't you see this man's been dead some time? The blood's quite thick. And anyhow I think we went over his waist, not his head. Your barouche has got a very high road clearance, and if the wheel didn't touch the head, nothing else would, would it?"

"N-no. Wh— you mean, I didn't kill him?"

"Help me to get his trousers down and I'll show you. Pull, you clot. Now look, quickly, because it's the last match. See that sort of dint? That's where you went over him, and if he'd been alive there'd have been… Oh, for God's sake!"

Tim had turned away with his face in his hands.

"Why the flap? I tell you, he was dead already."

"But the police won't believe that. Only an expert could tell."

"I bet I've seen more stiffs than any of the Oxford cops have. Why bring them in, anyhow? Why not just leave him?"

"But Nigel, someone may have seen us. And we've done all the wrong things, moving the—body—and making marks on the road. It's no good. I'm done for."

"But we can prove you didn't kill him—if you insist on bringing in the police. I can prove it and swear to it, too."

"Yes, but you're my brother. They won't believe you. And I've been in a car accident this term already. They're all against me. It's no good. I'm done for. I'm not like you, Nigel. My whole life…" It was terrible to be the younger brother of a hero.

Nigel's temper suddenly flared. He took Tim by the shoulders and shook him. Then he slapped him on the face, hard.

"You miserable little blubbering clot, stop! I'm fed up with you. Now, go home."

"Sorry … For God's sake, Nigel! What are you doing?"

"Obvious, isn't it?" said Nigel between his teeth, as he heaved the body up into the passenger seat. "Find me the rug and then go home."

"But—"

"Shut up. Listen. You didn't kill him. But you don't think the Oxford police will believe that—and they won't, either, with you weeping and jittering, blast you! Well, then, I'm going to dump him somewhere else. I'll ring you up from London tomorrow."

"But the risk! I can't let you …"

Nigel's teeth gleamed in the dark. "I like risks. Pick up those bloody little cold feet of yours and go."

The car rattled away in a Piperesque apocalypse of crimson and smoke and brass. Tim stood helplessly for a moment, and then began to run. The Oxford chimes were still at their leisurely midnight when he reached Pentecost lodge.

Nigel drove on, neither smoking nor snapping his fingers. For the first time in ten years he was not bored. In fact he felt almost grateful to Tim for exasperating him into forming a one-man Maquis; this job was just his cup of tea. He saw a police road patrol car in the driving mirror, beckoned it to pass, and courteously returned the driver's salute.

CHAPTER 2

"I see there's another of these arsons today, Praefect," Miss Pinfold remarked, as she brought in Dr. Burdock's letters to be signed.

She was a conscientious girl. When people said that her employer was lacking in public spirit, she resented it. She even felt guilty. For Dr. Burdock himself, Praefect of Pentecost College, carried his forgetfulness with an air, and when detected in ignorance of some burning question, would assume an injured look and complain that nobody told him anything. Miss Pinfold, as a good secretary, took these complaints to heart. And so, now, she remembered to remark that there had been another of these arsons today.

"Arsons?" repeated the praefect, passing two fingers over his capacious forehead. "Arsons? I don't remember any Arsons in my time. Did we have his elder brother up here during the war? Or is it a son? If so, the parental Arson was probably up before I returned to the college as a fellow. It's an unusual name, and I don't recall it. Still, if it's a Pentecost family I suppose we shall have to take him."

"It isn't a *name*, Praefect. I mean, it's a crime. You know, this person who keeps on setting fire to churches and things."

"Oh dear me! Yes, of course! Well, all I can say is, I hope the fellow makes a really thorough job of the town hall before they catch him. Even the best music, in a setting like that..."

"Well, actually, it was only a haystack that was set on fire last night, out by Wheatley. That's not so bad as a church, anyhow."

"It depends on the church. And they didn't catch him?"

"No. It just said that the cause of the fire is unknown and the police suspect foul play. I expect you'll hear more about it at your luncheon party."

"Luncheon party?" Then, as his secretary pointed to an entry in the engagement book, "Oh dear! How extremely tiresome! I thought it was next week. Just when I was hoping we'd have some time to catch up. You poor thing, I hate to think of you toiling away alone all the afternoon."

"Oh, I'll be all right." As if he could help me! she thought. Bless him! "But do bring me back the latest news about the arsons."

"Arsons? I don't recall the … oh, just so. Yes, I might suggest their getting in that Scotland Yard detective I met—what was his name? Bellman? Ranter? An Oxford man, quite a good classical scholar, I believe. Pupil of Costard's, I fancy, or friend, perhaps. He married Liddicote's daughter. He was up with me, I mean Liddicote, of course. He might have been a really good historian if only he wasn't so irresponsible. He never would take the trouble to interest himself in anything boring. I met the son-in-law once, and really, considering everything, he wasn't bad at all. Now what *was* his name?"

"Ringwood?"

"Ringwood! Yes, of course. Really, Miss Pinfold, you are simply wonderful! Now why did I think he was called Ranter? Ranter and Ringwood, what's the connection? Oh, yes, of course, Ranter and Ringwood, *John Peel*. You know," he continued with much animation, "those traditional names of hounds have a history of immense antiquity. In the twelfth century … Loyer, Beaumont, Latimer …"

"I'm awfully sorry, Praefect, but I see the porter's waiting for the letters. Could you just sign them?"

"My dear child, why didn't you tell me? Oh, but you did. I do apologize. I'll tell you about the hounds at lunch. I think we are on our own for lunch today, are we not?"

* * *

Miss Pinfold was waiting eagerly for the praefect when he returned soon after three; he was pleased, for generally he found her typing away at high speed, and felt like a slave driver or, worse, an intruder. The polite fiction that the college was administered by the praefect and that Miss Pinfold merely carried out instructions wore a little thin at times.

"Well!" he said, throwing himself into his chair, "You'll be pleased to hear that we've been talking nothing but arson. It's extraordinary, how often you mention something and then I go out and find it is the chief topic of conversation, isn't it?"

For the hundredth time, she wondered if the old man was as innocent as he looked. Did he realize how carefully she briefed him?

Did he *mind*? She asked quickly,

"Oh, do tell me! What's the latest? Have they caught him?"

"By no means. But, my dear, the plot thickens. It wasn't only a haystack that was burnt last night. There was a body inside it."

"What?"

"Yes, a man, unfortunately too charred for them to identify him. Only the feet were intact, curiously enough. Still, gray socks and black shoes are hardly a clue, are they? Though perhaps a chiropodist. ... My dear child, you're looking quite upset. I'm so sorry. I'm afraid reading all those thrillers has made me callous. I wonder if Elizabethan melodrama and the awful public executions link up in the same way? No, your humanity does you credit. Forgive me."

"It isn't that. But the—the chief constable rang up. He wants to get in touch with you at once. He wouldn't say anything to me, except that it was urgent, and he asked me our college laundry mark. And I can't help thinking now—was it a Pentecost man in that haystack?"

The praefect became businesslike and curiously awe-inspiring.

"Most unlikely, I should think," he said. "But I'll ring up the chief constable at once. Meanwhile, will you just take a note over to the college clerk and wait for an answer? They may not have it at once, and if so, you could perhaps be kind enough to cut yourself a few carnations while you're waiting; the plants need lightening. There are secateurs on the hall table."

Miss Pinfold departed, so amazed at being allowed to touch the carnations (the praefect's special hobby, which even the college gardener left alone) that she almost forgot how miserable and creepy she had felt a moment ago. That was what the praefect had intended; but his note to the bursar's office demanded a list of all personal laundrymarks in Pentecost.

On the telephone to the chief constable, the praefect agreed that the mark PEN was used by the college laundry. But the socks on the corpse, which bore that mark, might surely have been those of a different customer from another laundry? He promised, however, to look into the matter at once, find which undergraduate, if any, in Pentecost used the mark PEN 154, and make sure he was not missing. Yes, of course he would be extremely discreet in his enquiries. No doubt the police would not wish to expose the college to the publicity of a police search if it could be avoided. He would be pleased to save them trouble of that kind. Just so. Not at all.

Well! he thought. No policemen about the college for the moment, so the press wouldn't pester him. That was something. There were aspects of Pentecost administration this year which would certainly be misinterpreted by the outside world if they were publicized, murder or no murder. Yet he did not see how they could have arranged things otherwise.

The real mistake had been to elect Leary as dean last autumn. Poor Leary had needed the extra money which the appointment brought him, and he had seemed so keen. Too keen, that was the trouble. He had been a naval officer in the war, and now he tried to carry out his notions of naval discipline in Pentecost. He patrolled the gardens at night to catch people climbing in; he inspected beds to see if they'd been slept in; worst of all, he refused perfectly reasonable requests for leave of absence; and the praefect and fellows, having voted college discipline into his hands, were bound to support him.

The undergraduates might have caused a lot of trouble in the old days. The praefect could remember unpopular deans who had been put on bonfires or screwed into their rooms. The present generation had better sense and better manners, and the praefect was grateful. If he heard a bump on the roof of his garage at one o'clock in the morning, or saw the name of a Pentecost man listed in the social column of *The Times* as a guest at some London dance which he had not been given leave to attend, he took no notice. So long as the young men dealt gently and reasonably with Leary the other dons would turn a blind eye. Leary would not be reelected dean next year.

So far, the policy had worked. No one had complained. Now it was different. He did not look forward to having to confess to the police that almost any of his undergraduates might have been out last night without the knowledge of the authorities, because the dean was an ass and his colleagues were not disposed to help him. It looked bad, put so baldly.

Miss Pinfold now returned with the laundry lists. The praefect looked them over and sighed. As bad as it could be! The owner of the laundrymark was the Hon. Francis Clandon, who shared rooms and a car with Tim Dawson-Gower and was so often in trouble with the dean. The dean had a special mistrust for what he called "these society types." And to make things worse still, the staircase scout was Varlett, the oldest, idlest, and most venal of all the college servants; Varlett, who boasted that the dean could never tell if the beds in his staircase had been used or not, because they looked "slept in" all the time; Varlett, who adored titles and hated dons. There was nothing for it; the praefect would have to go over and listen to Varlett himself. The old villain would probably tell more of the truth to him than to anyone else, but it would take at least half an hour and be unedifying.

He returned at length wreathed in smiles.

"Will you take a letter for the chief constable, please, Miss Pinfold, and see that it's delivered by hand at once?"

He sat back and began.

"Dear Chief Constable,

*"In answer to your telephone enquiry this afternoon, the laundrymark in which you are interested, viz.—*wait a minute, I had it on a bit of paper somewhere. Where is it? Oh! thank you!—*PEN 154, is indeed used by the Hon. F.J. Clandon, one of our second-year men now living in college."*

"Oh Praefect! How awful!"

"On the contrary. Take a fresh paragraph, for we are about to give our correspondent the surprise of his life.

"But Clandon himself, I am happy to say, is still with us and in the best of health. I have just seen him. He was certainly in college all last night. There was a club dinner he attended which lasted till late in the evening and was finally dispersed by the dean; many people can bear witness that Clandon was there all the time. His roommate, T.J. Dawson-Gower, a character as candid as Clandon himself ..."

Miss Pinfold looked up, pleased. She had a weakness for Clandon.

The praefect saw her look up and reconsidered his phrase.

"No, perhaps that's not quite fair to Tim Dawson-Gower ... *a thoroughly truthful man, says that Clandon went to bed immediately afterwards as usual—*he ought to know, he undressed him—*and the staircase servant, Varlett, found him still asleep this morning.* For once, I thought Varlett was telling the truth. Tim Dawson-Gower is not looking at all well, by the way. New paragraph.

"The college is most grateful for the discretion with which you have conducted this (as it turns out) fruitless enquiry. Please let me know if I may help you further. Yours sincerely..."

The praefect mused, one hand held up.

"A postscript. He deserves it. *P.S. I wonder if you ever came across a Scotland Yard detective called Ringwood whom I met here last year with his father-in-law, an old friend of mine. They tell me that he is remarkably good on these unusual cases.*"

Miss Pinfold thought that the praefect was wonderful in a crisis, but he *was* a bit vague in ordinary life. Look at that for a postscript to a business letter! Amiable, but still…

The chief inspector ground his teeth; he understood the postscript very well. And, damn it, the old dodderer might be right.

CHAPTER 3

"Nigel Dawson-Gower here."

"Nigel! Oh, thank God!" No reply. Tim remembered to press Button A. "Nigel! Can you hear me?"

"You're practically deafening me, Tim," said Nigel's voice right in his ear. "Listen. Everything's O.K. I garaged the car after seeing the chap with the horrible tie safely deposited. It all went fine. Have you posted my electric razor?"

"Yes. But Nigel, something awful's happened. The pol—"

"Just a minute, I'll ask my secretary. Jane, would you go and see if there's a small parcel for me downstairs, marked fragile? Thanks. Go ahead then, Tim."

"They've—they've found him! They knew by his socks. His—his feet weren't …"

"I get you. Funny; I thought I'd… oh well! No concern of yours. Why worry?"

"But Nigel! They're on to me somehow. The praefect himself came over to our rooms and asked Francis and me a lot of questions about where we'd been last night. He said the police wanted to know. Only us he went to. Nobody else."

Nigel's voice changed suddenly from its deliberately tough drawl, and became warm and quick. Tim remembered that voice from old days, when he and Nigel were more on a level, before the invisible visor of war had closed over Nigel's face, making him more impressive and less approachable. This sounded like the boy Nigel—not bored or remote any more.

He asked Tim if he couldn't just bluff it out. He was not satisfied with Tim's answer, for he cut him short and said that he'd better get out. He could just go to France a bit earlier than he'd planned. Were the tickets, money, and passports in order? Good! Lucky he'd got them in good time. The college? Oh, Nigel would square *them*; he'd come down and see the praefect himself. Easy to think up some convincing reasons.

Privately, Nigel looked forward to this. There was no better sport than making fools of the brass hats … and it was a risk. Life was boring in peacetime, every day like the last, just being a dull good chap like the other dull good chaps … and anyhow Tim's nerve had gone, obviously. Tim could make quite a mess if he stuck around. Never could keep his mouth shut, poor clot.

Pip pip pip. Nigel's comforting, prewar voice said, "O.K., Timmy. You just go to the Defays and wait till I put you in the picture. Relax, can't you? This is the sort of job I'm good at. And besides, it's all my fault; I got bored and didn't stop to, er, clear up after the picnic. Lucky the parents are abroad, it gives me a handle with the praefect. Your what? Exam? Don't worry. I'll get you permission to take it next term. Just relax."

They were cut off.

Well, Nigel doesn't sound fed up with me any more, thought Tim as he pulled the cap over his eyes and ran the gauntlet of a queue waiting to use the call box. I'm glad he isn't. But, oh Lord! if this business mucks up my whole career and I don't get a job when my money's run out … or if I get put in prison or he has to keep me abroad … but he couldn't possibly afford to. He needs a lot of money, Nigel does, and I couldn't think of letting him do that.

He carried his heavy suitcase to the station, not daring to take a taxi lest the driver should remember him. His dark glasses took off the glare of the sun, but the cap, muffler, and mackintosh which completed his disguise were very hot, and, on such a day, rather conspicuous. After his ticket had been punched, he went into the lavatory and stayed, alternately listening and mopping off sweat, until the Southampton train came in. He was young to support such fright and misery.

So young, indeed, that he did not distinguish between major and minor disaster. The thought that he might possibly have killed a man, though Nigel said otherwise, and might be hanged, did not dwarf his other anxieties; anxiety about being sent down from Oxford and never getting a good job, and the fear that he had somehow involved his friend Francis Clandon in the affair, troubled him just as often. He even found time to worry about his car. Some garages didn't realize that she needed special care. Then he began to wonder whether Madame Defay would be put out by his arriving a whole fortnight early at Pontchâtelet, instead of going there when term ended as he had done last year. At this point his heart expanded somewhat; for he was young enough to be distracted, even from disaster. He remembered the Defay family and how pleasant it would be to see them again, especially Jeannette. He wondered if they would think he had changed—even improved, perhaps?—since last summer. He reflected that anyhow he wouldn't be sitting for his prelims this time next week, and that was all to the good, since he wasn't allowed to plow them again and easily might. He thought what a well-planned escape he had made—well, it was partly luck his having got the tickets ahead of time—and how decent it was of Nigel to say he would cope with the dons. And he thought of life at Pontchâtelet—the calm rows of poplars at Angennes, the long delicious meals in the shade, the breakfasts in dressing gowns with Jeannette on the terrace. Lovely. Perhaps he could get a job in France, and make a new life with … Anyway, he'd look into it.

But then he nearly screamed at a touch on his arm, which brought the present situation back to him. He managed to show his ticket with a steady hand, but his mind was running full tilt again round the squirrel cage of fear. Murder, arrest, sent down, unemployed, caught, murder, arrest …

But finding the boat, passing the customs, and feeling the first qualms of seasickness caused him hardly less anxiety.

CHAPTER 4

The fellows of Pentecost were assembled at teatime that day for their weekly college meeting, sitting round a table in a dark paneled room. A bee droned in a patch of sunlight against one of the deeply recessed windows; the estates bursar and the domestic bursar droned across the table at one another. The praefect waited until all present were reduced to somnolence or fidgets and then said vaguely,

"Yes. Well. It all seems rather controversial and I see time is slipping on. Perhaps the college would like to see the figures before we take a vote on the matter? There's one bit of business still to be settled, or rather perhaps taken cognizance of. It's about young Dawson-Gower."

There was a subdued groan, and Mr. Maddock, who taught Modern Languages and was Tim's tutor, tightened his lantern jaw and said nothing. The praefect continued,

"As you know, his parents are in Ceylon and his brother stands *in loco parentis*. Well, it's all very tiresome, though no doubt he acted in good faith, but the long and the short of it is—preferably short, for time, I see, is getting on—I'll tell you what, I'll read the correspondence, shall I?"

There were urmurs of "No, no! Just the gist of it!"

"First," said Dr. Burdock, shuffling his papers, "there was a telegram. Now where is it, it was yellow, I believe. Ah, thank you! *London, 11 a.m. My brother removed health reasons temporarily may I call three today Nigel Dawson-Gower*. Well, I duly informed the dean that Dawson-Gower was away and saw the elder brother an hour ago."

"What's he like?" said the classical tutor, waking up.

"What's supposed to be wrong with the boy?" added Jobson, the medical expert.

"Disgracefully high-handed!" muttered Leary, the dean.

The praefect gave them all his benevolent and unhurried consideration.

"Well, I must say, Dawson-Gower, the elder one, that is, impressed me very favorably, very favorably indeed. Of course I really think young Tim is a very decent young chap at bottom, too. As you know, he, I mean of course the elder, wasn't at Pentecost long, but he had a most remarkable war record, as no doubt you remember. The Resistance and parachutists and so on. I daresay that kind of background *would* rather give him the habit of making quick decisions… But he was very apologetic afterwards, and really I think he did the right thing. I was talking to him—the younger brother, that is— quite recently, and I thought he was looking very seedy. I suppose he was too shy to bring the matter up. Yes, I think he's got a very genuine sense of responsibility, the elder brother, that is …"

"Have we any decisions to make, Praefect?" cut in the dean in an exaggeratedly patient manner. "Because there are two pupils waiting for me in my room, and if…"

"Oh, please don't wait. I'm only, er, wising the college up." The younger fellows exchanged amused glances. Leary left the gathering. The praefect's manner became brisker.

"Jobson, your question, I think. The medical side. Well, I'm afraid I shan't be very accurate. It's a pity the boy didn't see the college doctor first, but I understand that his brother took him straight to a London consultant who said that it was a rather rare deficiency disease. A well-known man, one of these Central European names, now did it begin with an M?"

"Murkowitz? Merejowski?"

"No. I'm very sorry, but do you know, it's slipped my memory. We shall get a letter from him about it eventually, I gather. Just at the moment he's abroad on some medical conference, so I had only Dawson-Gower's account to go on. If I followed him correctly and he was not misrepresenting the specialist, which of course is quite possible, the boy is somehow failing to assimilate a vital element of his nourishment. He takes his food, but it doesn't do him the good it ought to. And it won't, apparently, unless he's exposed to a lot of natural sunlight. Does that make sense, Jobson?"

"Could."

"Well, as we all know only too well, you can't count on sun here, even in the summer term. In fact my carnations … but I mustn't keep you. The danger apparently is that if the boy didn't start his sunshine cure at once, he ran the risk, not only of increased lassitude and inability to concentrate, of which he had already shown marked signs …"

Mr. Maddock unlocked his jaw and then thought better of it.

"… but of a bone disease which is very difficult to check. So he sent the boy to a sunny climate at once. When he comes back he ought to be improved in every way."

"He hasn't passed a single exam since he came up," said Mr. Maddock. "Are we sure about having him back?"

"Oh well, of course I didn't commit the college in any way until you had been informed. I know there have been complaints about young Dawson-Gower. But one feels it may have been due to illness. One would like to give him the benefit of the doubt as he seems so anxious to have a place kept for him. His father and uncles were here, you know. I did say, provisionally of course, that if he did return it might be better for him to take a Pass school of some sort, and be taught by external tutors …"

"Oh! So long as I don't have to teach him, O.K. by me," said Maddock. "Then I'm in favor of letting him come back if he's cured."

There was a general buzz of assent. The bee at the window found an open pane and sailed out. The fellows pushed back their chairs.

"Then I'll write to the brother in that sense, shall I? That if Dawson-Gower recovers we'll have him back to read for Groups? Very well."

The meeting broke up or rather burst loose, and Dr. Burdock returned to the praefect's lodging. Miss Pinfold had his letter to Nigel Dawson-Gower already written and ready for his signature. As she tidied up her desk and prepared to leave, she remarked,

"You know that man in the haystack?"

"A local Diogenes? No. Who is he? A Balliol don?" Then he smiled shamefacedly. "Yes, of course I remember, really. The corpse that turned out not to be young Clandon. What's the news?"

"Well, they think now that it must have been a French undergraduate who's been missing since the Sunday evening—a Cat's man. Shall I leave you the paper?"

"Thank you. For goodness sake stop toiling away and go off to your party. H'm, this is very interesting. Goodbye."

He began to read with more attention.

"Too interesting by half," he murmured, and took up his pen to write a letter. But presently he exclaimed, "Oh, bother!" and went in search of his wife.

"Hattie, I'm writing to Peregrine Liddicote. Oh dear! You're washing up again! Let me do it. Only really I ought to … I say, can you remember the name of that chap, the detective, you know, that Peregrine's daughter Clare got married to?"

"Richard Ringwood. I had a letter from Nancy, and apparently Peregrine's in London with them now. Clare's having a baby. I'll tell you what, Batty, you finish drying up and I'll ring the exchange and get their address and telephone number. You know you hate enquiries."

"I do!" said the praefect, taking up a spoon and polishing it absently. It was a dry one. Then, as the door shut behind his wife, "My poor old Hattie! How right you are!"

CHAPTER 5

Richard Ringwood's superior officer, a veteran detective nicknamed the Bloodhound, sat in his room at Scotland Yard. He was reading a report that lay between two telephones on the desk in front of him. Sometimes he turned up his red-rimmed eyes; sometimes he sighed.

And as he read, the wrinkles in his forehead deepened, and the loose skin of his mouth and chin settled into ever grimmer folds.

"*Oxford* murder!" he thought. "That always means trouble. Letters to the papers. Getting at us via the Minister. Trying to teach us our job, like they always do, those Oxford blokes. Ringwood is typical … Ugh! Victim probably French … More trouble. Have to work in with those Sûreté types … Never liked 'em. Soft soap and parly-voo one moment, snap off your head the next. Ugh! And Ringwood says he likes them! He *would*. Likes showing off his superior French, I suppose."

The right-hand telephone rang.

"Eh? Oh! Yes, sir!" The Bloodhound's manner changed. He was never one to presume with the chief. But his face sagged more and more as he listened. So Oxford had got busy on the high-ups already! The chief was asking him to suggest a suitable officer. He did.

At this, the voice on the telephone became less sharp, and said yes, that had been his own idea too, actually. Ringwood was an Oxford man, wasn't he? Quite. And hadn't he been all set for a diplomatic career at the time when he'd suddenly decided to join the police? Funny, that; police work wasn't such an attractive job, really … Still, considering all things, he'd shaped well in these first ten years. Of course the Bloodhound's training was largely responsible. Improved him a lot. In fact, the Bloodhound might be interested to know that the Minister had actually asked if this particular officer was available. Yes, by name. This was in confidence, of course.

"Of course, sir." The Bloodhound sniffed. "If it leaked out, we know what people would say. *Jobs for the boys, eh?*"

"They never do say it about people who can pick boys for the jobs. Well, we all agree, it seems. Good. I'll leave it to you. Thanks."

The Bloodhound picked up his other telephone and spoke in his other voice.

"I want Inspector Ringwood. He's what? Ugh! Well, I can't help that. I want him here. Now."

Five minutes later, Richard Ringwood was listening to the Bloodhound, who had not offered him a chair, and reflecting that the nickname was a slander—on bloodhounds. The man was certainly down to form this morning. After telling Ringwood that the Oxford haystack murder had been assigned to him for investigation, pointing out all the difficulties and saying that Ringwood must take all sorts of care that he had been taking for years, he had gone on to remark that lack of success would reflect, not only on the force, but also on the various nobs who, as Ringwood probably knew, had been pushing him from outside. Not, he continued, that efforts like that ever got people anywhere. Still …

"It's the first I've heard of the case, here or anywhere," said Ringwood stiffly. "Actually, there's another reason why I was going to ask if you could send someone else. My wife's having a baby this week, so I'd rather hoped not to be sent out of London just now."

"Rather hoped, had you? Any reason why you should hope for different treatment to the others? For instance—" he paused to smile in a manner which did not really become him—"no help in the house? No doctor near, no hospital facilities, young family with nobody to mind them, danger to mother's life? We do consider giving leave on those grounds."

"I am not applying for leave, sir," said Richard. "My wife is well and has her father with her; the monthly nurse arrives on Saturday. All I'm saying is that it's a first baby and I'd be grateful if …" He stopped and made himself count ten.

"Well, I'm sorry, Inspector Ringwood." He was, too; sorry in a sullen, puzzled way. Why did a straightforward talk like this always seem to put Ringwood's back up? "I've nobody else I'd want to put on this case. But look here, why don't you *try* and get leave? No harm in trying. If you do get it, I'll go down to Oxford myself. It wouldn't be easy, see, on account of the office work, but I'd manage at a pinch. Now that's a fair offer, isn't it?"

The Bloodhound came of a class in which offers like this, made ungraciously, were never made insincerely. Ringwood, on the other hand, assumed that an ungracious offer presupposed refusal and was merely a way of spiking your adversary's guns. He simply repeated that he didn't wish to apply for leave. Both men felt angry and misunderstood, and there was an awkward silence.

"Mind you," said the Bloodhound, "we'll give you every help so you can finish it up quickly. Lab priority, free hand, etcetera etcetera. You can even phone me at my place on reversed charges if you want to. I'll try and get you a car, too."

"I have my own, thanks."

"Well, petrol. Repairs too, on this trip, within reason; it's an old car, isn't it? Anything else?"

Inspector Ringwood considered. Then, as if thinking aloud,

"Just the feet of the body left, you said. And the socks, which aren't a straight clue because they belong to somebody who's alive and has an alibi for the time. No fingerprints, no oddity of constitution revealed by the blood they analyzed from the feet. So there's only scent left to try. It's been a mild damp day. Might be a chance, even though the trails will be twenty-four hours old at least."

"Dog?" said the Bloodhound. "I could probably get you one of our Alsatians."

"I've got my own, thanks. Trained it myself."

The Bloodhound glowered, and fingered his dewlap. "What did you do that for? Ours not good enough for you?"

"Well, the thing is, they won't work for anyone but their regular handlers. And that means another man's time, and fares, and so on, even if he's free when I want him …"

"Surely you can trust me to give you any assistance within reason, like I said? You've got a right to it. It's public money."

"That's just it," replied his subordinate. "We don't want any more of these questions in the House, do we? when the police are accused of wasting it."

"More high-falutin'," thought the Bloodhound. "S'pose he thinks we all ought to spend our private means saving the force money. Talks as if he was assistant commissioner at least. Well, maybe he will be, too, when me and my lot are on the shelf. But he'll never make what I call a policeman." Aloud he said,

"Very well, then. You can try, but mind, you're responsible for the animal's efficiency. It's the first I've heard of such a thing. What sort of dog is it, anyway?"

Richard had looked forward to the question.

"Hound, actually. Quite efficient, too, though an ugly brute, obstinate, you know, and not all that intelligent in general ways. Marvelous on the job, though." (Pause.) "Eats nearly two pounds of meat a day." (Pause.) "A lot of people think bloodhounds are old-fashioned, but personally I always like to see them working."

His chief was silent, wrinkling his forehead, and Richard wondered if he had gone too far. This kind of joke was only funny if nobody saw the point except yourself. He was soon reassured. Facts, not implications, were what the man worried over.

"Must cost you ten bob a week, at least. You can put the meat down on expenses till you get back. Well, that's all." Then, as Richard turned to go, "Not savage, is he?"

"Gentle as a lamb, sir. She's a young bitch, actually. I must introduce you some time."

Half an hour later Richard Ringwood was bowling out of London in his roomy old-fashioned Lanchester. He had taken out the back seat cushions and put down sacks, but even so it was a tight fit for Ranter, his bloodhound; especially while she was awake and excited. Car rides always affected her emotions. She had spent the first part of the journey resting her heavy muzzle on his shoulder from behind and alternately slobbering and squealing down his neck. Now she was asleep, and Richard's thoughts turned to home. He had hated leaving his wife at such a time.

"Still," he thought, "she's really better with the pair of us off her hands. Ranter's so big to be barging about, and I'm so anxious till it's all over, we just bother poor Clare. Whereas she and her father, left to themselves, will keep having fun and not worrying. He never does worry."

Old Peregrine Liddicote, his father-in-law, was curiously detached, for such an affectionate man. His bright eyes took in everything but he never became involved. Now, for instance, he was aware that his presence in the Ringwood household provoked Richard's unconscious jealousy, but he had never worried. He had merely gone off to his club and from there helped Dr. Burdock pull strings and get Richard sent to Oxford. His son-in-law never suspected. And once alone, Clare and her father amused each other extremely and took things as they came, which is by far the best regime at such a time. If Richard felt a little left out in the cold, well—expectant fathers do. Peregrine Liddicote had been through it in his time.

As soon as he arrived in Oxford, Ringwood called at the police station, leaving Ranter outside in the car. The Oxford detectives had already made enquiries about the missing Frenchman. His name was Jean Despuys on his passport, but for social purposes he had apparently preferred the form des Puys, which appeared on Oxford correspondence found in his rooms. The police had questioned the professor who was supervising his thesis, one of his acquaintances, and his landlady.

He was twenty-four, born in Ponchâtelet, a town in the Loire district, and a graduate of the Sorbonne. He had come to Oxford to write a thesis about the influence of Versailles on English etiquette during some very short period in the eighteenth century. An amusing subject, if marginal; but in the two terms he had been there, he had produced no written work. His supervisor, Professor Upjohn, did not, he said, consider him a very serious student. He was surprised that the Sorbonne had thought it worth while to give him a bursary. He added that no doubt the young man had strong *practical* intelligence, for he had worked hard to become a social success. Despuys had evidently failed to charm the professor.

But his landlady, Mrs. Raymond Gyles, was devoted to him. She was no ordinary landlady, but the grass-widow of a distinguished sculptor; and it was by her invitation that des Puys, or Despuys, had come to live in her house in Priory Road. He had done well for himself there, obviously. She told the police that Jean "knew everybody" and was "frightfully popular." His mantelpiece was full of invitation cards. No, she didn't think he had any money problems or any special girlfriends. She had last seen him going out to a cocktail party about six on Sunday evening, and he had said that he was going on to dine at Melford House, which was a sort of club for senior researchmen. He had not returned. At first, according to Mrs. Gyles, she "hadn't said anything because she didn't want to get Jean into trouble." But today so many people had called or telephoned saying that Jean had missed dates with them that she became alarmed— "Jean is so terribly efficient and good about engagements." In the end, just before lunch, she had rung up the police.

They asked her about his laundry, and she told them that only his sheets and towels were sent to the wash from her house. He took his clothes "out somewhere" to get them done more quickly, since her laundry only delivered once a fortnight. The police examined his shirts and socks and found some of them marked PEN 154—a Pentecost college laundry mark used by the Progressive Laundry for the linen of the Honorable F.J. Clandon. They had not yet had time to go into the matter further.

When they called on Mr. Sansom, having discovered from Melford House that someone of that name had been entertaining the young Frenchman to dinner, he was quite ready to help them. He was a French-Canadian by birth and a fellow of St. Denis's college, a new foundation which at present consisted only of fellows. Yes, he said, Jean des Puys had been his guest for dinner. He had seemed to be in a perfectly normal state when he left—had had a good deal to drink, certainly, as the bill would show, but appeared none the worse for it. He had left some time between half-past nine and ten, his host seeing him to the front door, and then going home to his own lodgings up the Banbury Road almost at once. Sansom did not, he said, know the young man well, but he was quite amusing. He might have asked him to a meal once or twice before. He seemed unwilling to believe that harm had come to a young man who seemed, he said, particularly good at looking after himself.

"Well!" said Richard to the Oxford detective, Colman by name, "you've done me proud in that short time, and I shall follow up all the lines you've started. But the first thing I want to know is this. Was it really Despuys in the haystack, and if so how was it that he left Melford House on foot for home that evening and yet we next find him dead in a haystack ten miles out of Oxford? I think scent is our only hope of finding out his real movements. I've got my blood-hound outside and we'd better get her to work at once. Do you think we could get Sansom over to Melford House so that he can show us where Despuys started from? Oh, and by the way, would you get me one of the feet? You know, the, er, *remains*. In a box or something?"

Detective Colman, an innocent youth who looked like a bank clerk, was at once shocked and interested.

"W—will he? I mean, I thought there had to be actual drops of blood on the ground."

"Oh, no. It's not blood, it's scent. All of us leave a scent trail, you see, wherever we go, all the time. I grant you a barefoot man would leave more scent. It's better over grass or rough country, too, and of course the fresher the trail the easier it is to follow. Still, there's a hope. This trail is twenty-four hours old and I suppose some of it will be over pavements—but on the other hand it's been mild and damp today, which means that the scent will have kept fresher… They're bringing the foot? Good! You know, bloodhounds have the most amazingly keen noses. There was one bloodhound called Nick Carter who actually followed a trail a hundred hours old and got his man." He was well off on his hobbyhorse now.

"You don't say!"

"Of course that's a record—really quite exceptional. Twenty-four hours is the usual limit. Still, as I say, this particular bloodhound, Nick Carter, identified the criminal after a hundred hours—that's over four days—and the man confessed immediately Nick found him."

"Ah well! I suppose if he hadn't, the dog would have finished him off. Sort of Hound of the Baskervilles touch."

"Nonsense!" said Richard sharply. "Bloodhounds *never* savage their quarry. Never! They might attack a burglar—they're good watchdogs— or some stranger who was teasing them. But never the quarry. They just stand over it, or sit, and give tongue. A won-derful sound it is, too. Come along and watch, if you like."

They went out to the street, Richard carrying the cardboard box and the young detective following. A little group of people had collected near the car, and a uniformed policeman, who addressed Richard angrily on his approach, was standing beside it.

"This your car? Well, you're not allowed to park there as you know very well, and what's more you've left a savage dog not properly in control …"

Ranter's huge head, darkly mottled black and brown, was half out of the car window. Her eyes glared redly from her domed skull; her forehead was wrinkled in a fearsome frown; and her long ears, curling inwards at the tips, framed her face as solemnly as a judge's wig. Slaver dripped from her pendulous flews, and she was making a noise, or so Colman told his mother later, like a lost soul. She varied this by deep growls directed at the policeman, whom she suspected of designs on the car.

"Explain, will you, Colman?" said Richard, opening the car door. "There's a poor old girl, then! I say, just hold this box—will you? I don't want her to scent it yet. Come on out, then, old lady! Want to stretch your legs?"

The tearful grieving barks of the deserted animal had ceased, and she began to utter high excited squeals of welcome. The spectators found these sounds even more alarming, and retreated.

"Come on, then, if you're coming!" said Richard, bracing himself with his legs apart. A hundred pounds of incarnate feminine emotion is apt to be overwhelming even in human form. When it is on four legs, compact of solid bone and muscle, only a strong man can stand up to it. Ranter came tumbling and lolloping out with all her weight behind the enormous head that she thrust against her master's chest. He staggered, caught her under the front legs, and held her against him for a moment until she had panted out the first transports of her passion. Then he gently pushed her, saying, "Down!" and she sank quivering on her haunches. Even sitting, she came well above his waist, and he was a tall man. Her eyes were upturned to his face, so that the bystanders had a particularly good view of the haws, or red inner eyelids, which glistened a healthy scarlet.

"Innee awful!" said someone in a hushed voice.

"Gentle as a lamb!" her master said loudly to no one in particular. Then, turning to Colman, "Get in, won't you?"

"I, er … On second thoughts, wouldn't it be better if I took one of our cars and fetched Mr. Sansom?"

"Very well. I'll take the box. Down, Ranter! See you there, then. Sorry I parked where I shouldn't," he added to the other policeman, looking round. But he was gone. In fact, the pavement was quite deserted. Ranter looked as if she couldn't understand it all when Richard asked her what she'd been up to. For a moment she thought he was scolding her, and was very downcast, but then he took her long ears and wrapped them round her nose. This was a gesture of special affection. She lumbered into the car, moaning with pleasure.

CHAPTER 6

Colman and Mr. Sansom had not appeared when the old Lanchester drew up outside Melford House. Ranter slept. Richard lit a cigarette and sat pondering her chances of success.

She was a good bloodhound. Though young, she was experienced and highly trained already, and had inherited sagacity from famous forebears. One of her ancestors traced a lost child along a twelve-mile scent for two days after its disappearance. Another, after starting to track a poacher and losing his trail, scented the culprit some hours later in the village street, and bayed over him so terribly that he confessed at once. Richard amused himself by imagining that it was a remote member of Ranter's family who had tracked the rebellious Duke of Monmouth, for it was a bloodhound that at last delivered him to justice, but this was fancy. Human pedigrees were confused enough in those unchancy times, let alone bloodhounds'.

Ranter herself had begun life with a pack of staghounds in the Quantocks, whose master was something of an antiquarian and liked to hunt in the old Norman way. Ranter had been trained like the Norman *lymers* or bloodhounds eight hundred years ago, to "harbor the deer." The huntsman put her on a *lyme* or leash and made her discover by scent where there was a suitable deer for the running hounds to follow. Ranter did not run with them, she simply put them on the line, being trained to the work by a wise huntsman and a wiser bloodhound. Richard had watched them during a holiday at home and became fascinated by the elaborate and ancient art. At last he had persuaded them to sell him Ranter. His enthusiasm won them over, and they hoped Ranter would make herself a name in the force.

As soon as he had Ranter to himself, Richard began teaching her to follow a human quarry—first, his wife or some other familiar person, over easy ground and only a short time after they had trodden it. He would give Ranter a piece of their clothing to smell, put her on the track and help her to puzzle out the way they had walked. When she found them she was given a bit of meat or a biscuit for her reward. Gradually Richard lengthened the course and made it more difficult for Ranter by waiting a few hours before setting her on. The more puzzles he set her, the better she was pleased. Soon she was following the line over ditches. Presently she even taught herself to master the check of a tarred road, on which scent does not lie, by casting forward and trying the far side until she picked up the trail again. She was so eager now and so sure that Richard, a good runner himself, had difficulty in keeping up with her. Straining at the leash, muzzle down and tail up, she would pass over the roughest ground in elastic bounding strides, never tired and never out of breath while the scent lasted.

Then he brought her to London and set her harder tasks. Tramps and urchins and old Limehouse characters would be paid half a crown to cross Hampstead Heath in the evening by a given route. Early next morning Richard would put Ranter on the track. She was now teaching her master almost as much as he taught her, working out the sort of places where scent was likely to be bad, conjecturing where the line might be picked up again, showing more and more intelligence and developing also a conscientious pigheadedness which was usually justified.

Her brains for work surprised him, for in ordinary life she was rather stupid as dogs go. If he left her alone in a strange place she often wept like a puppy till he came back. On the few occasions when she had strayed a short distance from the London house, she always decided that she was lost and simply sat on the pavement, lifted her huge voice, and howled for help. Fortunately a solitary weeping bloodhound in N.W. does not go unnoticed, and one of the Ringwood menage would be summoned to the rescue—Ranter refusing to move for anyone else. She never spoke to strange men.

Yes, of all domestic dumb animals, Ranter was surely the dumbest. She had, it is true, a limited language for expressing her emotions—the tearful bark of desertion, the rapturous squeals of reunion, the deep baying that warned the household of an intruder after dark. Affection, too, she communicated, though her language of love was not refined; she simply laid her heavy muzzle on one's knee and dribbled. But she had never learned to ask for more water in her bowl, or to show when she had a thorn in her foot. And she still failed to realize that the swing-door into the kitchen premises swung both ways. Many times a day she pushed it open with her nose and yelped each time it swung back and hit her smartly on the tail. Only deep humility and a constant desire to please stopped her from being an irritating member of the household.

At work, however, she was a different creature. For the last month, Richard had been lucky enough to get the run of Regent's Park during closing hours, for there had been trespassing and thefts at night from the park side and the authorities had been glad of help. Not that Ranter had caught the malefactors, for as soon as word went round that a bloodhound was loose there after nightfall, the criminal classes simply melted away, in the erroneous belief that a bloodhound would tear their throats out by the dozen. But the little children of the local Sunday school knew better. They competed for the fun of being Ranter's quarry, and the vicar's stock joke, "Now, Tommy, behave yourself or I won't give you to the bloodhound," made Tommy mend his ways at once. Richard Ringwood and the children had great fun plotting out lines for Ranter together.

Last week, in the park, she had traced a scent eighteen hours old from start to finish—her record so far. Today's test was likely to be even more severe. Impossible, thought Ringwood, if Despuys had kept to paved roads. But if he had trodden over mud, grass, or moss—and the bye-roads of that part of Oxford were fairly rough going—there was just a hope, especially on a mild damp day like this. Scent was a queer thing, but Ranter knew more about it than her master, and the attempt was worth making. He would get Mr. Sansom to start them off at the right spot. Perhaps even take him along? A witness often remembered more if one conducted the interview casually.

Unfortunately it was clear, as soon as Mr. Sansom arrived, that he was one of those who are never at ease with large dogs. He flinched every time Ranter made a sudden movement or came within a yard of him, although one could see that he was trying hard to be sensible and helpful. Richard put Ranter on a short lead and tried to scan Sansom covertly as they began walking down the drive. It was a type of learned man he had met before—the Egg-bound Recluse. Research rather than teaching produced them—stiff, tidy creatures, rather formal in speech, and apt to be disconcerted by anything to which they had not adjusted their minds half an hour in advance.

Inelastic, punctual, pallid with a costive, indoor pallor. Such men always looked young for their age unless they were in their twenties; then, they looked old for their years. Sansom was fifty-three. But his hair was not gray; his face was not wrinkled; he had probably looked the same twenty years ago. The thick white nose had not sharpened; the rather expressionless hazel eyes had collected no crows' feet. When people pulled out from the mainstream of life, its currents did not fret their surface, for men only age if they live. The important thing with Egg-bound Recluses was not to rush them. Halfway down the drive, Richard halted and made Ranter lie down behind him. Then he began.

"Mr. Sansom, do you think we might stop and talk here for a minute? It's a bit public right under the windows. It is good of you to come along and help us like this—at such short notice, too."

"Not at all," Sansom replied politely. "Anything I can do, of course … if I *can* help at all. Only"—he seemed more puzzled than annoyed—"I have already been questioned by a police agent yesterday, who was searching for a certain Jean Despuys, and naturally I did my best to supply such information as I could … But excuse me. Perhaps this is something different?"

Richard understood perfectly. Sansom suspected an official bungle, two interviews where one would do. "No," he said. "I've been called in about Despuys too. And I did read what you told my colleagues yesterday. But one likes to—check and expand one's references, so to speak. Details can be so important. I don't need to tell a scholar that."

Sansom nodded. "You are quite right, of course. Quite right. I agree." He seemed pleased.

But just then Ranter half rose, with a low growl. Sansom jumped a foot in the air, and a cat came out of the shrubbery opposite. It took no time at all getting back. Richard quieted Ranter, apologized, and began again. "This man Despuys—do you know him well? Tell me what you think of him. How did you meet?"

Sansom collected his thoughts with a visible effort.

"Jean Despuys is intelligent and amusing. He likes to be in the current. I think he is not the type of person one knows well. Perhaps my own meeting with him will illustrate what I mean. We were introduced at some large party—I no longer remember where it was. Despuys talked to me for a long time, and even took the trouble to walk home with me afterwards. Since then, he has called on me from time to time, and I have invited him to meals occasionally. I have found him very agreeable. He is a most amusing companion, though not perhaps very profound. One enjoys his company. I hope there is no reason to be—concerned about him? Has he still not been—found?"

Richard decided to get it over in one. "Yes," he said, with appropriate gravity, "Despuys *has* been found. His body, that is. Didn't you see the newspapers?"

Sansom blinked and faltered. "No. I don't usually read the papers till just before dinner. His—his *body?* You mean, he is dead? A motor accident, I suppose."

"No, not a motor accident. Murder. He was buried in a haystack and burned. Only the feet were intact."

Sansom stared. He seemed very much upset. "In a haystack? May I ask where?"

"Ten miles out of Oxford, along the London road."

"And you are sure it *was* Despuys? It seems so—so improbable." Sansom's voice suggested as much perplexity as distress.

"Mr. Sansom, to tell you the truth, we aren't downright sure that those feet are the remains of Despuys, though there are certain indications ... and certain tests still to be made. But—forgive me—I don't think it's *im*probable. After all, Despuys is the only person so far reported missing in this district—and they're a young man's feet. Surely it's the likeliest explanation."

Sansom still looked dissatisfied. "Perhaps. Excuse me; but I find it difficult to adjust my mind to the idea. A swimming accident, a car smash—yes. But murder, no. Despuys is not the type to get himself murdered."

"Not the type?" Richard took him up sharply. "What do you mean? Too superficial? Or too cautious?"

Sansom made a little groping gesture. "Excuse me. My ideas are—not very clear. I am shocked."

There! thought Richard with annoyance. I've rushed him, and just when he was making a really intelligent contribution. Because of course he's quite right: ambitious young men whose chief aim is making useful contacts *don't* get murdered. They're too cautious to get into that sort of situation. But Sansom obviously can't say that to *me* without putting his friend Despuys in an unfavorable light. He's torn between decent feeling and a regard for accuracy. How can I put him at his ease?

"Let's walk on," Richard said. They strolled on in silence. Sansom was the first to break it.

"You spoke of certain indications by which you hoped to establish identification?"

"Yes," replied Richard. "I hope my bloodhound is going to be useful. And that's why I asked you to come here. I want you to show me exactly where Despuys was standing when he said good night to you. I'll put the hound on at that point. The hound won't take any notice of the trail he left, unless it corresponds with the scent she is following—the scent of the body in the haystack."

Sansom was quick to see a flaw in the detective's reasoning. "Excuse me. Your test would only prove that a *man* was at Melford House who was subsequently murdered and burned in a haystack. It would not prove that the body was that of Despuys. Have you no other means of establishing identity?"

Richard tried to joke off the question. "I didn't know I had to deal with a formal logician, but ..."

"I'm not a logician." Sansom did not smile. "I'm a military historian."

"... but anyhow," Richard went on, "I shan't give up hope yet."

"Nor shall I!" Sansom spoke with unaccustomed fire. "I shall not give up my hope that Jean Despuys is alive. I will not believe that he is murdered. It is a distressing and unnecessary supposition. To me, at any rate."

Richard apologized at once. "Sorry—that was a bad way of putting it. Of course I, too, hope your friend is alive—and I hope to prove it as soon as possible. Shall we get this business over? Would you come and show us the place where you last saw Despuys yesterday evening, please?"

He opened the cardboard box. The single human foot—its color, its isolation, the fact that it stopped at the ankle in a charred mess like an overdone Sunday joint—had its effect on the spectators. Sansom and Colman turned away. Richard said, "Find, girl, find!" And Ranter sank her muzzle over the box and inhaled deeply.

CHAPTER 7

"Here? By the front door?" asked Richard.

Sansom nodded.

"Here, Ranter, here! Seek, girl, seek!"

The hound dropped its muzzle to the ground right at Sansom's feet, and he stepped back so hastily that he was caught in a spray of rambler roses and lost his hat. Colman extricated him, for Richard was busy holding Ranter's leash as she cast about, methodically going over the ground in front of the house. She did not miss an inch and she sniffed hard all the time—so hard, indeed, that every now and then she had to stop, sit back on her haunches, and take in great gulps of air. Then she would nose the box again and resume work. She went over the drive, the circular lawn in front of the house, and the flower beds, slowly and in silence. Then she sat down again for one of her air-gulping interludes. Richard said:

"Well, Mr. Sansom, it begins to look as if you were right and our corpse wasn't Despuys after all. If that foot had trodden here, I'm sure my bloodhound would have … Oh, damn it, Ranter, behave yourself! Come here!"

She had jerked the lead out of his hand, broken away, and begun to quest round the side of the house. Richard ran after her and caught the lead, but she would not follow him back. At the third command, she raised her solemn head with a look of reproach.

"You brought me here to find that scent, didn't you?" she seemed to say. "But I've hardly had a chance yet. Surely you don't want me to stop? This is my job, you know."

Perseverance was her virtue, as obstinacy was her fault. Richard knew from experience that only force would move her. She was now too heavy to be easily dragged away, and in any case it would be bad training. The whole art of handling a bloodhound is to harness its natural powers, not to frustrate them.

"Oh, all right, go on if you must. Find, Ranter, find!"

He followed her round to the back of the house. Sansom appeared to be uncertain whether his role was finished, or not; he hovered just within call.

Up and down, round and round Ranter led Richard in wider and wider casts, no longer pausing for breath. They were now at the back of the house, outside the common room. He could see through the bay windows a vista of easy chairs, and a few men reading. There was a door into the garden just beside this.

Ranter suddenly sat back on her haunches, lifted her muzzle and gave three barks, deep and sharp. No sound she had uttered today was like this. The note was as deep as a drum and as thrilling as a trumpet. To a human ear it sounded mournful and full of uncanny menace. Alarmed faces appeared at the windows.

But Richard knew that voice. It was a cry of triumph. Ranter had found at last—found the place trodden by that poor charred foot when, only yesterday, it had been part of a living body. She was straining now to follow where it led. He beckoned, and Colman ran up.

"He came out at the back," Richard said under his breath. "Not the front. See if you can … oh, Lord! I can't hold her much longer!"

"Your dog has found something?" Sansom asked, from a respectful distance.

"Yes, she's found where that foot trod," Richard replied, hanging on to Ranter's lead with difficulty. "You're sure Despuys left by the front door? You went down the drive with him?"

"No, now you come to ask it. I had taken it for granted that he went out by the front door. Just as we were leaving I remembered that I had to speak to one of my colleagues before he left, and mentioned this. Despuys would not let me come further than the hall in case I missed him, so we said goodbye there. I suppose Despuys could have gone out by the back, but it does not seem likely. Perhaps your dead man was here, and left that way. But—perhaps he was not Jean Despuys."

"Well—perhaps. I think such a coincidence is unlikely. Come along with us and see which way he went."

Ranter barked and could be held no longer. She tugged him at a run down the garden to a wicket gate in the fence leading into the university parks, sat back, gave tongue again, and gathered her powerful loins to jump the gate. But Richard opened it in time and they sprang out together over tussocky grass that whipped against their legs. Someone had gone through that long grass before. Looking ahead, Richard saw it trodden in a swathe on the very line Ranter was taking.

"Slow, Ranter, slow! Slow!"

This was not to save his breath. In the ancient partnership of man and hound, it was the man's business to watch the track for visible clues. Even so the *lymerers* in Norman times were trained to notice the *fumes* and *slots*, the dung and footprints which told them the age and sex of the deer and whether it would be good sport and good meat. Here in the parks, however, the grass was too thick for footprints, and clues were hard to see. But the Noble Art of Venery had an answer. When the *lymer* runs fast over rough ground, say the books, let the *lymerer* peg out the line with "a pouchful of peeled twigs" and examine it again at his leisure. Richard had a bunch of wooden seed markers in his pocket, marked in indelible pencil PO-LICE. DO NOT MOVE, and he stooped in his run to jab one in every now and then. Ranter was heading south across the parks, in the direction of Despuys' lodgings.

They came to a cricket pitch being mowed by a man with a mo-tor-mower, and Ranter checked, losing the scent. Richard let her cast back along the way they had come, for he knew that she was not "hunting counter," that is, following the line the wrong way as silly young hounds will do. She was just making quite sure that the quarry had really come as far as the edge of the cricket pitch. Rich-ard was glad of the delay, for it brought the other two within earshot and a question had just occurred to him.

"Were the parks locked up when Despuys left you?" he shouted.

Sansom did not answer and he could see Colman repeating the question.

"He says he doesn't know."

The man with the mowing machine, who had stopped work to watch, told them that locking-up time was about nine o'clock. But just then Ranter found the line on the other side of the pitch, gave tongue loudly, and dragged her master away.

She took him straight to the park gate nearest Despuys' lodging. Only a short rough road, with a muddy turf-edged footwalk, lay between it and Priory Road. Richard noticed that the gate was not easy to climb and that there was a place in the fence nearby that looked usable and bore marks of having been used. He dragged Ranter off the path by the gate—she was reluctant and very heavy—and set her to seek by the fence. She tried it conscientiously but did not make a sound and kept edging back to the gate. Once back there, she gave tongue again and tugged to be off.

"Wait, Ranter!" Richard said, and pointed to the gate itself. "Here! Here!"

She sniffed it but obviously drew a blank. It was an iron gate, unlikely to hold scent or footmarks. Richard thought that if it had been locked, one would climb the easier fence. But Ranter seemed sure her quarry had gone by the gate. So it was probably open. So Despuys had come through it before nine. Or else—

"Colman! Ask him if Despuys had a key!" Richard shouted, try-ing to make himself heard above Ranter, who had accepted the de-lay as an opportunity for a short aria and was enjoying the sound of her own voice. He saw Colman nod comprehension.

"Forward, Ranter! Sue forward!"

Ranter was on the road now, more difficult ground than the grass and soft gravel of the parks, though fortunately not much used and still fairly muddy. She took her time, casting about to make sure of the line, and settled for the dirt path, which was divided from the road by a strip of turf. Presently she stopped, sat down, and lifted her muzzle once more.

"Very nice," said her master, "but why the concert? You generally run almost mute. Oh, I see. Good girl! Well done!"

Between her paws was a white handkerchief. It had been rained on and was muddy outside but the inner folds were clean. It bore the now familiar mark PEN 154, the mark of Francis Clandon, who was alive and accounted for. But wait! Richard looped the lead twice round his arm so as to hold in Ranter and have his hands steady. Here was another mark—a name, in faded marking-ink. F.J. Clandon. Not carried by Clandon last night. He had an alibi, of course. But more than that. If it had been carried and dropped by anyone last night *except* the murdered man, Ranter would have taken no notice of it. Once set to follow a line, she was oblivious of everything but what smelt of her quarry: literally, she had a one-track mind. Despuys, then, had dropped the handkerchief.

She led him now to the pillar box at the corner of Priory Road—that corner where the old lady had broken her leg, and cried for help in vain, on a freezing night last winter. The path was paved here with oblong grooved slates which did not show footprints, but there was moss and grass in the chinks between them and here, presumably, scent still lay. At any rate, Ranter bayed again. Had Despuys—if it was Despuys—stood here for some time? Why? Trying to make up his mind whether to post a letter? Arguing with someone? Odd!

Ranter was off again, running confidently, in an unexpected direction, and over unpromising ground. She went right across the tarred surface of Priory Road. He was surprised that she could find any scent there, especially the faint trace of shod feet twenty-four hours ago. So far, she'd never found a scent actually *on* the road, except once when an engaging urchin had lain down and rolled across it, on his own initiative, to see what would happen. Then, she'd followed straight across as she was doing now. Still …

And here was another strange thing. Instead of turning down towards the river, where Despuys' lodging was, she led him *up* the road, away from the river. Up past the church towards a row of gnarled elm trees. Even in daylight, the mossy ground under them was in deep shadow. Sansom had caught up and was plucking his sleeve.

"Your dog is going the wrong way," he said. "Would not Despuys be making for home? He lived down there."

Before he could answer, Ranter stopped, cast round for a minute and then, planting her forelegs like columns over a particular patch of ground and settling herself firmly, she lifted her muzzle and gave her voice full freedom. It pealed out, in deep, sobbing, throttled music, eerie even in daylight, heart-searching as the Last Trump. Richard knelt and looked between her round tawny paws. There were dark spots on the moss. He took a specimen for the chemists, but he and Ranter knew what it was already. It was blood—the blood of a murdered man. Still pouring out her unearthly music, Ranter looked at him with innocent pride and thumped her tail on the ground.

"Good girl!" he said, patting her and feeling in his pockets for her reward. "Well done! But how the devil did he get from here to Wheatley? Colman, look round and see if you can find traces of a car. Ask at the houses, too; see if they heard anything. Mr. Sansom, just stand still, will you? By that tree there. I don't want the ground trodden over. Yes, Ranter. In a minute! Good girl! Why, Ranter, what the devil's up with you? Come back!"

For Ranter had dropped her muzzle, lifted it, and strained to smell as a short-sighted man strains his eyes to see. Then she sprang—or so it seemed—straight for Sansom as he stood obediently by the tree. He cried out and fell. Richard rushed to his help. He hadn't been bitten, but he'd fainted. Leaving Colman to revive him, Richard turned back to his hound. She was on her hind legs against the tree trying to get her nose down a hole halfway up the trunk, and baying like mad. Richard hauled her off and put his own hand down the hole. There was a flutter, a noise like a child being strangled, and out flew two little owls.

"Ha! Ranter! Bad dog!" he admonished her. "Hunting owls at your age! Shame! And look what you've done to the poor gentleman!"

But then he relented. After all, she had done well on the whole, and it wasn't fair to scold her about owls. She had tracked her man, and now deserved a reward and her master's praise.

"All right, old lady. Good dog! There you are! Lie down now. Ha! Lie down! Well done! Down!" Richard managed to quiet her and tie her to another tree just before Sansom came round—which he did slowly and crossly, in French.

"*Qu'il me laisse tranquille, cette sale bête! J'lui ai rien fait, à lui!* Make this dirty beast leave me alone!"

"I'm frightfully sorry, but the hound didn't mean to hurt you. Look, she's tied up now, and wagging her tail to show how sorry she is."

Sansom began, unsteadily, to rise.

"*Elle me porte sur les nerfs*," he muttered, still in French, brushing his new and (Richard noticed) expensive suit. "She gets on my nerves." He asked for his hat. Colman held it out, and Sansom smoothed his hair, which was smartly cut, short at the back and longish at the sides and front, before he put the hat on. Evidently he dressed with care. Egg-bound Recluses often did; perhaps it was a timid unconscious attempt to get back into the contemporary world. And perhaps the dinners to Despuys were another such gesture. Poor Mr. Sansom!

"I'll go back for the car and take you home," Richard said to him. "Really I'm very sorry. Are you feeling quite all right, now?"

"I should like to sit down." Sansom was still brushing himself. "In the church porch, perhaps?"

"Of course. I'll give you an arm, shall I? Colman, you're in charge."

As they walked away together, Sansom asked if Ringwood had found any "indications." Richard tried to keep the triumph out of his voice as he replied, "Yes. A trail from Melford House to here; blood on the ground; tire marks in the road, of a car that stopped and started again. In fact, every sign that Despuys was attacked here and carried off afterwards."

"Despuys?" Sansom's face was not apt to register feelings, but his arm stiffened against Richard's. "You have proved it was Despuys?"

"Well, as a working hypothesis. Economy of explanation, you know."

"Ah!" Sansom stared bleakly, sighed, then spread his handkerchief on the seat and sat down. "You will require me again?"

"Not till the case comes up in court, probably. Why? Are you planning a holiday?"

"No. I am devoting this summer to my work. But I find that all this is too, too...."

"Distressing. Of course. Well, cheer up! As you say, nothing is proved yet. We'll get you home in ten minutes and try not to worry you again. I'll probably be in France for a bit, anyhow."

And he and Ranter hurried back across the parks for the car.

CHAPTER 8

Richard rang up the chief constable from the public box in Priory Road, eager to report Ranter's triumph. Yes, Despuys was obviously their murdered man, and had been attacked on his way home. Yes, his—Richard stopped. He had been on the point of saying, "Yes, my bloodhound has proved it," but changed gear just in time to regain control.

"Well," he went on, "it does give us a basis to work on. But that's about all. It's illogical to hope one can put dumb friends in the witness-box—after all, speech is the essence of witness—quite apart from the fact that identification by smell alone might turn out a tricky point at law. And we've still no indications of who killed him. Sansom, anyway, seems to be in the clear. His landlady's family heard him come in at ten, do some typing, and have a bath soon after midnight—just about the time your people say the haystack was set on fire. What's more, Sansom hasn't got either a car or a driving license, and I'm sure Despuys was taken out there by car. So I'm afraid I haven't done any good at all, really."

He listened for a moment to congratulations and reassurances. They seemed warm enough for him to come to the point. He asked the chief constable, who alone had the necessary authority, if he would investigate the bank account and other financial documents of Despuys. The poor man assented heartily, never anticipating that the enquiries were bound to spread to a French bank and a bursary committee at the Sorbonne. Richard said, "You can't imagine how much trouble that will save me," reflected that this was the literal truth, and felt like one stabbing a gift horse in the back.

"Colman's just returning Sansom to store. Then he'll record the tire marks here and go back along the trail in case we've missed any clues. Meanwhile, I'll get going on Despuys' private life. I'll start with this man Clandon at Pentecost. He must have known Despuys pretty well to lend him socks and things. No, he can't be a suspect, he was presiding at a dining club and I guess he was a bit drunk, too. What? Clandon's been in court already? Oh, I don't count Guy Fawkes. So was I, come to that. Dangerous driving too? Still, it's a long step from that to homicide. If we lumped dangerous driving in with attempted homicide, we'd leave no one at large to make our laws for us. Think of—But thank you for telling me. Yes, I'll try to see him alone. But as you say, the college has to be told, and they may insist on having somebody else there. Suppose I call on the praefect first and try to work it?"

The chief constable concurred heartily, and felt like one setting a ewe lamb to catch a Tartar.

* * *

"I don't want to discourage you," Dr. Burdock was saying a quarter of an hour later with his usual confidential charm, "but if Clandon is really the only person you can get to answer these questions— well, between ourselves, he doesn't *interview* very satisfactorily. *We* know him, of course, but a stranger might find him rather—confused. And his father, Lord Clandon, would be most upset if the boy, er, talked nonsense in public and made an ass of himself. That sort of thing counts so much more in the business world, you see, and Francis inherits the title, so he's got to go into trade—can't afford not to. Something to do with sewage, I believe. Perhaps I should get their lawyer to be present—an Exeter firm, I think. This is really the dean's province, you know, but—" brightening—"he's in London for the night. And the junior dean …"

Richard explained why he couldn't wait for an Exeter lawyer, the dean, or the junior dean.

"Just so, just so. I'm afraid we're giving you a lot of bother. Oh, by the way, I must apologize about the laundrymarks. These laundries are quite dreadful, indelible hieroglyphics splodged all over one's shirts, and apparently not even the *right* hiero- glyphics. One might be a prisoner or a patient in hospital for all they care. We used to have a dear old college washerwoman up at Headington, but she had to give up when her daughter mar- ried in 1927, I think it was, or was it 1928? The bursar's office could tell you straight away."

Countering charm with charm and delay with persistence, Rich- ard was not wasting his time. The praefect rambled on and his ramblings built up, stroke by stroke, a character sketch of young Clandon. A spender usually short of money; a liar, whose lies were ingenuous; young for his age and youthfully self-important, but easily dazzled by sophistication and easily flustered by authority.

"Another thing—I'm afraid you'll find young Clandon hasn't been seeing so much of your Frenchman lately. I'm told he's rather dropped out of the so-called cosmopolitan set since he's been sharing rooms with Tim Dawson-Gower. Do you know him? If I admitted the taunt that Pentecost men are picked for birth, worth, and brains, in that order, I'd certainly put Tim under worth. Such a pity about that sudden illness and being sent abroad. I expect you've met his brother Nigel, something of a wartime hero, I'm told; they say he's the Englishman in *Le Cri Sourd*, that Resistance book, you know, that all the French authors afterwards claimed to have written anonymously. He was here only yesterday."

With little prompting, the praefect told the story of Tim's sudden departure. Then Richard said that he must really get on and see Clandon.

"Of course. I mustn't keep you. Shall we send for him here or had we better save time by going to look for him in his rooms?" He rose and led the way to the front door.

That word *we*, so deftly inserted, made Richard want to howl. Fortunately Ranter, sitting outside in the car and hearing her master's approach, howled first. He let her out, thrust her lead into the praefect's hands, and begged him to harbor her, as dogs weren't allowed in college rooms. Perhaps he could spare her a drink of water. Ranter hung out her tongue pleadingly.

"In, Ranter!" he said, and Ranter, bless her, began towing the praefect into his own front hall. "That *is* good of you. I'll just run across to Clandon's rooms and be straight back."

The hound and the head both looked put out, and no wonder. But three-quarters of an hour later, when he returned, they were fast friends. The praefect was trying her with Norman hunting cries, which, he said, had a history of great antiquity. Ranter took to them well.

* * *

Richard was startled and embarrassed to find that Clandon had a girl with him. Embarrassed, because he hadn't foreseen that particular complication; startled, because, although she was a most elegant and attractive creature, she and the young man were apparently construing Virgil together for their exam. Oxford had changed since his time. Still, they made a nice-looking couple.

Richard introduced himself without explanation. Clandon introduced Laura Fenning, also without explanation. An awkward pause ensued. Then the girl rose and said,

"Goodness! I must fly! Don't forget the dentist tomorrow, Francis. Nine-thirty. I'll meet you in the waiting room."

She apologized to Richard for leaving so abruptly, kissed Clandon in a manner unembarrassing to third parties, and went off in pretty style. Richard sat down and began talking, and the big fair young man in the chair opposite gradually disintegrated into a sandy, gangling boy, whose anxiety to put himself in a good light made him stray constantly from the point, and inspired the listener with irritation verging on disbelief.

Yes, he had seen a lot of Jean des Puys last year, but not so much this. To be absolutely frank, Tim Dawson-Gower, his roommate, hadn't much cared for him, and besides there'd been this work crisis. He and Tim had been practically hermits this term. Well, practically. Of course there were some things one couldn't just drop. Exercise—you had to keep fit, didn't you? And if you had a car, it was false economy not to take time out to maintain it properly …

Oh, Jean. Sorry. Well, he was a terrific social type and very interesting in his way. These old French families seemed to be right at the center of things in Paris. Jean had met people like Sartre and Cocteau and had lots of stories about them. Some of the stories weren't terribly on-color, still—No, Jean's family didn't live in Paris, in fact Jean had taken this flat he had in Paris partly to get away from them a bit. No, Jean hadn't gone over there much since Francis had known him. People in England were always asking him to stay with them. Oh, no. He was sure Jean wasn't short of money. He'd never said so, whereas most people always did at some point, didn't they?

"Look," said Richard, "I've seen his papers. His name wasn't des Puys with the *des* separate, it was Despuys, and there's no noble family in France with that name as far as I know. His address wasn't a Paris one, it was a number in a street in a rather small town on the Loire. He was up at Oxford on a bursary. And his landlady, Mrs. Raymond Gyles, said she'd invited him to live there as a guest. He'd said, no, he must pay her something. But as a matter of fact no money has passed and he's been there three terms. Didn't you even begin to see through him?"

Francis flushed. To be absolutely frank, he was a pretty good judge of character, but naturally, one didn't like to run somebody down if he was—dead. And after all, Jean *did* know quite a lot of people, really *people*, and that made one wonder, though Tim was only remarking the other day that Jean was always going to people's parties but he never asked you back. And another thing. Francis and Tim had both been looking for a family to go to in France, and Jean had fixed it up for them. Tim had gone last summer and Francis this spring. Well, that was all right, in fact they were a very nice family though they didn't know Jean personally. But to be absolutely frank, when Francis had been about to go, he had asked Jean whether he could spend a few nights in Jean's flat in Paris on the way, and Jean had said, no, it was being redecorated. And then Francis had asked him for introductions to some of his distinguished friends in Paris. After all, it was all education, wasn't it? These French writers might be a bit off-color in some ways, but people here gave them honorary degrees, which just showed, didn't it? Yes, well, Jean had promised he'd write direct to some of these people and ask them to get in touch with Francis at his hotel. But Francis waited two days and nothing happened. So then he had gone to see an American girl he knew at UNESCO who also knew Jean, to see if she could help. She said that on the only occasion she'd met Jean in Paris—they had been introduced at Oxford—she had asked him in for drinks and he had made a great impression on the other people who were there— he seemed to know everyone in England like Graham Greene and Noel Coward and told a lot of stories about their private lives, but she didn't think he knew many celebrities in Paris.

"Well, nothing clicked just then. Mary-Lou was in the middle of a terrific family crisis and I thought she was just pushing me off. And anyhow I couldn't afford to stay in Paris more than a few days. But I did remember later on that last term I'd heard Jean talking to a man in Pentecost, a friend of mine, who knew Graham Greene very slightly, and simply begging him to introduce him. So he can't really have known him, can he?"

"Did you ask about those letters of introduction? Had he written them?"

"I found a letter from him waiting for me at Pontchâtelet about that. He said he'd lost his address book and apologized for not hav- ing done his stuff. And he said next time I was in Paris he would make a point of being there too, so as to take me round. Well, that part seemed all right, but ..." He hesitated. "This bit isn't terribly on-color, actually. I've never mentioned it to anyone before. Will you ...?"

"Don't worry, I'm discreet. My guess is that Despuys sent you some night-life addresses as a consolation prize, knowing what the English are brought up to expect of France. Was that it?"

Francis protested. "It wasn't like that, I mean I wouldn't, well … To be absolutely frank, he did give me the address of what he said was a very gallant woman. I swear I hadn't any idea, that bit was in French, you see. I thought she'd been in the Resistance or something. I thought that was why he warned me to be very discreet and not say anything to the family I was staying with."

Une femme très galante. Was it possible Francis had not understood this French expression? On the other hand, could anybody make up a story like that against themselves? Richard wondered. He was beginning to know Francis's range of expressions, and last time he had stared in that limpid, injured way was when he was claiming to be a hermit. Now, he was claiming to have come away, of course, the moment he realized what sort of woman this was.

"What was she like?"

"Awful. I can't tell you." The shudder was obviously genuine. "Absolutely the outside edge. As I said to Jean, being broad-minded is one thing, but one has to draw the line somewhere. I was pretty frank with him."

"You had a quarrel with him when you got back here, did you?"

Francis flinched from the admission. "Not at all, at least not exactly. I mean, he did apologize, but I felt quite differently about him, as if there was a—a moral gulf between us." He paused, pleased with the phrase. Richard waited for a definition of Despuys' particular kind of turpitude, and it was forthcoming. "A moral gulf, that's what it was. He'd showed me up as a perfect fool. As far as any ideas of decent behavior are concerned, I said, it's obvious that you and I have nothing in common."

"Splendid! And yet, as far as socks and laundrymarks were concerned, you apparently went on having everything in common. How was that?"

"Sorry, I don't … oh, ha-ha, I see what you mean. Very neat, that! Yes, he *did* go on sending his laundry in with mine, just as he always had. I thought it was a bit off-color of him, actually, but *I* couldn't say anything, could I? One may bar somebody, but one doesn't want to be vindictive. Besides, he didn't make it an excuse to come in and talk, like he used to. He simply handed it to Varlett, my scout. In fact, that was the last time I set eyes on him, when he was nattering about laundry with Varlett one day last week."

And had Despuys paid for his washing? asked Richard. Francis was vague. He didn't think so, unless he'd given the money to Varlett; anyhow, one didn't have to *pay*. It was "charged for." And it couldn't be much, could it? Ten shillings a week! Really?

Had he missed any of his linen since the arrangement with Jean? With simple fatalism he replied, not more than usual. When you weren't at home and hadn't got anyone to look after your clothes, *things*, he explained, *went*. Sometimes, of course, it was the other way round. Things, occasionally, came. There had been a Terylene shirt that turned up once, and he and Tim had both worn it sometimes; honestly, it was so electric that when you took it off and put it in a drawer, it opened the drawer and came out and put itself on you again. Amazing. That was unusual luck, though. On the whole, things "went." He took Richard into his bedroom, a dank little box in a state of great confusion, and sure enough, there were only two clean shirts, one marked with Tim's name and one not marked at all. There were also six dirty ones in various places, two of which Francis felt fairly sure were his own. None bore the name of Despuys. It became obvious that identification by laundrymarks was, in this community, a forlorn hope.

Returning to the sitting room, they found Colman, just arrived with a note from the chief constable. Richard read it, dismissed him, and settled down again with Clandon.

"Did you ever lend Despuys money?"

Francis stared, this time rather haughtily. "To be absolutely frank, I can't remember. My friends and I do borrow sometimes, of course, but naturally it's the chap that owes the money who is expected to remember about it. Personally I always make a point of that. In fact, I can definitely say that I never borrowed from Jean when we were friends. But I can't swear I didn't lend to him. I'd have trusted him to remember that—then."

"Anyway, you're sure you didn't lend him money this term?"

Francis opened his eyes still more candidly. "No, sir. I told you, from my point of view, he was definitely barred."

"In that case," said Richard, fingering the note he had just read, "can you explain why you've been drawing quite heavily on your bank account this term, despite an overdraft, whereas Despuys hasn't cashed any checks at all for ages, but has been paying in fairly large sums in pound notes? It seems to connect, doesn't it?" For the first time he gave Francis a return stare. It was like a sword unsheathed. But he said quite kindly, "What *have* you been up to?"

Francis was practically popeyed with innocence as he began, "To be absolutely …" But he couldn't stand up to the impact. He dropped his head and began picking at a loose thread in the arm of the chair. "It's no good," he mumbled. "I haven't given him any money but … Perhaps I'd better, er, tell you about it, sir. If you aren't, er, too busy?"

As he had guessed, it was a story of blackmail. At first Despuys had threatened to tell Francis' father about the visit to the *femme galante*. Francis had replied that his father was so hard up that it would, on the whole, be kinder to shock him than to make him pay. Despuys then invented a subtler form of threat. He said that he would get the woman to send Laura written evidence that Francis had visited her but had proved a wholly incompetent lover. Yes, thought Richard. That's it. His shudder when he spoke of her ought to have told me. At this, Francis would have done anything to shut the Frenchman's mouth; but he begged for time. He was overdrawn already. All right, said Despuys, he would take it in services—Francis could have him to stay, introduce him to people, put him up for election to certain clubs. In the end Francis consented, only asking for grace till his examination at the end of term. If he didn't pass this time, he'd be sent down, and that would be killing the goose that laid the golden eggs, wouldn't it? Despuys realized the force of the argument, and promised to leave him in peace, apart from the small matter of the laundry, until the end of term. After that, he would expect him to be at his service.

"And I thought, you see—well, Laura does know me better now. I'd hoped that perhaps later on, if I told her the truth, she might take my word even against that woman's letter. Then I'd be clear of the whole trouble. But I don't know. It isn't an easy thing to tell a girl like her. I mean, Laura's so completely on-color, you know. And besides, if she did believe me, she'd still think I'd behaved like a perfect idiot. Whereas up to now, you see, she believes in me absolutely. 'S matter of fact," he added in a final burst of confidence, "I sometimes think she's the only person who does. Even Tim—well, he and I get on fine, but he's always going on at me not to be such a bloody fool."

The less young Clandon tried to impress one, the more he engaged one's sympathies. Surely Laura would feel the same? She looked a nice girl and no fool. All the same, the information from the bank took some explaining. In a life where drinks, tobacco, stationery, meals—almost all normal day-to-day expenses—didn't have to be "paid for," as Francis put it, because they were charged on the end-of-term bill, surely five pounds or more a week was a high rate of petty cash for a man who was practically a hermit? Richard said so.

"Oh, but I didn't spend it on myself," said Francis. "It was for the Camel, you know, our car. She's a vintage Aurora, 1923 actually, and Tim and I are gradually getting her back to her original form. It *is* rather expensive to start with, I mean she only does eight miles to the gallon so far, and then there's the odd running repair. I know it *sounds* a lot, but Tim's going to pay me back half after his twenty-first birthday, and anyhow we reckon that when she's really running well she'll easily save us what we've spent on her. We never, even now, go by train anywhere."

Richard's sympathies were further engaged. He too was a Jaco-bite of the motoring world, clinging to an old car with loyalty that cost him dear (forty pounds on the gearbox, two new tires, and a rebore in the near future) and he could almost believe Francis. But he said he'd like to see the Camel.

"I wish you could, sir. But the bother is, Tim's brother Nigel borrowed her to drive home in on Sunday. They had her out and apparently Nigel missed his train or something—I know Tim only just got into college in time—and I think Tim was going up to col-lect her, only the doctors suddenly ordered him abroad the next day. I suppose Nigel will do something about it. I only hope she's under cover."

Was this the connection at last? Richard tried hard to make Fran-cis admit that the Dawson-Gowers knew of his trouble with Despuys, but he steadfastly denied it. Suppose he was lying? Suppose the brothers—one of them was an ex-commando, a trained desperado—had taken the law into their own hands? One could easily imagine a "beating-up" in Priory Road which had ended in a death and a body to hide. They had smuggled the body out of Oxford in the car, to the haystack, and but for two incalculable events—the wind changing suddenly so that the feet remained unburned, and a bloodhound be-ing brought to identify the feet as those of Despuys—they would never have been suspected. Now, of course, even Francis could guess something—enough to feel that he must at all costs deny that the Dawson-Gowers knew of the blackmail. Francis may even have told Tim and forgotten afterwards. But only if he was drunk at the time. That too was not impossible.

Well, Tim had bolted and could no doubt be caught. Meanwhile, it was more important to get the car; there was perhaps a clue in it that Ranter could find, but not for long. Scent was tricky.

CHAPTER 9

"Come on! We must go and see the praefect at once!"

"Oh, I say, sir, you won't—"

"No, of course not. I just want to get you to a telephone quickly. You've got to ring up Nigel Dawson-Gower at once and find where that car of yours is. Got his number?"

Ranter welcomed her master, full of emotion but not, unfortunately, too full for sound or foam. The praefect had time for a good look at Francis; and seeing him appear unaffectedly worried, not artificially self-righteous, sighed with relief. Francis sat and telephoned at one end of the room, while Richard, at the other, questioned the praefect in whispers about Tim's departure. They fell silent when the phone was answered.

"Is that Nigel Dawson-Gower? Oh! His secretary, I see. Well, I'm Francis Clandon. No, I don't think you can, really; sorry, but it's a personal thing. I'm a friend of his brother's. What? He left a message? For me? Well, thank you very much. At High Wycombe? Why? A breakdown? No, of course you wouldn't. Well, please thank him. Just a second, I'll write it down."

"Don't hang up; tell her to hold on. Praefect, would you ask about that specialist now? Speak to Dawson-Gower himself, if possible."

The praefect, who hated telephones, announced himself and his business and asked for Nigel Dawson-Gower in person. There was a long pause.

"Bother!" said the praefect. "The machine's gone orf."

Richard shot out his hand just in time to stop the "machine" from being put back on the stand; as he did so, it began to talk, The praefect again listened, clinging to the receiver with both hands. He looked up.

"She says he isn't there. She doesn't know anything about the specialist; he hadn't said anything to her. Shall I mention that it's a pol—"

Richard just clapped his hand over the mouthpiece in time.

"They can't hear us now. No, Praefect, don't say that. Just ask her if she knows where he is." He did so.

"She says she doesn't know. He only went out a few minutes ago and he said he'd be in early tomorrow. Which thing do I put my hand over? Thank you. I must say, for a business man's secretary, she doesn't sound much good. The telephone seems to fluster her. Our Miss Pinfold never dithers like that. Shall I ask anything else?"

"No, thanks." The praefect rang off. "Those pauses told me all I wanted to know at present. I must hurry. Let's just write down his number, and—have you his home address? Thank you. Now I must rush off and look at that car straight away. I'll have to take Mr. Clandon to tell me if it's the same as usual. Is that all right? We'll be back in a couple of hours. Could I look in on you then?"

"Do, do. Would you like to leave, er, Ranter, here? I find her charming company."

"Thank you, Praefect. But I'll be using her."

One could see the old man take the point; he ran away from it like a lapwing.

"Ah? Then I know what to say to her. *Ca sy avaunt, mon amy*," he said in Old French. "You see? She half understands. One is almost inclined to think in terms of race memory. Though surely verbal memory is—"

But the three of them were in the car and away.

*   *   *

At first Clandon talked secondhand cars to Ringwood. Then he began to make friends with Ranter, and it wasn't until several minutes later that he thought of asking what she was to be used for this time. Richard told him; he saw the cardboard box by his feet and heard what was in it. He turned very pale and shrank away from the box, but said stoutly enough, "I'm sure you won't find anything. Tim and Nigel wouldn't, I mean, it's inconceivable to anyone who knows them—"

"Then what are you so upset about?"

"Well, it's—when you just hear someone's dead, it's sort of— like if they've gone to Australia. You know, you think, well I won't be seeing him again. And quite often you don't really mind much. But—that—sort of brings it home. Poor Jean! He wasn't bad in some ways, you know, and I was awfully upstage with him. Goodness knows, if we'd all been nicer to him, perhaps—oh, I don't know! It's too late to make up for it now."

"No, it isn't." Richard slowed down. "I'm sorry about that rather gruesome bit of luggage, but I'm not allowed to let it out of my sight. Would you like to go and keep Ranter company in the back?"

Francis changed places in silence. But silence was not his natural state for long at a time. Presently he enquired of the back of Richard's neck, "I say, sir, do you believe in hell?"

"Well, yes, in principle. I can't say that I've ever known anyone who seemed genuinely qualified to go there. Why?"

They talked about hell for some time; Francis cheered up considerably. Then he began asking about the training of bloodhounds. He was very keen on all that, he said, and wished he could have just lived in the country, like his father. Richard, who had struggled bitterly with his own father against this very fate, soon saw that young Francis knew more about hounds than he did. No wonder. He was reacting the other way. On this subject Francis spoke with confidence, and by the time they reached High Wycombe and found the Camel safe in a garage, he had recovered his nerve, and did not flinch at the grim routine of setting Ranter on. He even helped to heave her up into the interior of the car, for the brass footplates were not easy for four large paws.

Once inside, Ranter seemed uncertain. Perhaps the oily machine-smells of the garage distracted her. She quested about obstinately inside the car, refused to be called off, and was not entirely mute, but the sounds she uttered were like those made by a harmonium when the air supply is inadequate. And though obstinate in her quest, she seemed strangely listless. Richard began to lose hope.

"Francis, get up and see if there's anything different about the inside of the car since you saw it last, will you? Anything missing that ought to be there—anything disturbed—you know. I'll just be making a cast of the tires."

Francis climbed up, out of his sight where he knelt half-beneath the front wheel. He heard him muttering something about a rug and having to take the seats up.

And then he sprang to his feet, for Ranter had given tongue unmistakably. Francis was crouched on the floor of the car, very pale, with one end of a damp, stained old rug in his hands. Ranter, with straddled paws, was holding down the other end and baying like Cocytus itself. There was no questioning that note. The rug had wrapped the body. It was spotted with blood.

Richard took the rug and gave Ranter a couple of biscuits for her reward, which she wolfed and then lay down, panting. Francis, still on the floor beside her, mechanically picked up a fallen crumb of biscuit, and she licked it from the palm of his hand. He stared at Richard.

"It can't be true!" he was saying over and over again. "It can't be! What? Oh yes, I'm all right. I'll come down."

He climbed down, leaving the door open, and Richard called to Ranter to follow. But she loomed over them and seemed afraid of the five-foot drop to the ground.

"Come on, Ranter! You've jumped twice that. Good girl!"

She jumped, but landed heavily and immediately lay down on her side, panting. Richard suddenly seized the young man by the shoulders. He could hardly speak.

"What have you done to her, you—you? Poisoned her? My God, if you have—! But she gave you away first, didn't she?"

"No. You don't understand." Francis sounded tired and hopeless. "The body may have been put in the car somehow, but I swear Tim and Nigel can't have had anything to do with it. As for the hound—" his voice suddenly took edge. "Let go of me. Let me look at her. Come on, old lady, there! Yes, I thought so." He looked up. "You'd better get a vet to come at once or we'll have her pupping here on the floor. What on earth did you joggle her about in a car for? How long had she still got to go? Less than a fortnight, by the looks of her."

Richard began to calculate in a stunned silence. Yes, it was possible. Ranter had been in her old kennels with the Somerset pack again over Whitsun. And he hadn't remembered. ...

"Oh Lord!" he said. "And my wife's having her first baby."

Francis came back from phoning the vet in time to hear this.

"Oh, er, is she?" Then, with a wicked, comforting grin, "One thing, women do give you longer notice. Bloodhound bitches only go ten weeks from start to finish. What about the sire?"

"A very good bloodhound indeed. But I told the man we'd wait till the autumn. Must have been an accident."

"Just as well, really," said Francis. "The pups'll do better this weather."

The vet arrived, and was comforting. He said that bloodhound pups were very small at birth, and even breeders had been taken unawares. Ranter had taken her injection well and would probably last out her remaining time, so long as there were no more journeys. He was willing to take her to his own kennels nearby. Francis agreed, but suggested that when the litter arrived they should all be moved to the home kennels in Somerset. Bloodhound dams were strong, but the pups were delicate and apt to catch things; they'd do better in the country.

He offered to take them down in the Camel; but then his jaw dropped, and he exclaimed, "Good Lord! I forgot!" and whispered, so only Richard heard, "I say, sir, am I under arrest?"

Richard stared. He forgot! Really, this young man's insouciance almost amounted to idiocy. If he were an accessory, he might have forgotten that, too. Suppose he'd given Tim an alibi, or destroyed clues? Well, time would show. Meanwhile the best way to keep tabs on him was to give him some jobs.

"No, Francis," he replied, "you're not under arrest. But you're not in the clear either. Despuys *was* threatening you. And you *are* very thick with the Dawson-Gowers. And—you've rather a reputation for breaking rules."

Francis looked very worried indeed, and said nothing.

"It will be in your favor if you pull up your socks now and help us. Try to pick up facts from Despuys' other friends in Oxford. See if he was blackmailing anyone else—they'll tell you more than they'll tell us. Find out—well, I'll brief you. And speaking unofficially. I'd be very grateful indeed if I may leave Ranter in your charge. I expect to be in France by tomorrow."

CHAPTER 10

Yves Kéhidiou, born in Brittany, trained in Paris, and—for Breton thoroughness earns rapid promotion to more southerly provinces—well content at thirty to be *Commissaire de Police* at Pontchâtelet, hung up the telephone and stepped out of his office to give some orders. Do not imagine those vistas of chocolate-colored corridor, lit by weak and naked electric bulbs, which you find in English provincial headquarters; nor yet the aseptic splendors of a California cooler. The Revolution in France, unlike the Reformation in England, put private property to public use, and the police headquarters at Pontchâtelet had once been a townhouse of the La Vallière family. The Commissaire stepped, therefore, out of his own study into a sixteenth-century quadrangle, of which his private apartments occupied the best side. The main offices were opposite, and an extremely primitive prison known as *le violon* filled up the space between. Behind the Chief, his own flowering window-boxes dripped water on his head; before him the gravel, freshly raked into shell-patterns, glistened in the sun. He shouted,"Toussaint! *Hé là*, Toussaint!"

Toussaint Painlevé, the *agent de ville* on duty, appeared like a Jack-in-the-box at the office window. He had round brown eyes behind round spectacles in a round brown face, and his mustache only failed of circularity after a gallant upward struggle.

"I'm coming, *Monsieur le Commissaire,* I'm coming! Right away!"

Not that he guessed at any special urgency. He responded to any call as though to a cry of "Fireman, save my child!"—from pure native vivacity. Kéhidiou, an undemonstrative Northerner, had never quite got used to it. In Touraine they kiss the joy as it flies—loudly, on both cheeks, with exclamations, like a brother-in-law encountered in the road. Perhaps that is why they so seldom reach the rank of Commissaire. Office duty, with its firsthand news, indoor comforts, and occasions, too readily seized, of chats with the chief always heightened the spirits of Painlevé, and today they were ebullient. For early this morning, he had cut a melon—his best yet, a fluted orange melon with soft springy flesh round the stem—and had put it in the cool cellar that it might be sappy and aromatic by midday; he was throwing himself into the morning's work with the object of lunching at leisure. He popped out of the office like a cork.

"For once," said Kéhidiou, not quite hiding his excitement, "we've got a real job. An English detective, from Scotland Yard, arriving this evening. He speaks quite decent French, don't worry. It seems he's after a young Englishman staying with the André Defays—"

"Ah! I've seen him, then! Getting his resident visa. And do you know, Monsieur, I felt even then a sort of—how shall I say—"

"*Bon, bon!*" Kéhidiou raised two fingers. "This Monsieur Ringwood. We shall be at his service. I've asked him to be my guest, and in preparation—"

"Of course! The honor of our department is involved. I saw some splendid crayfish in the market today. Should I—"

"*Merci.*" He raised three fingers. "He has asked us to make some investigations today. Here is a list. Do you know a Madame Brunet, 5 Impasse du Cher?"

"Bah! La Zézette! A very low type, that. She began with the Germans. No longer young, as you may suppose. Far from hygienic—"

"Don't worry. Monsieur Ringwood's interest is official. Past history, maiden name, any foreign letters or visitors lately, state of finances. On paper, please, and be as discreet as possible. Avoid a direct approach at present. Next, there's a man called Jean Despuys—"

Shrugs were exchanged. Despuys, Dupont, Latour. You might as well ask for Bill Smith.

"See if there's anyone on the list using it as a pseudonym. We won't start working through old directories till we've tried short cuts. But begin with the, er, lady. You can take my bicycle. The car's being greased today."

Toussaint saluted and bustled into the office. The chief turned round and shouted to his own house.

"Sylvie! Are you listening to me?"

A little blonde topknot showed for an instant behind the flowers.

"Wait till I finish my sauce!"

No point in spoiling a sauce, certainly. He waited, making plans.

"Toussaint!"

"Monsieur?" he replied, appearing at once.

"Do you think we shall have some drunks in the *violon* this evening?"

"Ah! To turn your ice-cream machine! Of course. I'll pass the word around. Though on a Saturday, and in this heat, and with the wine so good—"

"Only real cases, mind."

"We have enough of those. We'll pick a couple of strong ones. That machine needs—"

"*Bon, bon, bon, bon!* And now, my bicycle!"

Painlevé pedaled off, ringing the bicycle-bell continuously. It was a good, heartening noise. Besides, it kept his mind off the heat, and melons, and ice cream.

* * *

Richard was hot and tired when his train arrived at last. It was hot outside, too, but at least there wouldn't be all those highly scented Spanish businessmen going to sleep on one's shoulder and expecting not to wake up till Madrid. One could be private. Unless—oh, horror!

Unless they laid on an official reception. Too vivid pictures formed in his mind; cocked hats, tricolor sashes, rotund speeches, even, yes, even embraces: you pulled yourself in to avoid their tummies and held out a prickly jaw. Unaccustomed as he was (he would say) to the traditional pageantry of a Republic, such a welcome was— unexpected? Not really, though he might have had the sense to ask off on the telephone. Fantastic? Exhausting! It would be, too, and not only for personal reasons. Publicity might be a further hindrance in this already difficult case. He climbed down the awkward steps (he had been climbing in and out of tall vehicles ever since the Camel yesterday) muttering distractedly "We are hardly—"

A fair lanky man in a gray suit, more English-looking than himself, was approaching. No, he would *not* stop and interpret for him. He must get away quickly. He bolted for the exit. All clear, so far. And a taxi. He jumped in. But the driver did not shut the door after him. He held it open until the fair man had taken a seat too, and greeted him with a formal handshake.

"*Monsieur l'Inspecteur* Ringwood? Yves Kéhidiou, *Commissaire de Police. Enchanté.* My men wanted to stage a proper reception, but I thought it might be indiscreet. Besides, after the traditional pageantry of an ancient kingdom—"

Richard relaxed. So that was the French for traditional pageantry. He would know next time.

CHAPTER 11

"What a good day we're having!" thought Tim, as the children trotted off into the forest. He and Jeannette had taken Chantal and François, her sister and brother, aged respectively eleven and seven, up the Cher in a rowboat to bathe in a shallow sandy curve of the river under the woods. The heat and the effort of rowing had only made the bathing more delicious, and if François had been a bit annoying, arguing and showing off and then trying to drown himself—well, Tim's intervention had been successful and Jeannette had been impressed. The children had devoured their snack in silence, peeping with saucer eyes over the big crusty rolls of bread stuffed with chocolate, and now they were off in search of wood mushrooms. Jeannette and Tim had climbed up the bluff with them as far as the edge of the forest, and sat down there on a bank of what she called asphodels, though they looked more like wild onions to Tim. On one side they could see the river, grayish-blue in the heat haze, wandering, past islands of silvery willows and calm lines of poplar trees, back towards the town. On the other side, four paths radiating from where they sat ran wide and straight into different quarters of the forest. You could see down them for miles—nobody could get lost in such a wood—and yet you couldn't see where the trees came to an end. The forest was very big, very old, but somehow not altogether wild. It was a good place in which to have won his first kiss.

"Won" was perhaps a conceited way of putting it. He had begun by slipping his arm behind her—after all, they called each other *tu*, so perhaps she wouldn't mind. Timidly and then less timidly his fingers had slid up her forearm to her bare shoulder, so white and cushiony that the little drops on it seemed more like dew than sweat. Her head was half averted and the strands of dark hair that had escaped from her—bun? It seemed too pretty to be called that— were wreathing into spirals like the ones on the vine. He tried to speak. She turned her head and her eyes looked bigger and darker than usual. She said, "*Ah, non!* It doesn't need to be asked for," and he knew somehow that so long as he didn't ask, she wouldn't refuse. The sappy flower stems crushed and broke under them.

Then one of the children, shouting in the distance far down a ride, made him remember that this exquisite present couldn't last. He must know where he stood.

"Jeannette, darling. Do you love me?" She looked as if she did.

"I like you very much. Besides, it's so pleasant here."

"Yes, but—Jeannette, I want you always, not just here. Will you marry me?"

The spell was broken. She was sitting up and tidying her hair and calling him her poor friend, which she only did when she wished to imply that he was talking nonsense. It was impossible. He was too young.

"I'm two years older than you, anyway."

"Yes, but you're not serious."

He began to protest that he had never been more in earnest in his life. As always in their more intimate conversations, he was speaking English and she French, for it is easier to understand a foreign language than to clothe your own thoughts in it. But this time they were at cross-purposes. He took some time to grasp that what she meant by a serious man was a man you *took* seriously—a firm option, so to speak. Someone in a position to marry soon and support a family; a man of whom her parents would approve and with whose parents she would feel at home. Someone who had already proved himself strong and prudent. Tim sighed.

"Oh, please don't look so sad! I like you so much. Even when I'm suitably married, I'll still like you. And I *could* be your mistress then, only I wouldn't, because it's a mortal sin. But cheer up! If it wasn't, you'd be my first choice."

Tim had never envisaged this Latin alternative. Far from consoling him, it threw him into a guilty confusion.

"I—I'm sorry. About just now, I mean. Because I suppose you'd say *that* was a sin too."

"It isn't in my book. Anyhow—one can't help it, in the hot weather. I'm sure *le bon Dieu* won't be unreasonable. Still—where have those children got to?"

"Wait!" he said, clutching her. "Wait! I never told you. I did mean to, but you were so—it went right out of my head. Jeannette, I can't marry you. I never ought to have asked you."

"*I* told *you* that," she said half-angrily.

"Yes, but it isn't what you think. It still doesn't seem real, somehow. Oh, Jeannette! I think I may have killed a man in England. And I'm running away from the police."

"You!" Then she held out both hands. "My dear friend, come here and tell me all about it."

She listened, smoothing out her striped skirt, retying the striped scarf round her big knot of hair, and stroking her eyebrows back into line.

"My poor dear friend," she said at last, "you're tormenting yourself for nothing. Even if you did run him over—and your brother said not—well, that's not murder. He simply got himself run over. It was silly to move him, but it was your brother who did that. Really, this Nigel must be mad! Still, he sounds as if he could get away with anything. Does he look like you? ... Don't be silly. He doesn't interest me in the least, he must be a monster. If you really did get into trouble I'd make him confess, because it's all his fault. He's right, though. Now it's done, the best plan is to keep quiet and not worry. Don't get yourself all worked up about it. Listen, I know heaps of people here in Pontchâtelet who did much worse things during the Occupation. They blew up trains and killed people. But it was for their country and they didn't feel guilty; they just went on as usual, and nobody suspected them. There's no bluff like a good conscience," she assured him seriously. "One must pray. Heaven is often against the police."

Her practical logic, curiously like Nigel's, half convinced him; but she did look very young, and he thought it was a mistake to bring heaven into it. Seeing him hesitate, she grew warmer.

"It's been a hard time for you, I know. But it won't be, now you've got me. I'll do everything to distract you. I'll start a novena for you. And—in the last resort—I might even marry you so as to give you French citizenship. Only in the last resort, because one's first duty is to give one's children a good start, you know. Heavens! That reminds me. Where are Chantal and François? I haven't heard a sound for ten minutes."

At last they found the children, a long way from the river hot, sulky, and disinclined for the long walk back. Jeannette rallied them.

"Come on! We'll sing and march in time. Chantal, you choose a song first."

Chantal chose maliciously. The song was about an unsuccessful offer of marriage, and ended

> The boy who courts too long
> Risks wasting his time
> And that's all.

François underlined the point by singing the last line as "Just like you." But he had gone too far. Jeannette turned on him like a fury, crying, "Intolerable!" and smacked him till he wept. Then she walked on, panting.

"Don't listen to him. He's just crying to annoy me. Horrid little beast!"

The child plodded after her, merely sniffling now and throwing her pleading glances which she ignored. Tim was sorry for him. He was tired, and his sister had hit him as hard as she could, though probably that was not very hard. He had just opened his mouth to plead when the little boy forestalled him.

"Jeannette," he began in a small, sad voice. No answer.

"Jeannette, I picked you some flowers yesterday. No one told me to. Do you remember?"

She whirled round, and Tim expected a further outburst. But she was laughing.

"You little monster! Come and kiss me!"

She hugged him and told him to choose a song, and they all set off gaily, singing,

> Let's go for a walk
> In the woods
> While the wolf's not there.
> If the wolf saw us
> He would eat us up.

Tim thought it was uncomfortably appropriate. But when they arrived at the house, he did not at first realize why they were met with such a hubbub of question and conjecture. It was Jeannette who whispered,

"It's the police who've been asking for you. Don't worry, it's probably nothing. Where's your brother's address? I'll ring up Tante Dédée at Poitiers and get her to warn him. It's more discreet." She smiled. "I was too young to do much in the Occupation, but I know the ways they had. This is going to be fun!"

CHAPTER 12

Letter from Richard Ringwood to his wife.

Commissariat de Police
rue de l'ancien hôtel de la Vallière
Pontchâtelet (Cher)

My dear Clare (never dearer),

No telegrams, so I keep hoping that Dr. Fowler's guess of a week longer turns out right. I want extremely to be with you. I know how you're longing to feel less mountainous and to see the Ridiculous Mouse. But try to keep the infestation under control till I'm there to beat him when he sneezes. (*Do* they sneeze?) The nurse sounds good. I'm sure she's right to keep you in bed for breakfast, Papa or no Papa. It won't surely do him serious damage to eat one meal by himself. I wish extremely I were with you. Having woken at 3, I am now, at 4, sitting up in bed and taking the chance to talk to you, however remotely, before the day begins.

Kéhidiou (the *commissaire de police*) insisted on my staying here in his house, which is like one of the Canons' houses in Tom Quad but smaller and chirpier. He is a fair bony Breton with a colossal sense of duty. I like him a lot. His wife is a chic little saucer-eyed blonde straight off a P.G. Wodehouse dust-cover, tottering about on three-inch heels, and they also have a Ridiculous Mouse, a six-month saucer-eyed blonde, not bad, but socially difficult. You can't pat it like a dog or talk to it like a person. And this French custom of public suckling makes me v. hot under the collar. I try, however, to keep up the animated conversation as before, and avert the eye. They are very interested in our Mouse, and have asked me questions about your inside which I am still hoping to forget. They also enquire at meals about the state of my liver (personal, not edible).

Dawson-Gower was out picnicking when we called at six yesterday, so Kéhidiou and I returned to dinner first. Splendid dinner, starting with crayfish and ending with pistachio ice cream made in a Heath Robinson machine on the premises by two singing drunks out of the lockup. This lockup is a sort of human stable, with wooden floor sloping up to a communal straw-stuffed bolster, on which they lay them out side by side, as in the Great Bed of Ware. After dinner we went back to the Defay household and I had a long session with Dawson-Gower, a very Pentecost type.

His story is that he ran over Despuys in Priory Road but the wheel only went over his legs. He was lying half out into the road. The boy says he was alone in the car and the time was about ten. On getting down to look, he saw that the man was dead already of head injuries, but was afraid to tell the police because he was sure they would accuse him of manslaughter. So he put the body in the car, took it out to the haystack and cremated it, drove on to Wycombe where he garaged the car, and got a hitch back to Oxford.

An unconvincing story, but parts of it rang curiously true. For instance, his horror of the corpse. He'd never seen one before. Says he didn't recognize it as Despuys and thought the face was injured, but couldn't describe injury. Quite obviously, he had got the horrors and couldn't bear really to *look*. Also (to me) his assertion that he didn't kill him sounded all the more truthful because he was so dead sure I wouldn't believe him. I don't think he's clever enough for this to be a double-bluff.

But his story is full of holes. If he was so frightened of *looking* at the corpse, could he have borne to handle it? And why drive to Wycombe instead of Oxford? He says he was upset, started in the wrong direction, and found himself driving so badly anyhow that he dared not continue. I think this is bad psychology. To a man feeling hunted, his own car is a sort of home, a refuge—he wouldn't want to leave it. Also, his times are wrong. He got into college at 12 (porter confirms). But according to the fire brigade, the stack must have been fired *after* midnight, to be burning as it was next morning. I told him all this but he stuck desperately to his story.

My present theory is that he's shielding his brother Nigel—who is certainly "in" it, for he invented Tim's illness. Tim didn't know he was supposed to have seen a specialist and let that cat out of the bag in the first few seconds. I had previously thought that Nigel was shielding Tim. But really it makes much better sense as the act of an ex-commando, and I've telephoned to the Bloodhound to hold Nigel for questioning. The motive is still uncertain, though I hope to discover a connection between him and Despuys, as Nigel was doing his Resistance work here when Despuys lived in the district. I've left Tim at large. He is most surprised and inclined to attribute his luck to the intervention of his hosts, the Defays. They came in at the end and we had one of those polite but violent French screaming parties with everyone pouring everything out—emotion, logic, coffee and cognac. I helped Kéhidiou scream a bit and then we left and he sang to me all the way home. Perhaps I sang a little too—it was a lovely night, and as he said, if a *Commissaire de Police* can't sing in his own department, where can he?

My dear, you have unscrewed me. Just writing to you does it. I'll sleep a bit now. Today I have to see this awful *femme galante*. Keep well and consider yourself first, the Mouse next, and then your distant but loving Richard.

* * *

It was half-past eight when he woke to the sound of an animated French argument apparently right under his window. But when he jumped up to look, there was nothing in sight but white gravel in strong sunshine. The day looked as if it had begun long ago. After a hasty shave and wash in the little bathroom profuse of plumbing but niggardly of hot water, he dressed and hurried to the stairs. His hostess was just coming up with a breakfast tray and expressed horror that he should have dressed fasting. She bustled into his bedroom, put down the tray, stripped the bed, hung the bedclothes out of the open window, wished him a good appetite, and shuffled away leaving him rather stunned. She looked pasty and tousled in her dressing gown, as Frenchwomen so often do, and did not care a pin who saw her so. Odd, this convention of either dressing to the nines or slopping to zero!

There was a letter from Francis Clandon on the tray. He and his girl Laura had been making enquiries about Despuys' friends and sources of income, and especially about his relations with his landlady, Mrs. Gyles.

"We thought," wrote Francis ingenuously, "that she would be more forthcoming to another woman, so Laura went to see her alone. Mrs. Gyles admitted she was very fond of Jean, but when Laura asked if she'd given him money, she was annoyed and practically threw her out. So I tried her myself. I went along to say bad luck and could I help her with clearing up Jean's things, and so on. This worked rather well, in fact she asked me to go and live there free next term, apparently she's afraid of burglars. I thought she was genuine. I mean, a bit lonely and almost overgenerous. He wouldn't need to blackmail *her*, and anyhow I think she wouldn't have done anything bad. Even Laura agrees. Ranter is doing fine."

Under the letter was a telephone message from Scotland Yard. Nigel Dawson-Gower had disappeared, and they were still trying to find him. At the bottom of the slip the Commissaire added that his dear colleague would find him in his office if he wanted him.

In fact, Richard found him in the quadrangle, watching a seedy old man dab with a scrubbing brush at the floor of the *violon*. He thought poorly of the dotard, and was giving full expression to his opinions. Imbecile—yes, thought Richard, that's obvious. Animal, even, was true up to a point. Weren't we all? But to declare him inseparable from his native mud—surely that was going rather far! Clearly, no one had ever tried the soap-and-water treatment. Kéhidiou interrupted his tirade to shake Richard by the hand, but was still too angry to leave the subject.

"You see that creature? I find him wandering along the river bank with nothing but a sack of old crusts. He says he's out of work, no family, no home, lost his cards, can't get a job. Well! I bring him here, let him sleep in the lockup, feed here, earn a bit on odd jobs while I try to place him. And what does he do? Slips out first thing this morning and drinks the lot! Comes back stinking! Look at him! Already he can't tell the difference between the bucket and the floor, the disgusting old toad. Toussaint!" The jack-in-the-box sprang out. "When he's slept it off, give him a sandwich and see that he starts

walking out of town. There aren't going to be any tramps in
Pontchâtelet while I'm in charge. Excuse me, Monsieur, I'll just see
about that sandwich." He went over to his own house. Richard turned
to Painlevé and asked him a question about public assistance.

"*Ah, oui!* That's a possibility, but—You see, six months ago, Monsieur le Commissaire found a tramp down by the river who really
had lost his cards and really *did* want to work. He took him in here,
begged cast-off clothes from his own friends, got him new papers,
found him a job as a vine dresser. And he did well. He's in charge of
a vineyard now. Monsieur was so happy, and now he's always hoping for another miracle. It's an act of charity, but still—" He pouted
his lips and blew a little draught of incredulity. "Besides, there's the
asylum, the hospital, the League of the Mothers of France Against
the Effects of Alcohol ..."

At these words, the old man came to with a start and began si-
dling along the wall towards the gate.

"Look out! He's getting away!"

"Well, he'd better get away if he doesn't want those Mothers of
France after him. He's free, as far as we're concerned, but with the
Anti-Alcoholics—Ah! That's done it! What I say is, if people can't
treat decent liquor with respect, they don't deserve any food with it.
They wouldn't appreciate it. ... Ah! *Monsieur le Commissaire!* Excuse me, but he suddenly took it into his head to leave, and I didn't
think it was my place to stop him, as he wasn't on a charge. A free
member of our glorious republic has a right ..."

"*Bon, bon, bon, bon!*" said Kéhidiou, looking more grieved than
ever. "Get back on the job, then. Now, sir, about this woman Brunet
..." They went into Kéhidiou's study.

"We can't yet tell you anything about her before she came to
Pontchâtelet with her husband in 1939, because the registers were
destroyed by bombing and we haven't been able to reconstruct them
fully. But don't worry. When you see her—I thought it better not to
tackle her personally before you arrived—you'll be sure to find that
she's kept at least some of the papers she ought to have, *livret de
famille* or identity card or something. You'll get her maiden name
and birthplace, anyhow, and then you can let us find out the rest if
you need it. Of course you can't trust her word at all."

"Can't I?" Richard wondered. Bretons were notorious in France
for their almost Jansenist moralism—Celts were like that, whatever
church they belonged to—and Kéhidiou was just the man to put
principles before experience. "In England we don't find prostitutes

specially dishonest. Stupid, yes, and inclined to take the line of least resistance—"

"Ah, yes! But I'm not speaking of her as a prostitute. Many such women are truthful and even patriotic. And I've heard of cases where they've persuaded a young man to get on and work at his career, when the parents have almost given him up; really they have their social uses. Mind you, I only approve as a citizen. As a Christian I naturally condemn them."

Richard suppressed his surprise and his desire to contest the theory of two worlds. Thank God for the Establishment, for once.

"Why can't I trust this woman, then?"

"She's a low type," said Kéhidiou, all granite and icy water. "The lowest of the low. Imagine, she began with the Germans. Yes! In the Occupation, when no decent woman would look at them, and not even prostitutes unless they were desperate for money, this woman opened her house to the filthy *Boches*. And that, after they'd taken her husband for forced labor and killed him. She knew what they were like. She had every reason to hate them. But no—she invited them to her house."

"Perhaps she was afraid of them?"

"Bah! We all were, naturally. That didn't make us lick their boots, though. And anyhow, she wasn't just a common camp follower. She was Blancbec's woman. You've heard of that traitor—a Frenchman, an ex-schoolmaster who worked full-time for the Gestapo, tortured citizens, here in Pontchâtelet. Everyone knew. And yet that creature could …" He spat—really spat—and made the action curiously elegant.

"Blancbec? I don't remember the name on the war criminals list."

"It wasn't his real name, of course. People called him that, oh! partly to keep up their spirits, I suppose, and partly because it wasn't very safe to use real names then. But just go into the marketplace today and say "Maxime Fleurat" and you won't have to listen to hear the curses. He got away, you see, before the Liberation, and he's never been caught and punished. That was before I came here."

"Fleurat. Yes, I have heard of him. Didn't he torture some school children for taking round our leaflets? Mm. But what about this woman? Why didn't he take her with him?"

"The neighbors were keeping pretty close watch on her those last days before the breakthrough. Reserving her for proper treatment. Yes, she had her head shaved in the square just in front of the church. In Brittany they'd have whipped her out of the town with nettles, but people are soft here. Decent, you know, but lazy. I suppose it's the climate. Nearly all the Commissaires round here are from the North."

"I'm surprised she didn't leave of her own accord. She can't have enjoyed living in the place, after that."

"Ah! The motive for staying was pure avarice. She owns that house, you see. And of course she couldn't get much of a price for it then. Nobody was going to have it said that he'd put money in *her* pocket. She only advertised it once. Then she tried to let rooms. She did get one old man, but the neighbors soon told him what sort of house it was, and he left."

Richard marveled, not for the first time, at the strange results you get in France from mixing strong regional characteristics with equally strong national conventions. It produced a boss-eyed and incalculable morality. Kéhidiou was both devout and kindly. He tried to help old vagabonds, but believed that all Germans were irreformable; he agreed that promiscuity was a sin, but clearly he thought it worse not to hate your enemies.

"So she owned her house. How was that?"

"It's all in Painlevé's report, but I'd better summarize. Her husband, who was a plumber, got it cheap in '39. He'd got a weak heart which kept him out of the army, but he was a good workman and labor was scarce, so he did well. They say he and his wife improved the house a lot, too, in their spare time. Well, when the Boches arrived, they took him to work in Germany. I suppose they reckoned they could get their money's worth out of him before his heart gave out, as of course it did, in those conditions."

"What did she do, after they took him?"

"Like everyone else. Any work she could get. Then she had German soldiers billeted on her, and that's where the trouble began. She got very friendly with the sergeant, who sent, or at least pretended to send, parcels to her husband for her. Too friendly, people said, and when she had a miscarriage no one would have betted if it was one more Frenchman murdered or one more German out of the way. It was a great year for miscarriages. Well, she did have a kind of excuse while her husband was alive, I suppose, because of the parcels and keeping the home together. But unfortunately she was even more friendly to the sergeant after her husband died. The neighbors stopped speaking to her, but it had no effect."

"Well, if they wouldn't—sorry. Please go on."

"Presently this sergeant began to bring his friends in too. They had noisy parties, with wine they'd looted from Vouvray and Chinon. Before it had matured properly, too, and they drank it like beer. Well, after the shopkeepers heard about that, they stopped selling to her. The Germans had the stuff that ought to be on their shelves, they said. Let *them* feed her, since she seemed to prefer it. She stayed in a good deal at that time, and it was said that the Germans all took it in turns with her at the parties. But that wasn't the worst. The worst was when Blancbec got her. She was very pretty in those days.

"Yes, he turned out the regular soldiers and put a couple of S.S. into the billet, which kept off visitors, except for him. He went about four times a week, and she must have made a lot of money out of him, because the Resistance offered her a good price to pick up information they wanted, and she refused. Plenty of women like her were doing it for nothing. Oh yes, she'd saved money, certainly. She kept alive all that year after the Liberation, when her hair was growing again, and she can't have been earning then. First treason, then avarice. It's disgusting, isn't it?"

Richard could not share Kéhidiou's hatred. The woman seemed so helpless. She had lost husband and baby, the German sergeant was her only friend left, and without him she had simply given up. But why on earth, he asked, had she stayed in Pontchâtelet after the Liberation?

Avarice, replied Kéhidiou angrily. She owned her house and could stay there rent free while her hair was growing. Then, probably having run out of money, she had gone on the streets. He used the slang word *grue* to describe her; and Richard wondered for the twentieth time why the French language assumes that cranes have lower moral characters than hens. Kéhidiou continued.

"There seems to be some confirmation of the idea that an Englishman went to visit her last spring. The gossips say he didn't stay any time, once he'd had a look at her, though I don't know how they can be so sure. Otherwise, nothing out of the ordinary. Oh, except that the carrier delivered a trunk and some bits of furniture just after Palm Sunday. Not the sort of things she'd have bought, they say—more like a lodger's bits and pieces. But the lodger never turned up. They think he may be paying a retaining fee, though, because she's been buying meat occasionally, since then. She couldn't afford it before."

"So the shops have forgiven her now."

"They've got more to sell and prices are up," said Kéhidiou, without a trace of irony.

CHAPTER 13

It had not been easy to persuade Kéhidiou to let him make the call alone. Monsieur Ringwood would be imposed upon, he said, or need an interpreter, despite his excellent French, or rather because of it. These low characters did not speak except in the vilest slang. Richard's view was that M. Kéhidiou would paralyze the witness, despite his excellent intentions, or rather ... and so on. In the end they compromised on sending Painlevé to show him the house and wait outside in case he were needed. It was a ten-minute walk, down streets all built of white stone or plastered to resemble it, and reflecting the sun in a way that hurt one's eyes, but Richard liked the market with its piles of exotic fruits and vegetables and the smart little women passionately reasoning a few francs off the price, also the Romanesque church with a crowd of saints and apostles over the west door and a glimpse inside of dark chancel and tiny twinkling lamp. He was amused and pleased, too, by Painlevé's effortless, if predictable, flow of international courtesies; he was clearly determined to make up for the informal reception last night. To do him justice, he showed a nice choice of words, especially *buts* and *moreovers*, which the district produces in insolent profusion, and enjoyed his self-imposed task. He did not stop till they reached the poorer streets, when he suddenly showed signs of embarrassment, and Richard suspecting him of wanting to say something on his own account, gave him an opening.

"What is your own view of Madame Brunet? I mean, speaking as an ordinary Pontchâtelet man?"

Behind his round spectacles the man looked his gratitude, but did not of course leave it at that level of inarticulate communication.

"Ah! Monsieur has such delicacy, such tact ... Well, to tell you the truth, she is like everybody else, I mean, like all low-class people, only she got in wrong with the Resistance, and of course that's more serious in the poor quarters. I believe it was different in some provinces, where there wasn't this political bias, but here the Resistance were mostly the left-wing chaps. I don't think *Monsieur le Commissaire* quite gets that. We all hated Blancbec—who wouldn't?— but with la Zézette, well, it was more like strikers boycotting a blackleg. The boys expected it, so of course the neighbors couldn't afford to be friendly to her. But later on, when everything had blown over, it would have been all right. We aren't that mean, we *pontchâteletiens*. But by then she wouldn't say a word to anyone except in the way of business. She'd turned miser, you see. Here's her street. I see her bedclothes are out of the window, so she's up, anyhow."

Sheets and blankets were hanging from first-floor casements all down the street, and in several doorways women in carpet slippers peeled vegetables and scolded children.

Number 5 was a flat rectangular facade, with peeling white plaster and gray exterior shutters to relieve the plainness of the design. It was the sort of house that foreigners think is picturesque, though it is merely typical of an unfamiliar convention. 1880, at a guess, and badly built. Inside, the walls would probably crumble if you hammered in a nail, and the drains work sometimes in reverse. He posted Painlevé round the corner out of sight, and rang the bell.

It seemed a long time before the door opened. The woman might have passed by lamplight, but in sunshine her thick paint, dyed hair, and awful smile were sheer travesty. He just had time to wonder that she was dressed for visitors so early, when she began her patter, in a muddy underworld slang hard to follow. But the intention was clear. She was calling him her handsome wolf, her fat rat, and names whose meaning he half-guessed; she told him to come back in a quarter of an hour when the room was ready; she was asking fifteen hundred francs.

He had not expected this reception, and stammered that the room wasn't the point. He wanted to see *her*.

She hesitated (looking much better without the smile) and then, with a glance behind her, resumed her sales talk more loudly.

"In a hurry, are you? Come in here, then—" she showed him into the front room on the ground floor "—and in just a minute ..."

But Richard thrust her into the room and put his back against the door. She shrugged, half slave, half merchant, and turned on the smile again.

"A quick one in the corner, huh? Down here? Just as you like, dear. But we pay in advance. Fifteen hundred francs." Then, afraid he would bargain for less, "And for that, I'll let a handsome fellow like you do anything you want."

Thirty shillings, and nothing barred; and yet you could tell that she was only pretending desire. One understood Clandon's shudder.

At last Richard made her understand the nature of his business and asked her about Clandon's visit. She was as still as a lizard in danger while he spoke. Then she cleared her throat harshly and said, in just the tone of an unsuccessful commercial traveler who has to keep on pretending he sells things,

"I don't remember. You see, I have so many visitors. Hundreds of men come here—English, Americans ..."

"This man was important enough for you to write to Jean Despuys about him afterwards."

She did not move except to breathe painfully. Richard waited and looked round at the hard chairs, the deal table, and the scarred gramophone. What was that noise? It sounded like someone upstairs. But the house was one of a row and jerry-built at that. Probably next door. Surely she wouldn't have let him into the house like that if she'd already ... or would she? One just didn't know what to expect. Nothing barred! Ah, she was scraping into speech again; but it was only to repeat that she didn't remember.

"I think you do. You wrote Despuys a letter that he could—and did—use to blackmail Clandon. I can prove that. But I won't need to mention it, if you'll only tell me the truth now. Did you and Despuys play the same trick on another English boy—a boy called Dawson-Gower? It's Dawson-Gower I'm interested in at the moment. No one else."

"Not—" she moved a little—"not Monsieur Despuys? *He* isn't any longer in danger?"

"Any longer? It's true, he has been in danger. How did you know?"

"Oh ... when you began asking, I thought you must be—after him for something. That's all. Is he now out of danger?"

"Yes. And in fact, I'm on his side."

"Oh, dear!" She began plucking at the rows of colored braid on her dress and pulling at her crimson curls, like any nervous middle-aged woman. "I wish I could help you. Truly. Listen. I'll tell you one thing frankly. There *was* an Englishman last spring, as you say. But he—he didn't stay. He—he said he felt ill suddenly. I don't know what his name was—I never do. But he said he knew Monsieur Despuys, and he's—he's been kind to me, you know. And I did write him a letter, just that once. It was the only—it was my own idea. The boy was rich and ... I needed money badly. People don't like it when you've got a cough."

"Shouldn't you be in hospital? The nuns take people free, you know."

"Nuns!" She laughed harshly. "No thanks! If God wanted me he'd have paid in advance, like the others. First come, first served." Then she faltered. "Sorry, Monsieur. One believes, but one doesn't hope … Is that all, then?"

"Almost. Just the routine, I'll have to see your papers. Identity card, marriage lines—" she started. "I won't take them away. Would you fetch them?"

He opened the door for her and would have followed her out, but she said in the old strident way,

"Fifteen hundred if you want to come upstairs!" and he shrugged, returned to the sitting room, and banged the door. When she had stumped upstairs, coughing and muttering, he opened it soundlessly. She was bumping about on the first floor now, out of sight.

He looked about him. The plan of the house was simple. Outside the sitting room the passage ran up to a steep staircase; and past the foot of the stairs there was a door open into the kitchen. He could see part of a cooking stove. The kitchen was flooded with sunlight, unlike the room where he had been sitting. So there must be open ground at the back of the house—and probably a back door in the kitchen standing open now. No window would let in quite that flood of light, and he felt a draft, too, warm but stirring. He was just going to explore when footsteps on the landing sent him back, and the woman found him shut in where she had left him. Panting from her exertions, she held out the papers, and he examined them.

Zézette Brunet, then, had been born—born Denise Despuys! The address of her birthplace was the address already familiar from Jean Despuys' records. And the tiny photograph on the identity card — what a pretty face! Could the porcelain of Denise have really turned to the varnished plasticine of Zézette?—the photograph had the features of—

"You're his sister! Anyone could see the likeness. Why didn't you tell me?"

"I was like him then," she wheezed. "Not now. He's ten years younger. He must still be very handsome. I haven't seen him since '47."

Jean Despuys was twenty-six when he died. Was his sister really only thirty-six? She looked much more. But no, the faded purple ink said *date de naissance, 1918.* That was another famous year for miscarriages in France. She was a weak child of war, her brother a strong child of peace. How could he have left her to decay like this for nine years, and then only noticed her degradation to use it as a handle for blackmail? Richard passed his hand over his eyes, and the momentary blotting-out of vision made his ears alert. He lifted his head. But as he did so, the woman cleared her throat with a more raucous rasp than ever and broke out:

"I didn't say it! I didn't say a word, ever! I wouldn't bother if it was the others. They've treated me like dirt, anyway. But not Jean! Don't tell him! Don't tell anyone! He isn't like the others. He sent me that rich English boy—two thousand francs he paid me, for nothing, nothing at all! And Jean wrote to me once, too. Such a sweet letter. Oh, please don't tell anyone I'm his sister! Don't ruin him as well! You couldn't be so cruel. Listen, he's doing so well, he's so clever. Why, it said in his letter that just the papers here are worth a fortune, once he's got them ready to publish. And now, if he too is threatened—*ah! Mon petit Jean!* Give him time to make good!" She fell on her knees, rucking up the tight purple dress. Tears were making havoc of her cheeks. "Promise you won't say! You've got a heart, you're like—you're not like Frenchmen. Don't give me away to him! I was stupid, I ought to have realized you'd find out from the paper, but I'd never read it, I hadn't got time. But I didn't mean— I didn't mean you to know. You wouldn't persecute a boy like Jean, surely. He's only a boy. One day when he's rich, he'll make it worth your while if you keep quiet now. Just two years, the letter said, and I'll be in clover. It isn't long for you to wait. It's not so long for you as it is for me."

She grabbed at the legs of his trousers, trying to hold his attention. But he had heard a door shut stealthily; and this time he was sure that it was downstairs and in this house. He pulled his legs free and wrenched the door of the room open.

"Quiet! Who's in the house?"

"Nobody!" She clutched him desperately. "Promise! Promise!"

"I won't tell your brother," said Richard, and rushed out.

The front door was shut on its spring lock; no one could have shut it without an audible slam. The door in the kitchen was shut. He hurried through and out of the back door, now also shut, to where the sun glared on a derelict, rubbish-strewn garden. It was walled down both sides. He searched the bushes but no one was hiding there. At the bottom end, the garden ran down to the towing path, from which it was separated merely by two strands of barbed wire and a shallow ditch. Not a boat or a man to be seen, and it was all open and flat. Except—yes! asleep in the long grass of a hollow beside the path, a huddle of old clothes that Richard recognized. It was the tramp Kéhidiou had been scolding this morning. Richard remembered the faded blue scarf that had been round the dotard's neck. Now it was over his face, and perched sideways atop of it, that straw hat sprouting like a forkful of hay. Well! Let the poor old wreck sleep off his absinthe in peace! He wouldn't have noticed if a troop of horses had passed within a couple of yards of him. Whoever it was in the house must be still there, and hiding, for he could not have climbed those high side-walls of the garden. Richard hurried back to the woman.

"Madame," he said, "would you be kind enough to go out and ask the *agent*, Monsieur Painlevé, who is just round the street corner, to come here to me at once? I think someone's hiding in your house, and we must search it immediately. You'd better come back too, and keep an eye on us," he added lightly. "See that we don't carry off any of your property."

By the way she stiffened, he saw that the point had gone home. Kéhidiou was right; she must have a miser's hoard somewhere, so she could be trusted to come back and watch it. As he stood in the hall on guard, listening, he heard bumping and footsteps; but it was again impossible to tell whether they were in Number 5 or next door.

Painlevé made a dramatic entrance, demanding loudly whether Monsieur was wounded or robbed. Richard reassured him. He just needed help in searching the house. Someone was hidden there—at least he could not see how anyone could have got away unobserved. Painlevé became matter-of-fact and slightly roguish.

"Ah! Don't worry.He must be a customer who hurried off for the sake of discretion. And you didn't want to give him away, *eh, ma belle?*" He slapped the woman lightly. "Doesn't look as if *she* got much sleep last night, poor thing! It's too hot for double beds this weather, and that's a fact. My wife says the same. Well, I'm at your command, Monsieur!"

There was something sunny and solid about Painlevé's ribaldry; it exorcised even this house. Richard left him in the hall to watch the exits while he searched the back again. Painlevé began enquiring how business prospered with la Zézette (his tone was one of benevolent detachment) and saying that she kept the house nice and clean and the inspector should hear of it. But why didn't she keep the garden up? Nothing like fresh vegetables for the liver, and one saved money, too. Her hoarse answers were inaudible. Richard opened a door under the stairs and went down to search the cellar. He found nothing but household stores and two bottles of the cheapest local wine. So she didn't drink, anyhow. He climbed up the dank stone steps again. Painlevé was saying.

"You ought to save up and get a little café, my girl. That's the way to get a husband. You know, if you sold your house, it would fetch quite a bit these days."

She was smiling at Painlevé quite naturally, but when Richard sent him up to begin searching the bedrooms, she looked like a beaten dog again, half wary and half cringing.

"One more question, madame. About the luggage and things that the carrier delivered here last spring. Were you expecting a lodger?" He lowered his voice. "Your brother?"

"Oh, please, please! He'd kill me for telling you. Yes, they're Jean's things, as you'll see when you look. But of course he wouldn't think of coming here to live; how could he? It's like this. He used to live at my sister's in Châtellerault sometimes, before he went to England. *She* was respectable, you see, and her husband was quite pleased, for Jean used to pay them a bit, and they had the room … If only she'd let *me* rent it after the war … Oh well, too bad. The hell with it! Anyway, after nine years, I hear—not from her, of course, Justine wouldn't even look at me, she said I was dead as far as she was concerned—no, a letter from Jean. Justine's expecting her fourth child—I'd never been told about the others—and hasn't got room for Jean's things. He knows *I* have, so he's having them sent here, and encloses four thousand francs, hopes I don't mind. The things arrive—not carriage paid, of course!—still, there's a bit of change left over from the four thousand, and I'd got the things to look after. I already felt a little less lonely. But don't tell the people here, please, please! He'd never forgive me."

Richard reassured her and went upstairs, letting her go first. Painlevé had just finished searching her bedroom and complimented her on its cleanliness. Richard stared. The peeling walls, the frayed, stained curtains, the deal furniture marked by cigarette burns, were squalid. But Painlevé was right—although it needed renovation the room did not need dusting. And he was soon convinced that it held no secrets and no clues.

"Now! The—lodger's things, please."

The little room looked out at the back across the river and was furnished only with a bed, lumpy under a frayed old blanket. Piled on it he saw boxes of books and papers, a lensless camera, a tennis racket with slack strings, a reading lamp without a shade, a folded card table with moth-holes in the baize, and a pair of yellow corduroy plus fours, rightly rejected by Jean as a means of winning hearts in England.

"I'll have to look through these," he said. "Stay if you like. Painlevé will bring you a chair. Thank you, Monsieur. I wonder if you'd mind doing the *cabinet* while I do this?"

No doubt of it, the things were Despuys'—books with his signature on the flyleaf, notes of lectures, a few letters in English, bills or amiabilities … But wait! The letters were dated from August of last year. And some had envelopes with postmarks. Yes, Châtellerault, August 26th; that was the date and place of delivery.

"So your brother was in France last year?"

"With Justine? Do you suppose *she'd* tell me?"

"These letters prove it," he said. "I can see that they've all been disturbed recently, because the dusty ones are at the bottom. So you must have known, as you've read them."

"Never!" she said. "I wouldn't, he hates people prying. I swear I haven't touched them. It must be the rats. Besides, I don't know any English. All I did was brush the clothes, truly."

She sounded sincere. Still, the papers *had* been searched recently. He was wondering how easily one could find a fingerprint expert in these parts, when Painlevé burst in, dramatically offering a folded paper.

It was surprising to find it signed *Toussaint Painlevé*, particularly if one had not met that compendious Christian name before. The paper contained several unexpected statements. "In the bathroom there is an enormous sum under a loose board in the floor." Well, so far, all right. But see what follows. "The basin is full of hair, and there is a wet badger underneath." What on earth?—Better go and see.

No badger; he had simply forgotten that *blaireau* also meant a shaving brush. Still, it *was* sensational. A shaving brush used today, and short black bristles embedded in the soapy surface of the basin, too coarse to be the leavings of a woman's toilet, even Madame Brunet's. And also (this of less immediate interest) a sum equivalent to thirty pounds in hoard. But just as Richard was congratulating Painlevé, bumps in the next room sent him hastening back.

Despuys' sister had bundled half the boxes from the bed to the floor and looked terrified at being interrupted. He did not ask what she was doing, but merely said that a sum of money had been found in her washplace. With a hoarse wail of "My savings!" she ran out as fast as her thick legs would go. Richard turned back the blanket from the bed, and called. Painlevé bounded in.

"Look! This bed's made up and I think it's been slept in. You don't smoke, do you?"

"Rarely, Monsieur. It coarsens ..."

"I've smoked too much today and spoiled my nose. So yours is the only hope. Smell those sheets, please!"

Toussaint knelt and took a sniff—considered—took another, and pronounced, in the pontifical tone of a judge at a wine fair,

"In my opinion, sir, it smells of recent sweat and also strongly of ammonia. Therefore. . ."

Fresh sweat with a high ammonia content. As the man was saying, it was likely that the bed had been slept in last night by a man who felt the heat and was in a state of fear. Not a peasant, for the bed didn't smell of dirt, not a woman, for there was no trace of scent. Also, Monsieur would consider the badger—no, the shaving-brush ...

"How marvelously you reason!" said Richard, who had already drawn these conclusions for himself and gone on to harder questions. Whom would this woman be ready to hide at risk to herself; this creature to whom all men were the objects of fear or cupidity? To whom would she have given a separate room but her brother, the only person she seemed to care about? But he was dead! Yet who else but Jean would have known where his collection of things had been put, who else would have wanted to go through it? Appalling thought! The corpse might be somebody unidentified, and Despuys the murderer. He called the woman and tried again to get the truth.

Yellow-gray under her paint, coughing horribly and clutching at her chest, she swore again and again that no one had been there except a customer whose name she did not know, whose face she had not seen; who had given her a bit extra to make up the spare bed as he felt ill and could not sleep. He had left early. Oh, no! It wasn't Jean! No such luck for the likes of her. Richard tried another tack; it was time to let her know a little more.

"What would happen to Jean's money if he died intestate?"

"Half to me, half to Justine. Both our other brothers were killed in the war. Our parents, too, in an air raid. Justine for once would not be ... But why? Why do you ask this? Tell me!"

"Well, I have to tell you sooner or later, Madame. Your brother has disappeared. At first I was sure he was dead. Now—well, I'm not sure of anything."

"Dead! *Mon petit Jean!*"

"If he is *presumed* dead, you'll get about fifty thousand francs and be able to make a fresh start."

Her hysterics were painful. Both men were glad when she fainted. Richard stood guard while Painlevé went out for brandy and hot coffee.

He was in extreme perplexity. After all, Ranter's nose was his only indication that the corpse in the haystack *was* Despuys; and the authorities had shown that they did not care for such evidence. Suppose it *wasn't* Despuys after all? A fine fool he'd look, traipsing off to France on a wild goose-chase! But surely, surely old Ranter could be trusted? He'd never known her to lie yet.

Then he laughed wryly. He had never known her to tell the truth either. Ranter was a strictly *dumb* friend.

CHAPTER 14

Richard was amazed by the efficiency of the Pontchâtelet police. After the dinner and the singing last night, he had not expected it. The fingerprint expert was in Zézette's house within half an hour, and even before that the towing path and the riverside quarter were being searched for suspicious characters. The telephone buzzed with enquiries about the whole Despuys family. Red tape, routine, even traffic control went by the board as every *agent* in town competed for the honor of an international catch. And to judge by the screaming of the telephone, all the local stations were throwing themselves into the drama with equal verve.

Kéhidiou promised that most of the work would be done in an hour and a half. The fingerprints would take a little longer, as they had to be checked in the Criminal Laboratory at Lyons, where the police dossiers were kept. He explained that every single person arrested in France had a full physical record taken—it was called a *fiche anthro-pométrique*—and there were several millions of these records to check against the fingerprints found today. Richard gasped with admiration. But Kéhidiou went on apologetically,

"I'm sorry to keep you waiting so long. But these Touraine people can't be hurried. Talk, talk, talk! They're clever enough, but they get lazy in the middle of the day. I suppose it's the climate."

Richard felt hot and torpid himself. He couldn't find a phrase.

"And so," the Frenchman was saying, "knowing you'd dislike waiting about—the English are so active—I've ventured to arrange a little distraction for you. Monsieur Defay, Tim's host, whom you met last night, has invited you to lunch. He's a leading citizen, a wine merchant, and keeps an excellent table. I think he might be well worth talking to about the case. He was here in the Occupation and he knows the Dawson-Gower situation probably better than we do. He'll call for you in a car in ten minutes."

Wearily Richard went upstairs to wash and change. When he came down, Monsieur Defay was already in the courtyard, enjoying the sun under a broad Panama hat. His whole appearance was broad—shoulders, forehead, mustache, and his car too was of the wide shiny sort that looks like a stout fish with a head each end and no tail. He shook hands, bowed Richard in, and drove off very fast, hooting on both horns and keeping up a lively commentary on the sights of the town.

"That's the station, new, as you see. The old one was better-looking, but the English bombed it to bits in '45." He looked round impishly. "The buggers!"

"I'm sorry," Richard began, but he was boomed down.

"No, no, no, no! I intended a compliment. The Germans and the Americans had plenty of shots at it first, but the Germans always hit the hospital and the Americans the church. Your airmen got a beautiful direct hit their third try, and what's more, none of the railwaymen were killed, only some German soldiers who'd come too early for the train as usual."

Richard had met this attitude in France before. The gist of it was, "*You* fought, *we* suffered," and it was not only a face-saving device; there was truth in it, insufficiently recognized by foreigners.

"I did admire the French morale during the Occupation," he said. "The war would never have been won without. Still—a wrecked station doesn't quite call for drinks all round, I imagine."

Monsieur Defay slapped his broad thigh with a shout of laughter. The car swerved, bumped, and recovered. "That's just what it did call for!" he said. "The chaps from the station came down to my factory to shelter and I poured their drinks myself. Didn't want them running back to put the fires out too soon, you see, but one couldn't say so openly. One never knew whom one could trust. Well, here we are!"

The stone house abutted on the street, its tall windows veiled behind gauzy festoons. Richard was led through into a little paved garden shaded by a trellised vine, where the family was sitting round an iron table. As they rose to greet him, a servant came out with a tray of drinks; her dazzling white overall and submissive manner charmed one into unawareness of her mustache and dirty canvas shoes.

Monsieur Defay kissed each member of his family and passed them one by one to Richard.

"My mother, whom you haven't met. My wife. My daughter Jeannette. My son François. Keep still, can't you? My daughter Chantal. Hungry, darling? … *Your* criminal, Monsieur Tim." He much enjoyed reaching his climax.

"No! No! In English law everybody's presumed innocent till he's proved guilty."

"Yes! And the pedestrian is always right, and the Germans never meant to have a war. Pretty, but unpractical. Not very serious."

Richard was amused, but Tim began to defend his country with more warmth than tact. He said that the English might not go in for theories, but they always got there in the end. Character was the thing, not policy. Look at his brother Nigel, for instance; he hadn't trained for anything, but he was in a marvelous job, and … As for the war, well, it was the English, not the …

He was fortunately interrupted by the servant, who came out again. An out-of-work man was asking, she said, if he might clean the car, which he had noticed outside. Also, lunch was ready.

Monsieur Defay wasted no time.

"A local man, is he? All right, Rosine. Tell him he can have the job if he leaves the price to me. I pay by results. If he won't, so much the worse for him! Well, come on, let's eat! Where are you off to, Jeannette?"

"I've forgotten some things in the car, Papa. Shall I leave it unlocked so that he can do the windows inside?"

She slipped out and did not return until the others were eating *hors d'œuvres* in the dining room. Richard, as she sat down opposite, thought he would like such a daughter himself; mettlesome and soft at once, her sparkling looks only brighter for the extreme demureness of her behavior. Tim Dawson-Gower could look at nothing else.

The lunch could not have been better. Everything was in season, fresh from local markets, and most artfully dressed. But the master of the house was a perfectionist. He cut a tiny sliver from the melon, smelled it, and sent for another. "No aroma." And he passed his plate of meat back to his wife, saying indignantly,

"My poor friend, this veal has certainly been eating grass. You didn't examine the carcass. It is adolescent and quite uneatable."

It was white, tender, and stuffed with little yellow mushrooms. Richard refused to part with his plate.

"Well, eat it if you must. But I assure you, any veal that has to be cut with a knife has lost all edibility."

"My little Dédé," said his wife (asperity suited her classical features; give her an olive wreath and she'd go straight on to a coin), "you deceive yourself. It's true, I didn't see the head. But the feet—I guarantee to you, the feet were tiny. It was certainly a calf of milk."

"My dear, your feet are tiny, too. But…. Very well, see if you can find me a better piece. All the same, it's terrible veal! Jeannette, you're not eating. Aha! Yours is tough too!"

"No thank you, Papa, it's excellent. I was dreaming … wondering … Do tell us all about your case, Monsieur."

"No, no, don't bore our guest. Crime is the same everywhere. Food, luckily, isn't. These artichokes are from our place in the country. Notice the sauce, it's a speciality of the region." He shook his head at his eldest daughter. "Our poor Jeannette, Monsieur, is very unreasonable. All she thinks about is adventure. At four, she wanted to be a second Joan of Arc. At eight, a heroine of the Resistance. Now she wants to work her way round the world, silly creature. With her looks and a nice dowry all ready for her! Talk some sense into her while I have another artichoke."

Richard turned with pleasure to Jeannette and her mother. He talked of famous Frenchwomen, and talked well. The mother was all lively appreciation, but Jeannette, though she exclaimed and her eyes glittered, fell into fits of abstraction, when she gazed past his shoulder at nothing, or stole a look at Tim further down the table. Richard was perplexed.

"If that girl isn't in love," he said to himself, "I'll eat my hat. Nothing but new love gives them that—that pearly fire. And young Tim's head over ears, obviously. But if she's in love with *him*, why does she look at him like a pair of shoes that she can't get into a suitcase? On the other hand, if she *isn't* in love with him, why look at him at all? I'm a better proposition than that dumb mooncalf, surely?"

He was, and Jeannette at any other time would have listened. But now, she was anxious for a chance to warn Tim, and desperate—dying almost—for the moment when she could slip out again to the garage. It was not just love of adventure; it was love *and* adventure.

The children had begun lunch lively as robins, eating like their elders and drinking, as always, wine mixed with water. But either the wine was stronger today, or François had more than his due, for suddenly, in the middle of his favorite desert, the boy fell asleep with his head on the table.

"I'll take him upstairs, the poor kid," said Jeannette immediately. "Tim will help me."

The loose-jointed skinny little bundle in Tim's arms grunted and settled its head without waking; and his mother, placidly remarking that his bowels must be out of order, moved them all back to the garden for coffee. Richard loitered behind and asked if his host could spare him a few moments alone.

"Certainly, certainly. But we must have our coffee. And a liqueur, perhaps?"

"Or an orange, to help digestion?" put in the grandmother, who had eaten heartily but taken no part in the conversation beyond hissing at the children to sit up.

Richard thought that an orange would be the last straw. He sipped his coffee and wondered how soon his mind would begin functioning again; this sweet blank of midday had its dangers. Meanwhile Madame Defay's voice sharpened and rose.

"What are those two doing? Their coffee will be undrinkable. JEANNETTE!" No answer. She remarked (justly) that the girl must be deaf, and sent Chantal to find her. Chantal dragged into the house slowly; but she came out big with drama and galvanized into vivid pantomime.

"They've disappeared! I've looked absolutely everywhere!"

A splendid screaming party was developing when the pair strolled in from the back entrance. Or rather Jeannette strolled; Tim followed more self-consciously.

"Did you call?" she said. "We just stopped to see how the car was getting on. Papa, the man's done it most beautifully. He really works very well, and he won't make a fuss about the price. So I had an idea. Couldn't we let him mend the *Truc*? He does understand boats, and I *do* so want it. Rowboats aren't the same. I want to sail again. Please, please!"

She had both hands on her father's chest and was gazing up (perhaps a trifle too confidently, considering natural immunization) into eyes as bright and wolflike as her own.

"You want the boat, do you? Why? To start sailing round the world next week?"

"Oh no, no! I don't want to leave you, really I don't … only one gets bored sometimes. But if one can sail … Come on, daddy, be nice. No one else will do it so cheap."

"Oh? And what's he like, this man? Handsome? Young?"

"Oh, no, no! He's just an ordinary working man—" she smiled— "But good and cheap. He's very dirty, and talks like a peasant."

"That doesn't keep him from—oh, well!" Monsieur Defay gave his daughter a hearty kiss. "You won't be a bad businesswoman, my dear. All right. I'll see the man presently. But now I want to talk to Monsieur Ringwood alone."

His wife and daughter departed without visible resentment or slavish alacrity. Richard, idly gazing up at the vine-leaf shade, thought how easy life was with Frenchwomen. They never failed to look their best, flatter one's self-esteem, and feed one a couple of banquets a day. Still, perhaps it was humiliating and corrupting for a man to be pampered like a spoilt child; or why did Monsieur Defay seem so much more grown up when his women weren't there? His face now actually looked a different shape. Well, perhaps alone he would drop the big bow-wow and talk turkey. Richard began.

"You must know Dawson-Gower quite well by now; this is his second visit to you, I believe. And he's evidently very devoted to your—your family. Is it unfair to ask how you feel about him yourself?"

"On the contrary," said his host in a manner which would not have been out of place at the Quai d'Orsay, "I appreciate a delicacy which offers me the opportunity to define his position in my household. First," he held up a finger, "I must assure you that morally he is perfectly innocuous. But I believe you have yourself also formed that opinion.

"Nevertheless," a second finger came into the balance, "as a father, I confess that I find him a problem. He came to us last year simply as a friend of *l'honorable* Clandon, at his request. This year— well, he asked himself and one didn't want to be rude, or of course to offend *cet honorable* Clandon. But it was the latter whom we approved as a serious friend for Jeannette, not the former. In that respect, the poor young Dawson-Gower is less solid. You understand me?"

Richard understood. Solidity, in this context, meant a title and a future in synthetic manure.

"Still," he objected, "I suppose really she's friends with them both."

"Oh no! Let us define. Let us be exact. Dawson-Gower is unfortunately in love with her and *l'honorable* Clandon has retired from the field. He has conducted himself perfectly—he has natural sense, that one—and I bear him no grudge. He'll get a better match if he waits a few years, and we—well, we haven't wasted our time. He will remain an interesting acquaintance for the children. And of course one never cares for foreign marriages."

Richard looked his surprise at this apparent contradiction.

"Only when a girl lacks equilibrium—I mean, if she has a romantic desire for adventure and rebels against convention—sometimes one hopes she may accept security if it is disguised as adventure. Hence, you see. ...."

"It seems good feminine psychology."

"It was my wife's idea, in fact. But Dawson-Gower—that's something else entirely. We think of sending Jeannette to my sister in Poitiers for a time. But please realize that this is no reflection on the boy's character. I'm simply acting as a father."

"Absolutely. I see. By the way, how did you come across Clandon in the first place? Did you know the family?"

"Oh no! A friend, Monsieur Lévy, spoke to us of him. Not that he thought we should take an English boy ourselves, having no sons of that age—he just hoped we might know of someone that did. But as things were, we decided to consider him. One had, after all, heard of the uncle as a businessman."

"I see. Did your friend Monsieur Lévy know Clandon personally?"

"No, not directly. He teaches in the *lycée* at Tours. An old pupil wrote from England to enquire, I believe. Of course I wrote to Lord Clandon. It was more practical than dealing with a young man."

At Tours! Despuys had been at school there. Richard wrote down the master's name.

"Good! Now another question. Did you have any reason to think that the two young men visited a certain woman in the *Impasse du Cher* during their visits here?"

"*Tiens!*" He was surprised but tolerant. "No, indeed, I had no idea. They were very discreet."

"It may be serious. She was a Madame Brunet, generally known as la Zézette."

M. Defay said, with a shade of disapproval, that he had never heard the name mentioned among bachelors, even the merriest of them. She must be a low type, really rotten.

"She was the mistress of a man called Maxime Fleurat during the Occupation."

M. Defay went up like a rocket. That ordure, that foul beast, that filth, that traitor, Blancbec—*his* leavings! It was intolerable, it was vicious, it polluted his house. He had been deceived. Tim must leave at once. Hypocrites!

Richard begged him to calm himself. He thought that the boys had been led into a trap by Despuys, and had no idea of the woman's character; and he told Clandon's story, somewhat edited. Defay merely blew at him to begin with, but presently he said,

"Well, perhaps *cet honorable* Clandon was tricked, incredible as it seems. It at least explains why he didn't come back for a second visit to us. But the other—he must have known beforehand. I shall never forgive him, never!"

"Perhaps I ought to say that I haven't any actual evidence that Tim went at all. I know Clandon did; I merely suppose the same of Tim. Shall I tell you my present hypothesis?"

"I'd be delighted," growled the other.

"Dawson-Gower's elder brother Nigel was in this district during the war, working with the Resistance." Defay snorted. "He was here when Blancbec disappeared so mysteriously just before the Liberation. Well, now; suppose Dawson-Gower had something to do with that? And suppose Despuys' sister can prove it? What would happen if she told her brother, Jean Despuys, and he decided to blackmail Nigel Dawson-Gower? They would need to demonstrate to their victim that they really did possess damaging proof; but they wouldn't want to part with the proof or incriminate themselves by writing letters. I suggest that they'd do exactly what they did do— fix up an interview with one of Nigel's intimates, his brother or Clandon or both, show them how serious it could be, and use them to negotiate terms. Good! Well, last year, Tim, I think, but it might be Francis, has such an interview and returns to England with the news. Nigel takes it more calmly than they did, being, I think, a very much harder character, and reaches some arrangement with

Despuys. He persuades Clandon to play Despuys along—and they somehow keep him quiet till this summer. But then he renews his demands—perhaps increases them. Perhaps the snubs he has received make him turn dangerous. Anyhow, they can't pay him. Nigel decides Despuys must be killed."

"And then?"

"Nigel killed him in Oxford, took away the body in Tim's car and almost managed to dispose of it without trace. But the feet are found—wearing Francis Clandon's socks; and my bloodhound makes it clear to me that the blood-spots in the car are from those feet."

"My congratulations!"

"Thank you. Next, Tim gets alarmed and runs away to Pontchâtelet, leaving his brother to cover his flight, which he does by rather careless lying. I exposed the lies and telephoned London to hold Nigel for questioning. But he disappeared yesterday. And more thoroughly than young Tim did, which isn't surprising. For Tim has an alibi for the time of destroying the body, but Nigel has not."

"Exactly!"

"I visited the woman Zézette today. I found that a man, whose name she would not divulge, had slept in her spare room last night and tampered with her brother's papers. She was absolutely terrified. You guess my suspicions?"

"Naturally. That Nigel murdered Blancbec years ago, was threatened by the two Despuys with exposure, and killed Despuys, subsequently coming here to recover some bit of evidence from the sister. I guess your suspicions, my poor sir, but I can also dispel them. Blancbec was a declared public enemy, and has never been given an amnesty. To kill him would not be a crime, but the act of a citizen."

"To kill him, yes. What if Nigel had helped him to escape?"

"That would be vile, vile! But as a matter of fact it's common knowledge that the vermin was killed here, by patriots, privately."

"Oh? Someone actually came forward and claimed the credit?"

Defay's teeth showed under his mustache. "Plenty of people claimed the credit—and, I may say, their stories conflicted greatly. None of them could produce the body."

"In that case, you've no reason to believe the rest of the story— that Blancbec was really killed."

"You English! You'll never understand the Resistance. They were heroes, patriots, and so on; I agree there. But they didn't have to *go* underground when we were invaded. They *were* underground. You could trust them to attend to public enemies like Blancbec, but they lied to the police by pure habit. If they ever came in sight of them."

"But surely there were all sorts of people in the movement?"

"In other places, perhaps. But we're quite decent folk in Touraine. And a Marshal of France—that meant something to us for a long time. Pétain didn't get called *l'oncle Gaga* here till he'd more than shown he deserved it. By then, the Resistance had—taken on a certain character."

"You yourself, for example, wouldn't have worked with them?"

"I did in fact help occasionally. But you needn't believe me. Everybody made such claims, after the Liberation; it was prudent. My schoolmaster friend, Lévy, and my sister at Poitiers did much more, and their services were never recognized."

"But surely you could bear witness to one another?"

"Oh no! It was all very—individual. There were people working for both sides in so many families, no one dared to risk saying anything."

"So Despuys himself may have been a *résistant* even while his sister was Blancbec's mistress. Or was he too young?"

"No one was too young. The children still haven't recovered from the habits of deceit they learned then for the good of their country. Still, I doubt if they'd have risked using *that* boy. Ask his teachers."

"Yes. I will."

"But I think you're wasting your time, going back into the past. I hope you'll catch your murderer. But look for something more recent, and of course count on me to do my possible to help you. In return, I must ask you to remove Tim Dawson-Gower at once. I really now have every reason to expel him."

"Please, please, keep him a little longer. I'll have him watched. But I need him here; he's our chief hope of renewing contact with the criminal."

"What?" Defay's brown eyes sharpened like a wolf's. "With his brother, you mean? Do you really think he is in Pontchâtelet?"

"Well, someone was in the *Impasse du Cher* last night. The only difficulty is, if it was Nigel, how was he warned in time in England, and by whom? And how did he get past the checks at the ports?"

"Tim must have telegraphed. As for the ports—they learned that in the war."

"Maybe. But I still don't see how he knew what was happening here. We've checked with the post office. No telegrams to England left Pontchâtelet yesterday, nor were any foreign telephone calls passed through the exchange. That is why I do beg of you to keep the boy here just for a few days."

"Very well. But my children must go to their aunt at Poitiers. Or to our country property. I can't have them exposed."

Jeannette, listening behind the shutter of her room overhead, hugged herself and smiled.

CHAPTER 15

Nigel Dawson-Gower had returned to his old cave in the Forest of Pontchâtelet as easily as a man coming home from a holiday. Arriving before dawn, he had worked ever since; burying his parachute in a nearly natural landslide, stowing his gear, visiting the town to make contact with Tim and summon his old friends to help. Now it was evening, and he waited. The best or worst was to come. Blue-chinned and shabby, a Camel cigarette in the corner of his mouth, a greasy beret peaked over one eye, he lay on the ledge at peace, stilled by action as a top steadies with spinning; alert but relaxed, savoring his luck.

Lucky first time, to find that Jock was flying spare parts to Spain. Jock was a romantic. Nigel had always been a hero to him. So when Nigel asked for a drop, saying "spot of woman trouble," Jock conscientiously refrained from questions. The poor fish obviously thought he was on a secret mission. Jock had hidden him in the fuselage, and behaved so ordinarily to the ground staff that they wondered—Nigel heard them— if he'd got bad news or a hangover. Jock was a clot. Lucky.

At last Nigel heard what he was waiting for—steps along the path below and a voice humming the Maquis song, the bombastic words and the rubber-soled, unending tune that had kept them loping across country, once, through miles of darkness. The walker sang, "Oh, my countrymen, come down from the hills!"and Nigel answered by softly whistling the last line, his favorite, "Oh, miners, come up from the abyss!"

The footsteps turned uphill. They sounded like one man; but Nigel was not surprised to see three: Jeannot, Titi and Auguste. They gripped his hand and called him *tu* and good old Radar, his fighting nickname, but he felt they were holding back somehow. He produced a bottle.

"Have some whisky, chums. A present from my boss. He always tells me it's good for business."

"*Private* business?" asked Jeannot sharply. He was a meager man of fifty with a terribly scarred face. He got the scars under torture, ten years ago; Nigel had seen the wounds raw. "Listen, Radar," Jeannot said. "You're my friend always, but—I'm not doing any capitalists' dirty work for them. You might as well get that straight."

"How much do we get, Radar?" It was Titi, one of the two younger men. He still spoke almost without moving his lips, and he still looked as knotted and dry as a vinestock.

But the other young man was a pure, florid, Latin type, handsome beyond belief. Only fools do believe such men. He struck himself on the breast and declared that for him friendship came before money or politics. Perhaps Nigel had better speak to him alone.

Nigel, however—it was his acute ears that had earned him the nickname of Radar—merely grinned and replied:

"That's all right, Auguste. I heard you reminding Jeannot that the Commies might pay to hear my stuff, and him cursing you. But it isn't politics. I'm on my own, and the police are after me for murder. Five thousand now and more later if you help me out."

Then it really was like old times. They were slapping him on the back and calling him a madman. Nigel told them his story. Obviously they found it hard to believe that neither Nigel nor his brother had killed Despuys; otherwise, why bother to dispose of the body? They were sympathetic and critical. Why expect a haystack to burn properly in England, where it always rained? The bloodhound, though, was bad luck. One couldn't anticipate that. But why kill the man in the first place?

"I—oh well, never mind who killed him!" Easily Nigel gave up the argument. "The point is, who else but me could the police be made to suspect?"

Ah! They understood now. He wanted them to fix a frameup. He must pin it on to someone here in France, who might have slipped over to England, done the job, and returned. Because the clues, the motives, must be found here in France, where Jeannot, Titi, and Auguste could plant them. Besides, the English detective was here in Pontchâtelet. They were fertile of suggestions.

They named old enemies, rich men who'd been on the wrong side during the Occupation. Nigel cut them short. A respectable *bourgeois* wouldn't do. It had to be a man whom the police didn't trust; also a man they hadn't kept tabs on lately.

"Ah!" Jeannot's smile was ironical. "You mean—chaps like us?"

They ran over the list of local *résistants*. One had been deported for robbery with violence; another was a rich and respectable Trade Union official. It seemed hopeless. Then Jeannot remembered the mistress of an old enemy—Zézette. She wasn't respectable. Nobody was likely to rush to her defense. And she'd be no loss, eh?

"Excellent!" Auguste's teeth flashed. "But, listen—she might be able to prove an alibi. Wouldn't it be safer to fix her up as a suicide, and leave a confession or something at the same time? It'd be a risky job, of course, but one man would be enough to take care of it. We could toss for who did it. For my friend's sake, I at least am prepared to take my chance."

"Ah! But they're *your* dice." Titi merely stated.

Then Jeannot lifted his arms. "Listen, you idiots! What about Blancbec, eh? What happened to Blancbec? Nobody knows!"

They all began talking and laughing together. A grand idea! Blancbec! Even the police would like that. He was still listed as a war criminal, he was missing, wanted … Besides, if they used a fake Blancbec, they could exploit his former liaison with Despuys' sister, give him a motive for killing her brother. And Blancbec hadn't got any alibi, said Titi. Not unless the devil himself turned up in court to say he'd been personally roasting him at the time. (Loud laughter.)

They turned to Auguste to invent a plausible story. That, after all, was his *métier*. He was a confidence trickster, now specializing in American female tourists. Only Titi looked skeptical.

Auguste rose to the challenge.

"*Bon!*" His eyes flashed in the gloom. "Already I have an idea. Listen! A clever criminal—and Blancbec wasn't stupid in that way, was he?—will always take the initiative. He will exploit the element of surprise. That is, he'll do what you don't expect."

"*Merci!*" Auguste looked up sharply but could not tell whose dry whisper that was. Probably Titi, but they could all ventriloquize. It might be Radar. He resumed.

"Now imagine Blancbec making a getaway. I know, I know, but

imagine it. What does he do? Does he run to the place where he'll be safest? No! That's where they'll be watching for him. So he runs to the center, to …"

"Paris." The whisper had apparently shifted its source.

"Perhaps. But we'll say, England. Now, why does he not take his mistress, *la belle Zézette*?"

"Too risky. Wants a change." Auguste dared not show how the whisper annoyed him. It might be Radar. They could all do it.

"Perhaps," he said. "But we'll say—so she can send him money. How will she send him money?"

"Through a Spanish tourist agency."

"Perhaps. But we'll say, by her brother, who gets a job in England. I expect one of the collaborationist lot got it for him. But after a while Despuys thinks—why not take a bit before I pass it on? And then, why not a bit more? Anyone would. And one day, he takes the lot and pretends it hasn't come. Of course, Blancbec accuses him."

"And Despuys threatens to give him away?" Nigel suggested.

"Exactly! So what would Blancbec do?"

"*Not* kill him," said Titi, in his own voice this time. "Or how would he get the money through afterwards?"

"My poor friend! Which is more important, money or peace of mind?"

"Money. One can't eat peace of mind."

"Perhaps. But we'll say … Oh, very well! Make a better story yourself." Auguste stood up, his profile nobly averted against the night sky. "The point is, I could have got stamps, letters, postmarks, tickets—everything. You're not an artist, Titi, *mon pauvre vieux*. To an artist, construction is everything. Art, as somebody said, is the incarnation of impossibilities."

Titi merely grunted. Nigel interposed.

"Auguste's right in a way. It's the details that count, and we know Blancbec inside out. Can you still do his handwriting? And fingerprints? Auguste?"

"I can write like him, I think. But I never got his dabs. Did you, Jeannot?"

"No. I'll never forget his hands, though. I had them close to my face, all that night. A ring with a bee on it—something to do with Napoleon—a heavy ring. He kept talking about it. He pressed it into my eyes and then asked if I could still see the bee. …"

"Steady, my old friend!" Titi shook his shoulder. "Look, Radar, he gets these turns sometimes. Talk of something else and he'll be all right."

"The ring's a useful point," Nigel said, unmoved. "He was mad about Napoleon, wasn't he? He had a pencil with a bee on it too. Wonder if the boys took that off him? Oh, well, never mind. If we can't get a genuine souvenir we can fake one up. It all adds verisimilitude. Now, what about Despuys' handwriting? We'll need to fake a threatening letter from him. I suppose the quickest way to get a specimen would be from Zézette's house. I'll do that."

"No, I will. I'm smaller," said Titi. "Auguste can distract her. Make love to her. Incarnate a few more impossibilities."

"*Could* I? It would be a supreme test of my temperament. But if I failed …"

"Get her to confide in you," Nigel suggested. "Easier."

"I will. She can tell me all the little revealing details. I suppose we fix the evidence in her house, do we? Nice and handy, as the police are on to it."

"Naturally," said Jeannot. "And then, if necessary …"

"No!" Nigel said. "Better keep off 'suicide.' It might come back at us somehow. But if we get jammed up, we can frighten her into saying what we want. She might even be more useful alive. Well, let's get down to details. Come in the cave, we can have a light there."

Jeannot stayed after the others. His temperature had gone up and he wanted to rest. He had changed much since the last time Nigel saw him; it was worth making sure how deep the change went. Nigel let him talk a bit, and watched him narrowly as he slept. At last Jeannot stood up to go. Nigel lifted his eyelids.

"Well, good night, chum. And thanks."

"I haven't done anything yet, Radar."

"You gave us our big idea. By the way—what really happened to Blancbec?"

"The Pole—you know, the one they called *le Marteau*—said Blancbec was in that Boche staff car he shot up. He chucked the bodies in the lime kiln, on the road to les Tricheries."

Nigel remembered the Pole. *Le Marteau* had a fist like a club and pale, mad eyes.

"So it was never proved?"

"No. *Le Marteau* chucked the bodies in the lime kiln, he wasn't interested in getting a reward. Still, the boys could have cashed in, if he'd only thought to leave Blancbec's body somewhere safe for them. But he just chucked it in the kiln, pinned a note to the car, and went off. We never saw him again. Funny, that; he used to say that he was sure he'd croak when the Boches were accounted for. He said there'd be nothing left to live for."

"And—was there?" Nigel's shiny eyelashes hid whatever intent was behind the question. "Did you find there was?"

"Oh, yes." Jeannot walked stiffly towards the entrance. "There's always something. That's the bother." Only he used a stronger word.

"What, Jeannot—you mean you're still heart and soul for the Party? After—all this?"

"For the *people*, Radar. Like I always was. And I—mostly I get enough to eat. But I'm not so good when I get these turns."

Nigel whistled. "The people! You've never got a pennyworth of good from them, and yet you'd die for them?"

"I *am* dying for them." Jeannot was wryly matter-of-fact. "On account of what the Gestapo did ten years ago. No choice, see? But it's slow. I'm afraid I've a year's work in me yet."

Nigel's smile warmed him like a fire when he left; he felt less desolate, more like the Jeannot of the unscarred face, surer, than for a long time past.

As for Nigel, he curled up on his rock and went to sleep. His last waking thought was that, for present purposes, there was nothing the matter with Jeannot.

CHAPTER 16

"Baby's crying again," said Sylvie Kéhidiou. "It's these prisoners in the *violon*."

The two men sat over after-dinner coffee. Richard laughed.

"*Violon*. Yes, it's quite a concert."

"It'll be better when my men stop shouting at them to shut up. Still—six in custody here and another twenty sent off to Tours! You see what a problem it would be if we really enforced the vagrancy laws."

Richard asked if there were no institutions for tramps in France; Kéhidiou rather crossly admitted that there were almost none. Hence ...

"I'm awfully sorry," Richard said. "But I'm sure somebody got away from Zézette's house this morning, and ..."

"Don't worry. Picking up the tramps was clearly the first line of enquiry. If it doesn't yield results, we'll have a house-to-house search tomorrow."

"Tomorrow? Why not now?"

"It's against the law. We aren't allowed to enter any house between dusk and dawn."

Richard was glad he wasn't a French policeman. He asked if the batch of tramps examined by Kéhidiou were at all interesting.

"Not really. I expect the Bureau of Identification of Lyons have got their prints and so on already. Oh, there *was* just one thing. You know the old man I had in the lockup last night? That you saw asleep by the towing path later on?"

"Yes."

"Well, he's missing. And another man's got his identity card. We found it on him when we pulled him in."

"What was his explanation?"

"Said he'd been out for a walk by the river and picked it up in the grass. The man's known as Titi. He isn't exactly a tramp. I think his game is smuggling and undercover politics, but I can't prove it. He had a decent war record in the Resistance."

"He might have really picked it up, you mean? Intending to sell it to someone who was after false papers. Did you get him to show you where he said it was?"

"Yes. A bit further downstream than Zézette's house."

"Find anything?"

"No. The river runs fast, that side. Things could easily ... disappear there."

Yes. The broad sunny river was less harmless than it looked. Between the wooded islands were deep swift channels; the silver-brown sandbanks were soft enough to swallow a body, and the gray willows had tough gripping roots to hold one wedged under water....

"The inspectors are going round the likely places now. You can't really *search* this river, but it doesn't keep its secrets for long. The sand's always shifting. In the end, we'll find him. Poor old man. It's my fault."

Kéhidiou was surprisingly upset.

"I bet he's just asleep in a barn somewhere," said Richard. "No one would do murder just for a spare identity card."

"Perhaps. Most of the prisoners had no cards at all. But ... it was me cursing him like that this morning. Ah! Sylvie, my dear! Baby asleep?"

"At last. And I saw the dog of an inspector coming in. He looks pleased about something."

Kéhidiou hurried downstairs with a stricken look.

"I didn't know you had any police dogs here," Richard remarked, feeling he ought to stay and be polite.

Sylvie laughed. "Oh! Not real dogs. It's just slang for inspectors. They nose round, you see, spying in all the unsavory quarters. Don't you know the song ..." She strolled out, softly but with strongly marked rhythm and snapping eyes:

> Whoever invented that damned dog of an inspector
> Is a long way, believe me, from being an imbecile,
> Because a dog runs faster than an inspector,
> And he has the advantage of being intelligent.

"Sshh! Sshh!" hissed her husband, returning. "You choose your moment badly. Will you come down, Monsieur?"

The inspector had found the old tramp's body half submerged in a sandbank, naked. They could find none of his clothes anywhere.

"But their lack of success," said Kéhidiou on the stairs, "is no proof of a negative. One must admit that the intellectual level of our inspectors is rather low. You won't get much sense out of *him*."

"Oh? So that nice little song has the sting of truth?"

"I hope he didn't hear. It's a red rag to a bull. Like that one about stationmasters' wives."

"He's a cuckold, the stationmaster! That? But it's a classic. They *must* be used to it by now."

"No, I assure you. A trainload of students leaned out and sang it at a station near here and the stationmaster had apoplexy. He wanted to sue them for medical expenses," continued Kéhidiou without a smile, "but I persuaded him not to. This is our inspector."

The "dog of an inspector" was heavy, with flat eyes like a goat's. The body, he said, had been found by a fisherman stuck headfirst into a sandbank. The fisherman had shouted for help and the inspector had been rowed out to the place. It was towards the left bank, a bit out of town.

"North or south bank?"

"The left. I said."

"Above or below Pontchâtelet?"

"Outside. I said. There." He pointed in a direction well away from the river. Kéhidiou looked grieved and Richard continued:

"Is it still in the sandbank? Oh, you had it moved, did you? Was the sandbank in midstream? Could the body have drifted into that position naturally? Or had it been put there? How did look?"

The inspector almost seemed to think. "Like a crayfish, Monsieur," he replied at length. "But," he wagged his finger, "bigger, Monsieur. Naturally bigger."

"He means half sticking out and half in the sand," said Kéhidiou, chafing. "As we know already. We'd better go and look. You marked the spot, at least?"

"No, *Monsieur le Commissaire*. One sandbank's like another, after all."

"That's just why … *enfin*! Is the fisherman waiting?"

"I don't know. I told him to stay with the body, but he didn't seem keen. I told him, too, I said, it's your own fault, *you* found it …"

"*Allons*!" said Kéhidiou. "The car's outside. Inspector, you bring the doctor along when he arrives."

The car was the usual front-wheel drive Citroën and went fast. As Richard expected, they were taken to a part of the river downstream from where he had seen the tramp that morning—a place where the Cher flowed between gently rising fields and vineyards, a broad meandering stream tufted with islands. Even in moonlight one could see the surface rippled in the main channels and glassy smooth where there was dead water. They walked between strip plantations, following a line of poplars that marched towards the river. There was a little beach cutting a scallop in the high bank, and a boat was grounded there.

"Well, here's the body," Kéhidiou said, "but the man seems to have gone."

"Not at all, *Monsieur le Commissaire*." A man stood up on the bank around the bend, reeling in a fishing line. "Just waiting round the corner. It's more fun than over there. Poor old chap, he gives me the horrors."

Kéhidiou made a note of his name, Sylvain Tissier.

"You're a fisherman?"

"Yes and no. That is, I spend a lot of time fishing about here. It's right by my land. That's mine, third strip from the trees there— carrots, eggplants, beans, artichokes …"

"You're a cultivator, then?"

"Yes and no. Certainly I work my land. But we live in town,

the corner of the Rue Clémenceau, just handy for our paper stand."

"Oh! A news agent, are you?"

"Again, Monsieur, yes and no. My wife really does most of it. I have to go out to my job."

"Which is …?"

"Clerk in the gasworks."

Kéhidiou ceased to cross out entries in his notebook and introduced the Englishman. Tissier said he was honored.

Richard began:"When you found the body, did you happen to notice the time?"

"Oh yes! What a feeling! I shall never forget it. The church clock struck nine while I was looking at him, and for a moment it put me in mind of a passing bell. Death is always disagreeable, but like that! Ah, Sylvain, I said to myself, one day it will be your turn. Let's hope at least that you'll make a handsomer corpse. And yet you won't feel any better for that."

"However, that will hardly console you." Kéhidiou was fidgeting to get at the body.

"You go," said Richard. "I suppose we ought to leave it in the boat till the doctor comes, and I can join you then. Let's walk up and down here, Monsieur. Yes, it must have been nasty to find him. I don't wonder you feel upset."

"Now, I am almost calm. But the dead are always disagreeable, and this one—imagine, not only naked, but moving its legs, like this—really, that was too much."

"Moving? do you mean he was alive when you found him?"

"Oh no, poor thing. It was just—well, it's difficult to explain if you don't know the river. You see that island with the bird flying just over it? Well, the right bank of it is steep and the water flows fast there; just below, but you can't see it from here, there's a bar of soft sand. Evidently, this poor fellow was carried past the island rather quickly and his speed plunged him headfirst into the bank like a spoon in a *purée*. He was jammed in right up to his armpits, you see, but his feet were still out in the current, sort of dancing— Oh! It was horrible!"

"Dreadful. But I wouldn't have thought the current was strong enough actually to ram things into sand like that. The Cher is surely a very dangerous river for boating?"

"Dangerous? No, no, not if you know it. It's a lovely river, the Cher. You can come down on the mainstream without any work except steering, and then row back easily by keeping to the dead water. It's splendid."

"But aren't the sandbars always shifting?"

"Yes and no, Monsieur. They shift, but we know what they will do by the weather. More rain, bigger sandbanks. More wind, sharper edges. More heat, less depth everywhere. Why, you can calculate just how far your boat will float in a given time on a given stretch, if you know the river."

"That's very interesting. Tell me. If this body entered the water from the left bank just past the station, how long would it have taken to get to where you found it?"

"Let me think!" said Tissier briskly. "The Cher's deep there, and without islands. It would take him along quite fast if he didn't stick on a pier of the bridge. Good. Well, then, round the bend, but he'd be on the outside edge so he'd probably be carried right on round. Next comes the bathing place. It's true there's a little barrier there where things sometimes jam, but surely with a body someone would have noticed. There's another bend after that on the edge of the town, he'd be on the inside of that one, so he'd take a bit of time passing it. It's slower going from there, too; the obstacles are worse outside the town, you get islands and odd humps of sand and roots sticking out under water. And he couldn't steer, the unlucky fellow. He'd have been bumping and sticking all the way. I'd say it would have taken him all day to get as far as this. And yet, you know, with the water pulling at his legs like that, he'd have been on his travels again by tomorrow, probably. What a deathbed! Quite takes away your appetite for fish, doesn't it?"

"But what you say is enormously important," said Richard. "According to you, he'd go past the town quite quickly, and only begin to slow up where the houses thin out? And he might have stayed undiscovered for any time, almost, according to you."

"Not according to me, Monsieur. According to all Pontchâtelet. That's where our children's toy boats get lost. Many a Sunday I've spent looking for them with my boat. Sometimes with success, sometimes …"

"But a stranger wouldn't know, unless someone told him."

"No, but—Excuse me, you're not suggesting that any of *us* would do an awful thing like that! Drown a man so as he'd be lost forever! Listen. We're not that bad around here! And anyhow, he may have fallen in. Or drowned himself. Besides, how do you know he took the plunge in Pontchâtelet at all? Much more likely up-river at Pontpoupon. They had a murder there three years ago."

"Calm down. The criminal I'm looking for committed a crime in England. Ah! Here's the doctor at last, so we'll have the body out of your boat in no time and see that it's all cleaned up and decent. Shall I bring you your basket of fish?"

"Ah, no!" He shuddered dramatically. But then he said, "Or perhaps, yes, if you would be so kind. I needn't tell them at home, and it's a pity to waste good fresh fish. But *I* shan't touch it. No, one course less for you, my poor Sylvain. But, too bad."

Kéhidiou held a torch and the doctor began his examination. Richard sympathized with the "emotion" of that eupeptic man Tissier. The body appeared very old, very dead, and very naked. The creature had looked decrepit enough this morning too—you wouldn't believe that clothes and a soul could have made all that difference to him—but even allowing for that …

"Are you sure it's the same old tramp?" Richard asked the Commissaire. "I wouldn't have recognized him myself."

"He simply got the dirt off. The sand and water have given him a good scouring, that's all. We can check by his anthropometry in the office if you like. Found any injuries, Doctor?"

"Well—these scratches and bumps seem to have been picked up in the water, by the look of them. Ah! Here's a swelling on the temple, though. Was he knocked about at all while under arrest?"

"Of course not!" replied Kéhidiou hotly. "Why, we … that is, no, Doctor."

"Well, he received the blow quite lately. Help me turn him over, please. Can either of you do artificial respiration?"

Richard volunteered. The ribs under his fingers felt as cold as doorknobs.

"Hmm! It looks as if there were no water in the lungs. *Bon!* If so, he didn't die by drowning, though there is still the possibility of heart failure and a fall. Oh well! I suppose I'd better have him up at the hospital for a postmortem, Monsieur, if you would be so kind as to transport him."

Kéhidiou muttered mechanically that the kindness was all on the doctor's side. The doctor replied that it was his job, also there was an extra fee for postmortems, also it would not be possible for him to perform this one until ten next morning. Richard could not make out if he were being rude, facetious, or merely factual.

At last they got away, taking turns to stumble with the body in an improvised stretcher across the long field. Kéhidiou had beached the boat as though to withstand a tornado; that was how they did things in Brittany.

CHAPTER 17

"Psst! Psst!"

Nigel did not answer, though he had woken at the snap of a twig a minute ago. He held his finger on the button of the torch and waited in the cave till Auguste's voice quavered,

"Radar! It's me, Auguste! Wake up!"

"Then why the hell couldn't you say so?" purred Nigel from the cave. "I was just going to—well, come inside! What's wrong with you?"

"Radar, they've copped Titi."

"Had he got the letters first? So that you can do Despuys' writing?"

"I—I don't know. He and Jeannot were going to the *Impasse du Cher* by the towing path. I said I'd wait near the bridge, on the main road."

"Well?"

"Well, I had finished one cigarette and started another, and then I saw the cops coming, and they'd got Titi. I just managed to nip over to the opposite side of the road."

"Nothing like standing by your chums. So?"

"But Titi saw me. He didn't say anything, but he did this." Auguste drew his fingers across his throat.

"Meaning he'd had it in a big way. But Jeannot wasn't there? Well, so what did you do about it?"

"What *could* I do?" Auguste talked faster and with more gestures. "Radar, I can't go on with this. If Titi *had* got specimens of Despuys' writing, we shan't see them. And if not … well, housebreaking isn't in my line. And you'd be a fool to try it now. We'll have to call it off. It's hopeless."

Auguste felt himself gripped. It was not only the strength of the grip that alarmed him. It was the voltage. Nigel was angry and enjoying it. Auguste blinked as the torch was turned full on his face.

"Sure that's all you came to say?"

"To warn you, yes. And I thought you might like to leave some money for poor old Titi. Compensation, you know. I'd see he got it, you can trust me."

"Always trust a boy from Marseilles. Nothing for yourself?"

"Well, Jeannot and I shared the risk. And though we'd never turn against an old pal like you. ... *Aïe!* What are you doing? Put the light on!"

"In my left hand," purred Nigel, "I've got a whisky bottle. In my right, your knife. It's silly to keep it in your sock suspender, because it bumps when you sit down. Well, which is it to be?"

"I'm your old friend—" his teeth chattered— "what do you want?"

"That's better." Nigel switched the torch on. "Have a drink. Now, listen. We can't call the operation off, and leave Titi in jug, and me in a mess. Can we?"

"N-no. But I can't bear to let you run risks, Radar."

"So first we contact Jeannot. He may have got the letters, and if so you can still do your little forgery job. I'll plant it in the house. Secondly, we get Titi out."

Auguste moaned, but he drank too.

"Look," said Nigel suddenly. "Suppose Titi *wasn't* caught burgling that house, or he'd passed the letters to Jeannot. Could they have had him up for something else?"

"I did hear they were pulling in tramps. Titi never carried his cards. He lives with his mother, and didn't want her upset, or something. They may have thought he was a tramp."

"No, he wouldn't have given the cutthroat sign if it was only that. Was he carrying anything hot? Dollars, or watches? Party stuff?"

"I wouldn't know." The knife glittered. "I mean, well, yes. It was really mine in a way. I'd promised him fifteen hundred for it. An identity card he found by the path. Nice one, too. A man with a beard and an ordinary name. Titi wouldn't part with it till I'd paid him. I bet he's sorry now."

Nigel still did not think Titi would get into bad trouble just for having someone else's card on him. He began to ask questions.

"Lots of cops, you say. And just questioning tramps? Nothing else?"

"Wait. Yes. Just after they passed with Titi, one of the inspectors went off and started talking to the man at the ferry. Pointing down river to the islands, they were. People still hide there sometimes. I wouldn't myself, unless I had a nice girl in a boat to bring me my meals and keep me warm at night."

"You've got something there. I'll remember that. Well, come on!

We'd better have a look at Titi's jail before there are too many people about. I've got an idea about getting him out, but we must finish our little frameup job first. Also see what the cops are up to. You can walk down with me. It looks better. You're not afraid now, are you?"

Auguste threw out his chest and attempted a swagger. After all, only a very brave man could bear to feel as frightened as he did. Lesser spirits would collapse. And Radar was mad. After stealing letters, he planned to plant false evidence—and that involved house-breaking—and then to burst into the town lockup.

It took courage to walk with a man like that.

CHAPTER 18

In pale early sunlight, Jeannette arrived at the empty bathing place and shivered as she hung her clothes on the peg in the hut. Thank goodness Tim and the family hadn't heard her leave the house.

Her first assignation, her first adventure, her first love. The last was all she thought of now, gasping as she entered the water. The group of bushes was some way along, but he would be waiting there. She wished she had a prettier bathing dress than this schoolgirlish black woolen thing. She came to the bushes, and he was not there.

"Oh God! I shall get gooseflesh and be all blue and horrible. Still, at least he won't see me in a bathing cap."

She pulled it off and bent over the water trying to see her reflection and arrange her hair. Two hands came out of the bush behind her and closed round her waist. She knew the feel of them. He was here, pulling her into the hollow center of the bush, a perfect hiding place, and turning her towards him.

"Careful, darling. I'll make you all wet and cold."

He pulled out a ragged shirt from his bundle and began drying her, but soon dropped it. The front of her bathing dress was warm and half-dried when he let go of her.

"Still think you'll make me cold?"

She shook her head, unable to speak.

"Jeannette. You'll marry me. Soon?"

"Yes, Nigel. Oh yes, soon! Now make my back warm. Ah, that's a lovely way to be. As if we were specially made ... Nigel, what's the matter?"

He had pushed her away and was taking off his shirt and trousers. He stood in his pants, looking at the ground. She half-understood, half-shrank from the look on his face. But he was Nigel, and turned away from her.

"Are you angry? Look at me! Even in my awful old bathing dress, darling."

He did not look at her. He began filling a pipe, and said, "Put those things on, or you'll catch cold. We mustn't waste time."

She put on his clothes, which engulfed her and smelled of him. Suddenly she resented the pipe. She snatched it and was going to throw it when he caught her wrist. She could feel the blood in his finger veins and was glad of his strength and his anger.

"So what happens next, Jeannette? Don't you care? Or—don't you know?"

"I'm sorry, darling. Of course, you want us to arrange a plan. Well, Papa says—"

"Oh Lord. Yes! Plans. I'd forgotten. Keep talking." He sat down and lit his pipe. She wished she could comfort him. She asked if he was hungry.

"*Hungry!*" He lifted his face and looked full at her, and she dropped her eyes, fully understanding. She tried to keep talking, as he wished.

"Papa says that the children and I and my aunt are to go to Angennes, that's our little country place, tomorrow. To keep us safe from *Tim!*"

She laughed, because however shaken you are by passion, a joke is a joke. He did not laugh.

"Go on, quick. It isn't too safe here."

"Well, I and my aunt between us are to supervise your work on the *Truc*, the boat that wants mending."

"Is there a shed or something I can sleep in? Can you feed me? Good. Now listen, darling. You're friendly with the Commissaire of Police? His wife! Better. Well, go and see her this morning, and find out—Are you listening?"

"Yes." She listened.

"And get yourself invited there this evening. When you arrive ..."

She listened, with horror and exaltation, trying to be as brave as he.

"I understand, *mon lapin*. But I'd better repeat it back to you. They always did in the Resistance. I'm to ask ..."

She repeated his instructions; he checked them with his hands over his eyes.

"Right. Oh, Jeannette! You know everything and nothing. We can't *not* be married."

"We mightn't be," she cried, losing control, "with all these mad risks you're going to take. Getting yourself into prison … If you really loved me, you wouldn't—"

He sprang to his feet.

"Come here. I'm mad about you, and you know it. Don't you? Yes, take them off, right off. Give me my clothes and go. Because I've got to do this, and do it my way. So go, before … Oh, come here! But now go. Quickly."

There had been no gentleness in his farewell. But when she had gone, he buried his face in his clothes that she had worn, sitting on the ground, forgetful of danger.

Richard Ringwood also rose early. In dressing gown and slippers, as French convention demanded, he walked over to the *violon*, that primitive prison. There was a gap above the heavy door, too high for a spy hole; it was probably an air vent. But on tiptoe, he could just look in. The prisoners were lying in a row on the communal leather bolster; the young and strong brutally spread-eagled in the middle, the old, dribbling toothlessly, by the wall. One small man, finding no place on the bolster, crouched with his head on his bent knees, like a body in a prehistoric barrow. And yet, in spite of their discomfort, they slept: the defenseless look of oblivion cannot be assumed. But they muttered in their sleep, and Richard listened.

"'Tisn't fair. Wasn't doing anything. Can't …" A senile, thick voice from the shadow by the wall.

"Ah, what they after? Eh? What they want, the bastards?" That voice came from the middle. It might have been the sturdy rogue with his head pillowed on an arm so covered with black hair that the skin was invisible. But he hadn't moved.

Then came a whisper, clear and curiously unplaceable—an old lag's trick of speech which Richard had met before.

"Must be Blancbec. He's been about again, they say. Blancbec! Remember Blancbec?"

An old man who had been snoring moaned, twitched, and awoke as though from nightmare, with a loud, choking "No! No!" His gummy eyes were struggling open as Richard ducked out of sight. He heard the old man's whimpering drowned by curses from the

others. Then there was a sharp warning *Psst*! and total silence. Someone must have seen his shadow falling across the cracks in the door.
When he looked again they seemed asleep, though not so soundly
as before.

Kéhidiou met Richard on the stairs. Contrary to all custom he
was already dressed, and in strict uniform. He listened skeptically
to Richard's story of what the prisoners were saying.

"Blancbec—Maxime Fleurat! Seen here? What a hope! Still, if
you like, I'll get his physical record sent here. I know there is one,
though the fingerprints got lost somehow. I'll be on the telephone to
Lyons in any case."

"Well, thank you. But how on earth did they get a physical
record—what d'you call it, a *fiche anthropométrique*—for Blancbec?
I thought he was bossing the police, not the other way round."

"In the war he was. But this record dated from before the war. It
was some very minor cause of arrest, a traffic offense or something.
But, you see, we have a rule that every single person who's arrested
has a complete physical record taken. I'm just going to have our
prisoners put through the *service anthropométrique*, and then ring
up Lyons to see if any of them is a likely suspect for the murder. It's
a long job measuring them up, even with the special callipers."

"Anthropometry." Richard looked interested. "That's the Bertillon system of body measurements, isn't it? I learned it once. Big-
toe joint, joints of middle finger, length of earlobe, mm? Is it sound?
I can see that everyone's got different proportions—even a tailor
knows that. But don't they vary a bit from year to year?"

"Not really. Sometimes certain kinds of illness—gout, for instance—produce local variations. But the all-over measurements
don't change, once a man's grown up and his bones are set. We
regard it as the most infallible identification. You see, no two sets of
measurements are alike."

"Nor are two sets of fingerprints."

"But suppose your criminal loses his hands?"

"Mm. There's something in that. Has the post come?"

"Any minute now. I'll have yours sent up to you."

When the post was brought him by a very superior policeman
known as a *secrétaire* (who explained that his rank was due to having passed Matric) Richard opened his wife's letter first. Their child
was still unborn.

Next he opened the telegram from his chief, which told him that

Nigel Dawson-Gower had disappeared. The BBC were broadcasting for information about him, and the Bloodhound was calling at the War Office to enquire about his record as a commando. Poor old Bloodhound! He'd hate being diplomatic with the army brass hats! It was good of him.

The third letter was from Inspector Colman, the young Oxford detective who had helped him the first day, and a conscientious youth he was. Remembering that during the run across the parks Richard had told him to ask Mr. Sansom if Despuys had a key to the parks, and remembering after Richard left that in the excitement of the chase he had never put this question, he had called on Sansom. Finding he had gone out, Colman left a written question with the landlady. Sansom replied immediately, as the postmark showed, but he had addressed his letter to the police at Cambridge, not Oxford, and there had been a couple of days delay. Colman said that the mistake was common; he had asked the post office. He enclosed Sansom's letter. Posted on Monday night, redirected from Cambridge on Tuesday, it had arrived in Oxford on Wednesday, and merely said that Despuys could not have had a key to the parks because he was not an M.A. Richard reserved judgment. Ranter was quite sure that her quarry had passed through a gate normally locked at sunset. And Nigel Dawson-Gower was quite capable of stealing a key if he wished.

Kéhidiou came in, having measured all the prisoners and telephoned to the office at Lyons. He said that the fingerprints found in Zézette Brunet's house yesterday had not been traced to anyone with a dossier. Didn't they probably belong to some stray visitor who was, from the police standpoint, innocent?

"It's possible," said Richard. "Or they might not be a French criminal's prints at all. I'll send them to Scotland Yard. What about the prisoners? Did Lyons give you any lines on them?"

"Not really. Some of them are recorded, some aren't. But they're all petty convictions, apart from this man Titi who had the old tramp's identity card. He's been in prison twice: once for assault and damage in a labor riot in 1937, and once during the Occupation for suspected sabotage. I'm inclined to keep him here, and release the others. Not that I can prove anything against him—and he won't talk so far. Nor that I'd consider the sabotage as anything but honorable to the fellow. But the fact remains, he's the only one we've got so far who might have drowned the old tramp."

"I agree. Though I still think that the tramp's murder is tied up with my English one. And Titi wouldn't have gone to England for that, would he?"

"I'll try to check. You still suspect the elder Dawson-Gower, don't you? Disappeared, you say? Well, we must look out for strangers. What's your next move?"

"I'm going to go and grill Tim Dawson-Gower. You work on Titi."

"Jeannette, I can't do this corner." Chantal was learning drawn-thread work, as all properly brought up little girls must, in a province where wedding linen is still hand-sewn. She spent half an hour grimacing over it in the garden every morning.

"All right, give it to me. No, watch, stupid, or you'll never learn."

"But François and I are writing our epic." The children were composing a poem about the Gaulish hero, Vercingetorix, and Julius Caesar; a subject at once so patriotic and so educational that their parents felt bound to approve. It was a splendid means of evasion. "What rhymes with *glorieux*?"

"*Amoureux, dangereux*," Jeannette smiled as she spoke, "lots of things."

"And *pas chez eux*," put in François, watching his elder sister flinch slightly. "And *honteux*, and *trop heureux*. Where did you go so early today?"

"Bathing. But it was too cold; I shan't go again. You two must wash your hands if you want to use Papa's book. Don't argue. Go!"

But just when the children were disposed of, Tim attacked her with all the pent-up force of a turning worm.

"Well, who did you swim with? Got a serious boyfriend this time?"

She blushed, confirming his instinctive feelings of jealousy. "I didn't swim with anyone, truly. Look, I have to go out for five minutes. Will you keep an eye on the children?"

"Where? Can't I come with you?"

"No. I'm going to police headquarters to find out if there's any more news. Why are you so horrid all of a sudden?"

"I'm not. Only lately you've been looking so, so … and it's our last day today."

"Listen, *mon petit*. I promise you, we'll have many, many days together when this is over. See you soon!"

She ran off, almost colliding with François, who asked where she was off to.

"An errand. Back soon!"

The little boy came and quizzed Tim.

"She rumples my hair, too. Never mind, it's a sign she's in a good mood. Listen, I've made another couplet:

> "And on the Seine of that time, which resembled the Styx,
> He paddled on, the bold Vercingetorix.

"Chantal said you couldn't rhyme his name. Bah!"

"You've never seen the Seine," said Chantal, who had.

"And you've yet to see the Styx. Unfortunately." He scored.

"It's my turn for a couplet now," said Chantal, "Listen!

> "He skimmed the waves to see his homeland
> He ran to the aid of ... of ...

"Wait a second …"

"The people of Gergovia?" suggested Richard, showing himself. "Or is that in the wrong direction? Tim, I want a talk with you. We'll go up to your room, shall we?"

"What's the point, if you'll excuse my saying so—" Tim was polite even in his desperation—"of you keeping on like this? I've told you all I know. If you don't believe me, well, arrest me. I don't care. At least the Defays wouldn't be involved then."

"Why, are they objecting?"

"Oh no! Madame Defay is very kind. But, but the children are being sent away to Angennes, so you see …"

"That's natural. They're a bit young to be in the middle of a murder enquiry."

"Little children, yes. But Jeannette … she's eighteen."

"Well, she's going to keep house, I suppose. Oh, her aunt's doing that? Which aunt? The one from Poitiers? She worked for the Resistance, didn't she? Tell me, just where is this place Angennes? Three miles downstream, past the islands. Hmm! Have they got a boat?"

"Not at the moment. There's a sailing boat, but it needs mending. Why?"

Richard put aside the question with another, gently asked. "This isn't just curiosity, but I have to know—is Jeannette in love with you?"

"No," said Tim, glowering. "I'm not *sérieux*." Then, with a ray of hope, "Why? Did you think she was?"

"I don't know. Is there somebody else, do you think? Just recently?"

"Why, do *you* ...? No, I've no idea. And if I had, I wouldn't discuss it."

Good boy, thought Richard. Good boy, bad liar. What a beast one feels!

"The point is, don't you see, that if Despuys had been threatening your security—he *was* a blackmailer, you know—well, you might feel more strongly about security if you were just getting engaged. Even strongly enough to ..."

"Kill him? Well, I didn't. And he wasn't blackmailing me, actually. But that won't make me pretend I don't care for Jeannette, because I do. Oh!"

"What? You look very pleased all of a sudden."

"Nothing. Only I thought she was—going off me, being a bit aloof and going out by herself and all that. But now you may have hit on the explanation." His face fell again. "Still, what's the good? If you think I ... I say, will my parents have heard?"

"Probably not. We haven't told them and we've not given your name to the press. We did try to get in touch with your brother in London, though." Richard paused. "He seems to have disappeared completely. Have you any comments?"

Tim was ready for this. "Oh, er, has he? He does go off on business sometimes without leaving an address, you know. After all, you hadn't specially asked him to hang around, had you? I expect he'll be back very soon. I certainly hope so, because he can tell you about the body better than I did."

"You honestly don't know where he is?"

"Not at the moment, no." It was true in a way.

"Did you write to him?"

"Well, er, yes, but I expect the letter's still in the post." He glanced round the room, and Richard watched carefully. Yes, he was making sure he had everything ready to write this letter as soon as possible, for his eye came to rest on the writing pad and then ceased to rove.

"Written to Francis?"

"Oh yes, and I had a card from him today. Would you like to see it?"

"Don't bother. Now, to go back to last Sunday. You and your

brother went on the river at a quarter past eight, I believe. Were you with him before that?"

"Oh, yes! We had dinner together."

"And before dinner? I noticed you were down to read the lesson in college chapel that Sunday. Was your brother there too?"

"No, actually he waited in the bar of the King's Arms for me. It couldn't have been more than half an hour."

"Hmm! And when you both found the body, it had been dead some time. I see. I still don't understand why the car ran over it at all. Had your brother been doing anything to the works that day?"

"N-no," said Tim, suddenly remembering. "NO, HE DIDN'T TOUCH IT. She always did swerve if you braked too hard."

"Yes. And that place, of course, is just where you might want to brake suddenly, after accelerating for the slope. Do you still stick to it that it was you, not your brother, who drove to the haystack?"

"Of course. I said so before." Tim was rigid with loyalty.

"Well, I'm sorry, but I don't believe you. We shall be broadcasting your brother's description tonight as a man wanted in connection with the murder, so your parents and his firm will have to know, I'm afraid. Sure you've nothing to add?"

Tim's usual healthy color had quite gone, but he was perfectly steady as he replied, "Neither of us killed Jean. But I moved the body. As I said."

On the way back Richard saw Jeannette on the other side of the street, and she passed him without a sign.

Back at the police station, they discussed it.

"And another reason I don't think Tim can be guilty," Richard was saying to Kéhidiou. "He actually finds time to be crossed in love. *Phillida flouts me.* Or rather, Jeannette's slipping out to meet a friend, the little beast. And he's wretchedly upset. Incredible, isn't it, with all this against him! Were you ever as young as that?"

"No. But if I were clever, I might make people think so," said the other drily. "In any case, he needn't worry. Jeannette was here with my wife, and left just before you came in. You must have passed each other."

"We did. When did Jeannette arrive?"

"Shortly after you left. You see?"

"Yes. But still—did you *look* at her? She looks so—how can I put it?"

"Blossomed out? My dear friend," the Frenchman kindled. "That is, if I may say so, a very natural mistake for an Englishman, or even for a Breton who hadn't moved about. One must realize that the typical young girl of Touraine is very coquettish; it's summer, she's wearing her pretty dresses, she knows that she's contributing to the general happiness, she's almost intoxicated. She glows with happiness. It's instinctive, like a flower opening to the sun. How shall I say? Like the bloom on the ripening grape. Like a child smiling at her mother Nature."

Richard would have been pleased to do without the stock phrases. Frenchmen talking in the abstract about women were as bad as Englishmen on politics. "Must lead to a lot of trouble." he remarked.

"But no, no! One must make a distinction between the desire to please and the desire to be loved, which follows later. Take Jeannette." Richard nodded. He would always exchange a general for a particular. "To look at her, you'd say—just a pretty flirt. But to us who know her—ah, no! She's ardent, yes, poetic, responsive. But also, she has intelligence, she has ideals. That's what she argues with her parents about, not about young men, I assure you. She sees herself as an Antigone, not a Phaedra. In fact, her father's quite annoyed that she won't have anything to do with the suitable young men of the district. In my opinion, she takes after him. He's wilful enough, heaven knows … One day she'll be a marvelous woman. Beauty, character, intelligence, temperament, and innocence—and still, very much the young girl."

"With a woman's equipment. No wonder my compatriot Tim is baffled."

"If he's baffled. Oh well, talk to her yourself, if I don't convince you. She's coming to see us this evening." He broke off, a little embarrassed by his own warmth, and looked into the courtyard. "I couldn't get that Titi to talk. He's tough, that one. Says he picked up the card on the towing path, and that's all he knows."

"Could it be the truth?"

Kéhidiou shrugged. "If it is, the truth must be worse than it looks. A type like that's bound to be up to no good."

"We have a phrase—I don't know how to say it in French—about 'the benefit of the doubt'."

"Benefit?" Kéhidiou stared. "Why is doubt considered a beneficial state of mind?"

CHAPTER 19

La Zézette was plodding along the main shopping street with a striped cardboard dress-box under her arm. It looked as if she had just bought herself a new dress. But in fact the box was heavy with food, which the man in her house had sent her to buy.

"If only my chest didn't hurt me so! … If only he'd gone away, that first day, as he meant … If only I could just go to bed! Why did he have to take my bed and send me out like that? It's cruel! Who's going to notice if I'm about the streets every single night? 'I won't have carelessness. Details are important' …

"If only he'd let me go to my usual shops! Oh, I'm so tired! And he said never to go to the same shop twice. I'll have to walk even further next time. If only he'd let me take a basket! 'Take a dress-box, it's more in character. People expect tarts to be always buying clothes.' Beast! Beast! As if I could afford.…"

She changed the loaded box over to the other arm—it was unsafe to hold it by the string—and wondered dully how much longer she could endure. One thing was clear; if she really broke down, *he* would leave her to die, and without calling a doctor. *He* wouldn't risk discovery. She'd just have to keep on and hope *he* would be able to go away soon. And then … there would be Jean's money. Or perhaps even Jean himself, about to make his fortune. The police might, after all, be lying when they said he was dead. Hadn't Jean's letter told her, "Don't worry, whatever you hear. Just keep the papers safe and in two years we'll be in clover."

Well, she had kept them safe. And yet, when the English policeman looked, he assured her that they contained nothing of value. Could *he* have got at them first?

"But no! *He* doesn't need money. He gave me ten thousand, and it didn't make the roll much thinner. 'A little holiday for you; you can stop trying to be glamorous. Just cook. That's a thing you *can* do.' Brute, brute! If it wasn't for his being in with Jean—if only he'd come, *mon petit Jean! Mon petit Jean!*"

She sat down on a bench on the edge of the main square, coughing.

"Yes, and I *can* cook, too. The *agent* was quite right, I ought to buy a little café and ... the English detective was polite, yes, but he didn't appreciate me like the other. Of course I'm not looking my best just now, still, *he* could see I'd got it in me. I'm not just a—He said. 'A little café and a husband.' That was nice. I wouldn't mind an older man if he was young in heart ... we'd work up a clientele ... a little café and a husband. His friends would all say when they saw me ..."

She coughed violently. When she had recovered, she saw the red spot on her handkerchief and came back from dreams.

"What's the use? If only *he'd* go, if only Jean were here! I never had a chance, if only, if only ..."

It was then that Auguste sat down on the bench. His teeth, his wavy black hair, and his cigarette case glittered in the sun. He offered the case, and she, pulling in her waist and throwing out her chest, tittered that just this once, maybe ... She sidled along the bench for a light, stifling her cough.

"On second thoughts," said the glittering man, "no!" He took the cigarette out of her hand and tossed it away. His manner was both masterful and tender. "A cigarette isn't *you*, somehow. It sort of coarsens a woman, don't you think? Would you have a drink with me instead?"

She hesitated. At any other time, it would have been amazing luck.

"Don't say no! I've watched you go past so often"—he picked up the dress-box by the string, felt its weight, tucked it under his arm, and offered her the other. He was a smooth mover. "But till today—I'll tell you."

He waved aside the traffic, brought her solicitously across the square, and seated her under an umbrella at the third best café of the town. She was going to be easy! But he hadn't expected so quick a result—after all, she was practically a fellow professional. She couldn't ever have been good at her stuff.

"What'll you have? Cinzano? Dubonnet? A shot of Pernod, with soda? My favorite drink. Strange!" He gave her his headlights again; she was dazzled but vaguely alarmed. Why couldn't this have happened a week ago? If only ...

"I—I can't stay long today. What do you mean, you watched me often, but till today you—you shy or something?"

"You'll laugh at me. Well, laugh, then!" He flashed his eyes. "Till today, I was poor. I'd have had to take you to cheap places.

Well, I'm proud, I admit it; I like to treat my women right. Even if you hadn't turned me down—and you wouldn't have, would you? But now—" Auguste paused dramatically.

"Now?" Zézette was torn between fascination and uneasiness.

"I've been left a nice little business. A restaurant in Nice. You know Nice? I'll take you one day. When can I come and see you? Alone, I mean? Tonight?"

"No, I'd love to, I mean, I'm terribly sorry, dear, but it's the doctor. He says I've got to rest this week. Only a week, he said, it's nothing serious. Just overdoing it."

"I understand," he said. "It's someone else, isn't it? Well, send him away! Or—but no, my poor Zézette, you're not lying to me! You're pale. What a brute I am! You *are* ill, too!"

"How do you know my name?" She spilled her drink.

"There, look, I'll order another. But of course I know your name. Didn't I worship your photo in Jean's room, in Paris?"

"Jean? My—my brother? He—he had my photo? You noticed it?"

"But yes, I pestered him to tell me all about you. My poor, poor child! Somehow you seem like a child to me. What martyrdom! To be the victim of that monster! And afterwards, the insults, the refusal to understand. What you must have gone through! And yet, you know, it gives women charm, suffering does. I don't care for happy women, I'm funny that way."

"Why," she half rose, alarmed. "Are you—?" She had met that theory before.

"Don't go. Listen. A rich young girl—what can I give her? A little pleasure, yes. But I'm proud, that's not enough for me. I want to give a woman happiness, life. I want to be everything to her, do everything for her. Do you think that's—silly?"

"No. No, it's wonderful." She relaxed.

It was, he knew, a sure winner; at least, he had tried it on middle-aged female tourists with invariable profit. He was surprised that it also worked with Zézette. But she might be pretending. He decided to be sure she trusted him before he went any further; though really, he need not have bothered.

Zézette had no real sense of masculine character. To her, a "nice man" was a man who admired her, whose looks did her credit, whose company excited, whose purse sustained. If the only thing that interests you about a man is whether he will make you happy or let you down, he never becomes a person to you—you don't see things

from his angle. Perhaps that is why women like Zézette are unsatis-
fying companions and easy dupes. At any rate—always provided he
could pay—she was not worrying about Auguste. She had worries
enough, but she thought he was wonderful. So the second half of
the program was—well, perhaps not wasted on her, for it gave her
pleasure.

"I can read your thoughts, my little Zézette!" he continued vi-
brantly. "You're saying, so many men have talked to me like this—
how do I know he's on the level? You see! You can't hide anything
from me, can you? Look in my eyes!"

She was already goggling like a bird before a snake.

"Listen, I'm going to show you I'm not like the others. *I* won't
rush you. Just let me see you, that's all I ask. Take you out, give you
some fun—behave myself. Oh! It isn't easy for me, I won't pretend
it is. I'm half Spanish, you see, and passion and pride are in my
blood. I don't like rivals, I don't tolerate suspicion. In fact I wouldn't
take it from any other woman but you."

That always went well. Odd, how they ate out of your hand if
you said you were Spanish. He now never admitted his Italian ori-
gin except to maternal types who liked *naïveté*.

"All I ask is, let me see you again soon. This evening? Sshh!
Don't tell me when you've got—dates! I'm a proud man. Just say
when you're free. To—talk about Jean, eh?"

"*Mon petit Jean!* I didn't know he'd got my photo. Oh, sorry!
I could meet you about six, only I couldn't stay very long, because …"

"Hush!" he said. "Don't make me jealous. At six. Do you like
that place by the river, Le Poisson Complaisant?" It was near her
district, new, and flashy.

"Oh yes, Monsieur, it's lovely. Sort of—romantic, isn't it?"

"Monsieur, indeed! Say, 'I promise, Jules.' "

"I promise, Jules." She gave full emphasis to the intimate second
person singular, and the Christian (or rather, stage) name. But then
the church clock struck midday. She looked down at her dress-box
and saw a trickle of olive oil oozing from one corner. She snatched
it and stood up, holding it to the side away from him.

"Till six, then. You're not joking? You—you won't … ah! That's
nice!"

For he had kissed her hand with an ardent flourish. He even—so
thorough was he—remained standing until she had turned the corner out of sight. Then he sat down, kicked off his shoes, and yelled

for a double martini. He needed it, for his temperament had only just managed the supreme test. Those legs! That skin! That hair! And why the devil did she carry olive oil about in a dress-box? Oh, but of course; she probably did a bit of shoplifting on the side.

He smiled with tolerant pity. After all, only a high-class operator could afford to specialize.

As soon as she was indoors, and clearly unaccompanied, the hidden man spoke gratingly from the cellar steps.

"Have you locked the doors? Where have you been all this time? Met a client? My God! Can't you think up a better story than that? Here, what's this on your box? Olive oil! Idiot, it could have given you away. Did anyone notice? You don't know? Well, you'll just have to cut the box up and burn it in the stove. But do the cooking first, I'm hungry. Yes, cut it up with scissors and burn it, carefully. Details are important.

"Hmm, I see you've been drinking. Don't do it again. Not for fear you'd talk, for I don't suppose anyone cares to drink with you. But it's a waste of time. You can soak away to your heart's content later. I'll leave you with enough to booze for a month. What, you haven't? Prove it! Say *un chasseur sachant chasser sans chien*."(This tongue-twister is the French equivalent of *the Leith police dismisseth us*.) "You see? You can't say it. Well, don't stand sweating there; cook! What've you got? This all? How about dinner tonight?

"Idiot! Why couldn't you shop for the whole day? Can't bear to stay off the streets, I suppose. Any use telling you that persistence doesn't always bring success? You see, you neglect the details, and details are important. Just little things like dyeing your hair the same color all over, and remembering that women are supposed to have waists and ankles. Your brother, now, was—he's quite a natty dresser. He'd pass anywhere.

"Well, get on! You won't have a lot of time if you're going out shopping again, will you? Pity you don't think ahead. Still, the more you hang around the streets, the more the police'll think that everything's normal. And there's no real risk of you bringing anyone back with you, is there?"

He was smiling and rubbing his big hands together, as he always did just before what he called analysis.

"When *do* they come, then? Weekends, yes, from the military camps. Americans. Of course they're not particular, are they? What do you make per week? Four thousand francs? Five thousand! Well, that won't get you meat twice a day like you're having now, so aren't you lucky? Go on, then, cook! That's a thing you *can* do."

Zézette had made a great effort to finish the housework and be dressed to go out by five. She was not what is called an executive type; but at ten past five she was nearly ready and in a pleasant flutter.

"Yes, I look better in a hat. Lots of girls do, I think. A pity I've got to lug that box around, perhaps I could leave it somewhere before I got to the *Poisson Complaisant*. This dress needs cheering up a bit. I wonder if I'd find a rose in the garden; there was a bush once … That *agent*, he was quite right, it's a pity to let the garden go. Later on …"

She went out at the back, but there were no roses in her wasteland. A man walking along the river path looked over the fence at her. Just an ordinary working man with a scarred face, but she scurried back indoors.

"Ugh! That face—it gave me quite a turn. Well, but I won't say I saw anyone; *he'd* only ask questions and I'm late already. I can't stick it, I can't. I'll just slip out quietly. Oh dear! I've left my bag upstairs. I wonder what the time is."

But he caught her as she came down the stairs and the questions began again—this time on a sharper and more dangerous note.

"Locked the doors? Back and front? Fastened the windows? Done the stove?"

Oh dear! She'd left the damper out when she went up to dress, and now the stove was red-hot and almost burned out. And she hadn't destroyed that box, either. Too late now; she wouldn't say anything, just put it inside the other and throw it away in the street somewhere. Clumsy with haste, she spilt coal and dirtied her hands, so up the stairs again she went to wash, and down to the front door. His voice and hands terrified her.

"Got your key? Well, get it, then! Idiot! Hmm! You've got yourself up a bit smarter this time, I see. Details better."

"Don't! Don't! Your eyes—I can't bear it when you do that."

"All right, go, then. And mind you're back in time. I'd hate those fatal charms of yours to hold up my dinner. Well, *now* what have you forgotten?"

Too late. He'd see if she went to her money hoard now. "Nothing. I'm, I'm going."

"One more thing. Bring some ice in with you. The butter's too soft."

She slammed the front door and went her way.

Her thoughts went round like a lighthouse, bright and dark, hope and misery. The glittering young man, Jean's friend, seemed to offer a way of escape from the house which had become so terrible to her. But her money was still there, hidden under the loose board upstairs. When she had thought of taking it, *he* had come out and begun those terrible questions. So there was no help for it; she must go back. She couldn't leave her money. For even if the glittering young man was rich as well as keen, even if he *did* take her to Nice—well, she had no illusions about men. When they lost interest they left one flat, and then where would she be without her money? Still, Jules was so kind, so romantic. ... Suppose she fixed things up with him for late tonight, and made sure of having her money on her by then? After all, he had Spanish blood. He might prefer not to wait.

"Perhaps I'll slip back now, very quietly, and see if I can get my money. If *he* hears me, I can say my shoes hurt and I've come back to change them. They do hurt, too; and uncomfortable shoes bring out the lines in one's face, they say. ... Oh! *Pardon, Monsieur l'agent!* I didn't see you."

Painlevé had just come off duty and was anxious to water his garden. But politeness, as he often said, cost nothing and bought much.

"Everything all right with you, Madame? You people down by the river ought to be careful at present. After that drowning case yesterday. You might have some queer visitors. Why, didn't you see in the paper? A poor old tramp was fished out of the river stark naked—not a sign of his clothes anywhere—and between you and me, the paper said that foul play is suspected."

Zézette stared The news frightened her, but also hardened her into caution; she froze like a lizard.

"So if you take my advice, you'll pay a little visit to the bank." He laid a finger to his nose and lowered his voice. "Banks are safer than loose floorboards, eh? You understand me?"

She relaxed. "Oh, dear! Why, is there one of those gangs about?"

He shrugged. "Time will show. What d'you think of the writing on the walls today? Didn't see it? Why, it was all over the place! Just like in the Occupation. 'Look out for the traitor' was one of them. And a picture of a bee; I expect you know what that used to stand for— 'Blancbec's on the warpath.' There's quite an upset going on."

He noticed that she was looking terrified. Of course, poor thing— she had reason to remember how the last upset in Pontchâtelet had ended for her—with a shaved head and no friends. Toussaint, you have no tact!

"Ah, no, Madame! We no longer play politics here! No one's going to blame *you!* I expect someone did it for a bet or when they were a bit drunk. But what I always say is, if there's any sort of disturbance going on, the first thing to do is to look after your valuables. That's just friendly advice from one citizen to another. As a matter of fact I'd meant to warn you anyway, it was on my mind. Property's property, and it's never a good plan to keep such things in the house. People ought to be told."

She was trying to go, but he held up one hand.

"And specially during a crime wave like the one which is rife, if I may so express myself, in our own dear city. Better safe than sorry. Mistrust is the mother of security. And if you're on your guard, you won't need to call in the *Sûreté*, ha! ha! I must tell that to *Monsieur le Commissaire*. Good evening, then! And *do* pay a little visit to the bank." He bustled off.

She stood hesitating and heard the clock chime. A quarter to six! And she'd promised to meet Jules at the *Poisson Complaisant* at six o'clock! Suppose he got tired of waiting? She hadn't even done the shopping yet. And her money … even that nice policeman had thought … did he suspect the truth? Ah! It was terrible, terrible! What should she do?

But all the time her feet were carrying her along the line of least resistance, towards the *Poisson Complaisant*. He was there already, outside, and came hurrying to meet her, vivid in a suit of wide black and white stripes. Like a tiger, she thought admiringly, as he convoyed her inside. You can see he's a man of the world.

It was so easy to talk to him. She asked him about the drowning and he at once bought her a paper and found the place for her.

"Last seen wearing old straw hat, blue scarf, brown jacket and black evening trousers. Anyone finding such garments should take them to the police at once. Reward offered."

As he read the list of garments, she turned gray under her pink powder. He ordered her another drink, said he could see she was sensitive—and waited.

Well, she *was* nervous, she said. The police had warned her that there were bad people about, and the crime had happened in her district. She was quite often alone in the house. Really, she had half a mind to go away for a bit. She waited, playing for an escape.

With even greater solicitude than before, he applauded the plan. They would go together. He'd have liked to take her tonight but the banks were shut—he chafed as he said it. She could see he was proud— and with a girl like her one didn't care to skimp things. He waited again.

"I could—lend you some money, just till tomorrow," she ventured at last. It was an extraordinary thing for her to say. Ostracism and poverty had made her almost incapable of parting with money; and the effort of making her present offer was so great that she did not notice the sudden brightening of his eyes as he replied, half-angrily, that he'd never borrowed from a lady before. Quite the reverse. Still, in the circumstances … perhaps just six thousand francs?

Six thousand, for one night? All her experience rose up to warn her.

"I haven't that even in my house," she said. "I could manage two thousand, maybe. But I'd have to go home and get it." Then I can make sure of my savings.

Two thousand? thought Auguste. It isn't much. But I can lose her once I've got it; Jeannot and Radar will have finished by then. And I'm like that: always sacrifice myself for my friends. A generous nature.

"I'll come and help you pack," he offered.

"Oh, no! Please don't! I mean, I need a little time to—find it."

Aha! So she *had* got a hoard. What a fool she was! Well, patience! Two thousand was already something. More might follow.

He told her grandly that he was always discreet where a lady's reputation was concerned. He would wait at the corner of her street, and not force himself upon her. After all, she could only get away past that corner. And if she stayed too long, he could always rout her out.

As he waited, he thought, well, if you help old comrades, heaven rewards you for your courage. If he was lucky, he'd offer a candle to Sainte Radegonde. But he wouldn't mention the two thousand to Radar and the boys.

When Zézette parted from him, she hurried to her house with the key all ready. But the door, she saw, was already a crack open. She supposed she had not secured it properly when she left in such a hurry. Still, it was lucky, really, for she could get in without noise. She crept upstairs to the lavatory and lifted the floorboard. The parcel was there; really, that talk of burglars had made her quite nervous. But once she had the money safely stuffed down the front of her dress she felt, for her, brave and resourceful. Even *his* footsteps on the stairs did not terrify her now; they set her planning. She'd say she'd brought one lot of shopping and was going back for the rest. She'd take the clean box and leave the oil-stained one, which he had told her to destroy, and say it was the first batch of purchases. Quickly she took the one box out of the other and tied them both up, while he called again.

"Zézette? That scent of yours carries a mile. It *is* you, isn't it?" His nervous tone gave her confidence.

"Yes, here I am. I couldn't get all the shopping home at once and my shoes were hurting me, so I've just brought the first lot and—" Oh! Now she must remember to change her shoes. Details matter, *hein?*

She changed them quickly in the bedroom and took up her box. Oh! It was the stained one; she had left the other in the lavatory. Never mind, she could think of a way out. She snatched a coat from the hook, draped it over her arm to hide the stain on the box, and came downstairs. Nearly out of it now!

"How long have you been in?"

"Oh, only a minute, it was just my shoes ..."

"Yes, I'm not blind, I noticed you'd changed them. But I heard you moving round at least a quarter of an hour ago. Ah! Drinking, eh?"

"No, really. Just shopping."

"Shopping? Where are the things you bought, then?"

"Upstairs, but they won't spoil. I didn't bring them to the kitchen because ..."

"What's that coat over your arm for? It's hot enough, today, isn't it? I said, what's that coat for?"

"I'm taking it to the cleaner's. Now I must be quick or ..."

"Leave the coat here. You can take it another time."

He snatched it away and the box was exposed. She shifted it to the side away from him, gabbling,

"Well, I'll just slip out and finish before they shut. I got a bit help up, because I met that policeman who was here, and he said ..."

"What have you got there?" The big white hands came up, clawing.

"Oh, don't, don't!"

"The box. The box I told you to burn. And you not only dis-
obeyed my orders. You took it out with you." His hands closed round
her throat and shook her backwards and forwards, banging her head
against the wall. "Do you think—I'll have my plans—upset—by
one—careless—lazy—instrument? There! That'll help you to remember that details matter. You hear? Details matter. Get up, then.
Or stay there if you like, but answer my question. What did the
policeman tell you? Go on. D'you think I don't know the difference
between punishing people and putting them out of action? You
haven't had an injury, you can talk perfectly well. What did he say?"

She raised herself a little, and he thought she was clearing her
throat. But then the blood spouted from her mouth. He sprang back,
just in time to avoid being spattered—and watched. When she fell
back, he heard a sound more familiar to him ten years ago than now.
The death rattle.

And yet, he mused, he had only pressed hard enough to—punish.
Not hard enough to kill. There should have been no injury. Well, he
had made a mistake. He had thought her story of illness was just an
excuse. Otherwise—invalids, he remembered, were always tricky
to punish.

Still, she wouldn't have lasted him much longer, anyhow, if she
was ill. And there'd have been the risk of infection. Besides, a careless fool like Zézette was never safe to use. He was well rid of her,
really.

Now he must move on, and by now, a move was the correct tac-
tic; his luck was giving him a lead, as usual. Yesterday, when she
told him the police were rounding up strangers, he had waited, not
caring, just then, to turn out his pockets. Now he had a better plan.
Simply to post the—private—things to himself at a poste restante
address in Paris.

He put his clothes in the clean dress-box from upstairs, with the
papers tucked inside them. Then he slipped out when the street was
empty. In the old straw hat, a blue neckerchief, brown coat, and
ragged dress trousers, and with nearly a week's beard, he could defy
recognition. Details mattered.

CHAPTER 20

Jeannot was still patrolling the towing path. When he saw Nigel's face at Zézette's lavatory window, he took off his beret and scratched his head—their old "all-clear" sign. Nigel climbed on to the sill, hung by his hands, and dropped into the back garden. Neither he nor Jeannot had seen the boy in the beanstalks next door, playing Viet Nam with a green paper mask over his face. They began to saunter away.

"All right, Radar?"

"I think so. I put Auguste's masterpiece in a place where she'd hidden some other things—a loose floorboard just asking to be lifted up in the lavatory floor, with a parcel underneath. People never learn, do they? Look, take my gloves and tools before I forget. *Sacré nom!*" He stopped. "I forgot to relatch the front door. I put it on the latch ready for a quick getaway. I'll have to go back and shut it. Doesn't do to be careless about details."

"You're mad, Radar! The woman may be back by now. One can't rely on Auguste to keep to schedule. You're just playing with danger as usual."

"No. Details matter in this job. The police have more reason to suspect a plant if I don't leave the house as I found it. That's a good little gadget of yours for windows, by the way. I'll tell you what; we'll compromise. Let's turn at the bridge and walk up the street past the front door. I can shut it in passing. No need for you to come at all, actually. Go on, and I'll meet you in the café later."

"Unprint the unprintable café, misprint!" growled Jeannot (more or less) and walked back with him. It was a long detour, but they dared not attract attention by hurrying. Outside Zézette's front door, Jeannot stopped to roll a cigarette, putting his tool bag down on the step. Nigel picked it up for him, and they moved on, slowly, because the cigarette was still in the making. Nigel had found the door locked.

"Funny," said Jeannot. "I suppose the door shut itself. Well, you were always lucky, weren't you, Radar?"

Nigel shot a brilliant look at him. "Just like Napoleon's generals, *hein?*"

"—Napoleon!" Jeannot spat. "That was the start of the Fascist rot. Look how Blancbec was always on about Napoleon—"

But Nigel interrupted the homily.

"There's Auguste. Looks pretty pleased with himself, doesn't he? Give him the O.K., Jeannot!"

Jeannot did so, and received an answering signal he did not expect.

"See that?" he whispered. "That means 'keep off me and I'll get in touch later.' What's he up to? Is he going to split on us?"

"No," replied Nigel, easily. "He's not drawn his pay yet. Now come on, or I'll be getting behind schedule. Where shall I go to get myself had up as a drunk? The square?"

"Too expensive and noisy. Let's go to the café between the station and the post office. There are always some cops round there."

"Good!" Nigel was enjoying himself. "And if public drunkenness isn't enough for them, I can start grabbing mailbags or assaulting ticket collectors. Or even injuring the company's servants working on the line. A thing I've never tried yet."

Jeannot had protested when he first heard of Nigel's plan to get himself arrested. Now he sighed again, and said, "Radar, you're mad!"

"No, I told you, it's the best plan. If I get into the jail, I can get Titi out. And also, if the English police *are* after me, the last place they'll look is in the local *violon*. Now, Jeannot, you go and find us a nice conspicuous table on the pavement. I'll just post a letter and then come and join you."

Auguste, after half an hour of mounting impatience, went down the street and rang Zézette's bell, gently first and then with violence. This had happened before, women coming to their senses once his eye was off them. "I'm too modest," he told himself, "I underestimate the charm of my physical presence." But this time he had thought he was safe—the road being a cul-de-sac—in mounting guard over the open end. The old trout must have slipped out by the back. Well, she couldn't have got far; he would try the bus stops first and then the station. Once he'd picked her up again, he'd restore her confidence in no time.

Not long after he left, Painlevé came along leading his youngest boy, Victor, by the hand. Victor Painlevé had asked if he might invite his school friend Justin to join the family in their usual Thursday outing to the café. Now Justin's house was next door to Zézette's, and it seemed a kind of omen. Painlevé couldn't forget her poor frightened face and all that good money so ill hidden. *Bon!* he would call and offer to lock it up in the *Commissariat* safe overnight. If she refused, never mind; he would have done his possible. But the bell was not answered.

"You're wasting your time," said Justin's mother, watching. "She won't open it. Another visitor was ringing and ringing just now till I thought my head would split; and I know she's in too, because I heard her screeching and quarreling—but there! Such people are best left alone, I say, and specially when children are listening. What is it, then, Justin?"

"*Maman*, I saw a man getting out of her back window. He hung down by his hands and jumped. He jumped such a long way, all from upstairs."

"Be quiet! Little pitchers, eh? He's just making it up."

"No, I was playing in the garden. I couldn't help seeing."

"It shows he's clever, Madame. Well, and when did you see this, Justin?" asked Painlevé encouragingly. The child's mother sniffed.

"He hasn't been out there above half an hour, Monsieur. Well, speak up, Justin, can't you? You're lying, aren't you, dear? Just a game?"

"No! I'd only just started playing when I saw him jump all that way. But he didn't hurt himself. And so I went on playing. I was busy."

"What sort of man? What was he wearing?"

"I don't know. He wasn't stylish, but he jumped very well. Like in the cinema."

The matriarch took command. "Go on then, you little gangster! Run into the gar—no, take Victor in the kitchen while you wash your hands. One must consider their morals. This is getting interesting, Monsieur, isn't it? All this screeching and coming and going, there must be something behind it, and it can't just be love, surely, at her age? Someone's after her money, that's what I think. They say she's got piles hoarded away. If you want to investigate, I'll mind Victor for you. And you could take our back door key; they're all the same in this row. Yes, my husband and I have often wondered what it's like in there. You'll come back and tell me?"

But Painlevé, when he did come out, looking very unlike his

comfortable self, ran straight to the nearest telephone and called his chief.

Richard Ringwood was sitting at his table considering the second post from England, a pile of *fiches anthropométriques*, and his own notebook. The time was ripe, he thought, for a dressing gown and an ounce of wet shag tied about the temples; the moment of truth, like Mr. Attlee's target, was just round the corner. But it had not arrived when Kéhidiou burst in and announced the death of Zézette. And, as if that were not enough, just when they were getting into the car, the *secrétaire de police* ran out with a second piece of news. A man described as wearing the clothes of the murdered tramp had been seen—and lost again—somewhere near the station.

The *secrétaire*, that man of superior intellectual level, spoke feelingly of Scylla and Charybdis, and being caught in a dilemma. The driver tooted his horn and hissed for action; two or three *agents* joined the screaming party and began to back up their personal suggestions with general truths. The Breton and the Englishman drew aside.

"*Your* corpse, this time," said Richard. "You go to the *Impasse du Cher*. Give me someone who remembers faces and is quick on his feet, and I'll do the station."

"Admirable! And whichever of us gets through first leaves a message at headquarters and comes to join the other."

He gave his dry, quiet orders.

"*Ah, Messieurs!*" said the *secrétaire*, "at last you have cut the Gordian knot!"

Sitting with Jeannot at a table on the pavement outside the *Café de la Gare et de l'Univers*, Nigel drank a lot, partly for fun and partly so that the police could smell his breath and class him as a drunk. Jeannot drank enough to lessen his reserve, and began talking about his past. From a pinched childhood till now Jeannot had fought and suffered for the working class; lock-in strikes, street demonstrations, pickets, sabotage, and above all the Resistance. He had never known peace, never married, and since Blancbec tortured him in the Occupation had never been well. Not that he was complaining; if you believed in anything you couldn't let it down. Still …

He went back to the story of his torture.

"And Blancbec knew—oh yes, he knew, he'd calculated—just what you could take before you passed out. 'Can you see my hand?'

he'd say. 'I know you can. Now I'll give you a brandy. It's bought out of my own pocket, and I only give it to the brave ones. I respect brave men. You can see my ring now, eh? And the bee on it? Well, talk, or it will be the last thing you ever do see.' "

He was pale except where the scars stood out angry red.

"The last thing … and it's come true in a way. Radar, I can still see that hand and that ring. I wake up in the night seeing it. Sometimes I think I'm going off my head. That's why I haven't been to a doctor. He might cure this pain in my chest. But he might have me put in the asylum. No, as long as I can work …" Gray-faced, he stumbled to his feet. "Just going inside the café. Feeling sick. Keep my place and wait here at the table, Radar."

"Wait at table nothing!" shouted Nigel thickly, jumping up. "Waiter, keep my table in place! Think I'd let a sick pal go and be brave all by himself? Can't be brave straight without a sick pal to hold your head. Waiter, where's the puking hole?"

He and Jeannot wove their way through the dark interior of the café to the farthest corner, and then saw that there was a table pulled across the lavatory door with a man sitting at it. Nigel approached threateningly.

"Hey, you, get out of the light! What's the idea, blocking up that door? Important door, that. Must keep open communications. Haven't you heard of Napoleon? An army marches on its stomach. Boots bought off the enemy, so couldn't march on those. Too unpatriotic. We never marched in boots, did we, Jeannot?"

But Jeannot was staring at the man who sat at the table, and his teeth were chattering. Nigel could not fully grasp what he was trying to say.

"What's up, chum? You don't like his—*what?* Never mind! Explain afterwards. I don't like any part of him, and I'm going to chuck him out. *Allez-houp!*"

And he plucked the stranger from his seat by the scruff of the neck, punched his nose, and began to drag him out towards the street. Jeannot did not follow; he sank into a chair and fought for breath. Waiters ran up to Nigel, but he glared and they retreated, shrugging their shoulders. Big drunks were better left alone. And so Nigel and his victim reached the pavement unopposed.

Nigel looked round for his table, and let out a roar when he found it occupied. Richard Ringwood had just sat down there.

Now Nigel and Richard had never seen each other before. Nigel took Richard for a prosperous Northern Frenchman; Richard, for his part, thought Nigel was a drunken workman.

Nevertheless, Richard stood up quickly. For the man Nigel was holding by the scruff of the neck—the seedy-looking fellow who hung in Nigel's grasp like a coat from a peg—was wearing a blue scarf, a brown jacket, and dress trousers! The clothes of the murdered tramp!

"All right! Put your sick friend in a chair," Richard said. He preferred to humor the drunk and avoid a scene if possible, and he could see the two *agents* whom Kéhidiou had sent with him coming up the street to help. Nigel saw them too; he was also aware that Jeannot had slipped out of the café and down the street in the opposite direction. He glared at Richard and answered truculently,

"Don't you try to give me orders! Get out!" He held his captive still in one hand, almost absentmindedly.

"All right! I'm going. But do put your friend in a chair. The poor chap'll choke."

But Nigel would not be pacified.

"Friend! You unintentional by-blow of a paralytic miser, he's no friend of mine! I'm just chucking him out. I don't like him. 'Poor chap,' you said. So you're in with him, are you? Well, then I don't like *you* either, so—*allez-houp!*"

And Nigel suddenly pushed his captive against Richard. Richard was almost knocked off balance, but he caught the man in dress trousers, who had now gone quite limp, and put him into a chair. Nigel, meanwhile, was coming at Richard again. But the two *agents* were running up and seized Nigel's arms from behind. They could hardly hold him.

"Never mind the big drunk!" Richard ordered them. "It's the one in dress trousers we're arresting. He's our enemy."

"NO, HE'S MINE!" shouted Nigel, twisting free. "MY enemy, MY table, MY waiter! Keep off, you grabbing bastards!"

He knocked one *agent* out cold with a blow on the jaw, and made for Richard again. Richard glanced, for a split second, at the man in the tramp's clothes, and saw that he was still in a dead faint. Then Nigel's arms closed round him, and it was all Richard could do to remain on his feet. He had just breath to gasp at the second *agent*, "Handcuffs! Quick!" And then he was wrestling with all his might.

Richard was surprised to find an ordinary French workman, as he supposed Nigel to be, such a clever wrestler. Richard realized that he had met his match in strength and weight, and was relying on his police college skill to finish the brawl quickly. But to his amazement the workman broke hold after hold. He had, for a drunk, amazingly quick reactions, besides knowledge; only, as he wrestled, he laughed—laughed so enormously that he lost breath by it. Still Richard couldn't quite beat him. They banged into the chair where the man in dress trousers sat limply. The chair went over, and the man lay slumped on the ground instead.

"Handcuffs! Quick!" shouted Richard again.

Kéhidiou's man was having trouble in getting the handcuffs open. It was long since they had been used in Pontchâtelet, and the lock was stiff. The workmen sitting at the other tables were mocking openly, and not stirring a finger to help.

So it was that no one commented when the prostrate figure in dress trousers began wriggling toward the curb edge. And to make things worse, the *agent* misunderstood his instructions. He thought the handcuffs were needed for Nigel, who was so much bigger and more violent than the man in dress trousers. So he rushed up and got a shackle round one of Nigel's wrists, where it clawed for a hold behind Richard's back. Still laughing, Nigel brought his other wrist round beside it, and the *agent* triumphantly snapped the second shackle home, so that Richard was imprisoned in the bear grip of Nigel's fettered arms.

It was from within that circle that Richard looked and saw the man in dress trousers stand up in the street and run. He cried,

"Idiot! That's our man! Catch him, for God's sake!" and he struggled to get clear of Nigel's arms. But Nigel raised them of his own accord. Richard did not waste time in being surprised. He simply ran after the man in dress trousers, and soon outstripped the *agent*, who was already in pursuit. But—he did not pause to think it strange—heavier footsteps were behind him, and presently "the drunk" caught him up. Nigel seemed to know in advance where the corners would be. At last they both came out on the waterfront together—too late. The man in dress trousers had disappeared.

The alley they had taken ended in a quay on the river. On the left was a warehouse, and on the right a row of cottages. Richard was just looking into the warehouse when he heard a splash. Nigel—or, as Richard would have said, "the big drunk"—had flung himself into the river.

Richard was afraid that he would drown, deprived of the use of his hands. Blast! Must he lose the man he was really chasing because it was his duty to save the life of an obstreperous drunk? He hesitated; and saw with amazement that the drunk was swimming—

even using his still fettered hands. It was a queer-looking stroke, but not slow. He seemed to be making for a mooring post towards midstream, round which a raft of floating rubbish had collected.

As Nigel reached the rubbish, it stirred, and Richard saw a head— the head of the man in dress trousers! And then he saw Nigel's hands, still fettered, come up and fall like a noose over that head. Then both men disappeared under water, and only a patch of floating bubbles showed where they had submerged.

"They'll drown for certain, tied up in a knot like that," thought Richard, as he stripped. Calling over his shoulder to the *agent*, who had just caught up, to get a boat and follow, Richard dived. He hoped to keep the two of them afloat till help came.

When one is swimming fast, it is difficult to see what is happening on the surface of the water. Richard could not tell how many times, if at all, the struggling and entangled pair had come up; but when he reached the post, they were certainly submerged. He dived after what he hoped were their air bubbles, and swam open-eyed through the greenish-brown water light. It was another world. In the dancing shimmer were real objects, but their outlines wavered with the ripples; it took Richard a little time to adjust his vision to things without fixed edges. Then he picked out a velvet-furred tree stump, the white skull of an animal, and an old bucket black against the sepia-brown of the river floor. Suddenly he was over a patch of gravel, dazzling bright in the gloom. A shadow was passing over it—his own? No, there was his own, a little behind his knees. He rolled belly up and rose like a fish to the legs waving above him. Next moment all three men were gasping on the surface.

Richard saw at once that the big drunk was not (at any rate now) trying to drown the other, but on the contrary was doing his best to hold him up, though the clumsiness of that noose-like hold made it difficult.

"It's all right," said Richard in English. "I'll get behind and help you. There's a boat coming." Then he suddenly realized he must talk French. He found the words by degrees; luckily the big man seemed to guess the plan and did not resist Richard's hold under his arms, and he kept his legs clear of Richard's as they both trod water and got their breath. Then Richard slanted his body back and began swimming with his legs half-horizontal. The other tilted his own body to match and kept time with equal leg strokes. It did not work very well; now one and now another of them failed to keep his face clear of the water—and especially the man in dress trousers, who seemed quite passive—but still, they did keep afloat, and were even moving, though slowly, towards the bank when the boat reached them.

Richard's eyes were hurting (the river-water was full of sand and probably sewage as well) and his breath was short, but he tried to assess his two captives. The drunk was still obstreperous, cursing and trying to hit out at the *agent*, but missed every time. He must have drunk a great deal for the wetting not to have sobered him. A splendid twopence-colored fellow, in spite of his red eyes and dripping clothes. Richard hoped they would be able to let him off. The other man—the wanted man—looked wretched. He was bleeding from the nose, which had been punched out of all normal shape and color, and his rather long hair was plastered in wet rats' tails on his white face. His pale-rimmed eyes had the queer unblinking stare of an epileptic's, and his nose dripped blood on to the knees of his dress trousers. Richard doubted if he was fully conscious. The drunk, however, was rutilant.

"What about the reward?" he shouted. "Reward for saving drowning man, rates increased this year. Come on, hand over!"

"Be quiet!" said the *agent* sharply. "You haven't proved you did save him. Monsieur Ringwood probably saved the two of you. Anyhow you've got to come along with us. Drunk and assaulting the police."

"Still, he did lead us to the man we wanted," said Richard. "Twice. Once in the café and again when I didn't spot that he'd hidden in the river. Couldn't we take that into account and let him off with a warning?"

"Well, sir, but he did knock out poor Gomard, and surely he's a threat to public safety in that condition. Of course it's for you to say, sir."

This made the drunk roar again. Trust the police to suck up to a dirty American, they were all over France like lice. Traitor, lickspittle! Take that!

And he planted a surprisingly lucky blow on the *agent's* temple. After that he burst into tears and said it was all up with his dear country—invaded, betrayed, sold. Nobody contradicted and they had little further trouble with him. The question of his release was tacitly dropped.

CHAPTER 21

After his two prisoners had been given some rough first aid, searched, and locked in the *violon*, Richard was for going at once to join Kéhidiou in the *Impasse du Cher*. But the French policemen screamed him out of it. To take a walk in wet clothes was the height of folly; he risked a congestion; he should take grog, brandy, *café au rhum*, a camomile infusion, be rubbed with olive oil, camphor, alcohol; be purged; or, if he had swallowed river water, take an emetic. The suggestions were kindly meant, but Richard fled before they should pass from words to action. In this old-fashioned province, for all he knew, they might still believe in blistering and clystering as safe homely remedies.

He had just got into dry clothes when Kéhidiou returned, and came up with calvados in hot water and a dose of quinine. Under his host's concerned eye, Richard drank the medicine down before a worse should appear. There might be someone with a jar of leeches downstairs.

Kéhidiou bustled away again in high spirits. He had brought along the child Justin, accompanied, of course, by his mother, to identify the man he had seen climbing out of La Zézette's window. Obviously it would be—it *must* be—Richard's prisoner, the man in dress trousers. The case was practically over.

But after some time, Kéhidiou returned disconcerted. He had lifted the boy up to look through the chink at the top of the prison door. Silly man! thought Richard. With a child on his shoulders, how could he observe the prisoners' behavior? Why hadn't he got a stepladder? And the boy had given all the wrong answers. At first he said: no, it wasn't the nasty little man in dress trousers with the plaster on his nose. It was the big guy. That was the man who'd been so brave and jumped so far. The "big drunk."

Kéhidiou set him down and begged him to be sure he wasn't lying. The man who'd jumped out of the window was very wicked—perhaps a murderer—so he must be sure to tell the truth. Then he hoisted the boy up for another look. This time, after a moment of silence, Justin gave a laugh and cried, "No! No! It wasn't the big man! It wasn't either of them."

From that, nothing could shake him. They all tried to bring him to his senses—including the mother—but even when he was reduced to tears, he stuck to his story. Kéhidiou didn't know what to think of it.

Nor did Richard. He had seen the prisoners searched, and knew therefore that they possessed nothing with which to bribe or intimidate the boy. Then why his about face? And above all, why had he laughed?

Richard had forgotten the swiftness of a small boy's hero worship. And he had never seen Nigel smile. That was the whole explanation. Justin had simply become Nigel's ally.

"Well," said Richard, "we'll just have to go over the other evidence again. What do we know about our prisoners?"

Kéhidiou summarized. Big Drunk possessed an identity card and enough money to keep him for a fortnight. He claimed to have been a maintenance man in a well-known circus which had been broken up in the spring after a fire. Kéhidiou and Richard had both read of the fire in their respective national papers. Since then he had been moving round doing odd jobs. At present, he said, he had landed a job in Pontchâtelet for a week, doing some repairs for Monsieur André Defay.

"Did you check that?"

Kéhidiou snorted. "I telephoned Monsieur Defay. First he was cagey—I suppose he was afraid of trouble over a labor permit—and then admitted it. But would he come down and identify our man? Not on your life. It was *l'heure de l'apéritif.* And anyhow, Jeannette was visiting us after dinner, and could just as well do the job for him."

"Outrageous man, Defay," said Richard. "Still, it does look as if Big Drunk was *bona fide.* What about Dress Trousers?"

The second prisoner was less convincing; though Kéhidiou began to think he might be simply soft in the head. He had no identity card. Well, that was a common enough complaint. But he *was* wearing the dead tramp's clothes. He said that he had got them from another tramp on the towing path in exchange for his own less shabby clothes and the price of a meal. Why did he need the price of a meal, asked Kéhidiou, when he was carrying fifty thousand francs in notes, a large sum? The man babbled some story about saving up to emigrate. Whatever happened, he said, he made it a rule never to break into his savings. Once you started, they were gone in no time.

"It sounds just mad enough to be possibly true," commented Richard. "He's got queer eyes. By the way, what was that little bottle of stuff in his pocket? *He* said it was gargle."

"So it was, of a primitive kind. Simply salt and water." Kéhidiou rose and began to prowl up and down. "You know, when I saw those documents we found on Zézette's body, I made sure that this man in dress trousers was the criminal, and would turn out to be either Blancbec or one of his gang. But he isn't. The oldest policeman in Pontchâtelet has never set eyes on him before. And yet … the documents were so convincing."

Richard had not yet handled "the documents." They were being tested for fingerprints and then going on to a handwriting expert. But he had noted the gist of them. They were three in number, and were found *inserted* into Zézette's parcel of paper money. They had not been there at the time when Painlevé discovered it under the floorboard.

First, there was a letter from Jean Despuys, dated December of last year and addressed to his sister. He told her that he had by chance discovered and recognized Maxime Fleurat, living under a false name as a prosperous businessman. Fleurat had grown a beard, wore spectacles, and looked very different; but an intimate would still know him. Furthermore, his identity could be proved by his handwriting, seal, and certain mannerisms and peculiarities which Despuys described. The local police said that the description fitted. The letter continued. Despuys did not intend to denounce Fleurat while there was still money to be made out of blackmailing him; but later on, it would be necessary to denounce him and so gain the government reward. So he begged his sister to keep the written evidence safe. While Fleurat knew that a collection of proofs existed, and did not know where it was, he was in their power.

The other two "documents" were evidently part of this collection. There was an envelope addressed in a hand which some had already recognized as Fleurat's, the postmark London, the date illegible except for the year, 1955. It was sealed with a curious seal in the form of a bee—Napoleon's emblem, which, as everyone remembered, Fleurat liked to use. Third—and most interesting—was a note in the same hand, unsigned and unheaded, reading "This is all you'll get. Don't try any more or you will be in danger. My patience is exhausted."

Naturally, when Kéhidiou made this find, he thought that the rumors were true. "Blancbec was back." He had killed Despuys in England to stop his blackmail and then crossed to France and killed Zézette because he discovered that she was in the plot.

Auguste would have been delighted to see how well his bait was taken. But now the police were having second thoughts.

To begin with, it did not look as though Zézette was *purposely* killed. There were slight pressure marks on her neck; but she had not died of strangulation. She had died of hemorrhage from the lungs. And her attacker had left without taking away the papers that should have damned him.

"Look!" Richard suggested. "Can't we reconstruct a bit? The woman is by the front door, dressed to go out. As she's carrying all her money besides the papers, it looks as if she didn't intend to come back. Someone catches her giving him the slip. There's a quarrel. The neighbors heard it. She gets roughly handled, and she dies unexpectedly. Surely that looks much more like the work of an accomplice—someone she was going to cheat out of his share of the reward! An accomplice *would* drop everything when he found with horror that Zézette had died on him. He needed her alive to cooperate with his plan. Dead, she's horribly dangerous. He dared not search her, because of the blood. People might think he'd killed her! He drops the whole scheme and runs, not touching the body. That's why he left by the window. Natural death in a house locked from the inside—that's what he wanted us to think. The boy in the beanrow was pure bad luck for him. He should have got clean away."

Kéhidiou muttered ambiguously. He was unhappy until more concrete arguments were available—especially prints and an expert's analysis of the "documents." Richard distracted him by bringing out the two latest communications from England in answer to his own questions: one from the praefect of Pentecost, and one from his own chief, the Bloodhound.

Richard had asked the praefect to find out who, among Despuys' acquaintances, possessed a key to the university parks which Despuys or his murderer might have used on the fatal night. The praefect, *ex-officio* one of the curators of the parks, had sent Richard the complete list of keyholders. It was not very long, but it included Mr. Upjohn (Despuys' supervisor), Mr. Sansom, and the praefect himself. In his covering letter the praefect remarked, in his random manner, that if you gave dons keys, they usually lost them and didn't own up for fear that they'd be made to pay for new locks and keys, as the rules demanded. He hadn't seen his own key for some time though he was sure it was somewhere in the praefect's lodging.

"I see that this information pleases you," said Kéhidiou, "but I don't quite understand why."

Richard smiled. "Never mind now. Look at this from my chief. He says that there's £930 in Despuys' bank account, paid in cash during the year, and he's hardly drawn anything out. What d'you say to that?"

"It looks like a blackmailer's bank account, certainly. But tell me, is there any more news of Nigel Dawson-Gower?"

"They haven't traced him. But my chief seems to have got the army to talk. I'll read out what they said about him."

It was in telegraphese: "W.O. report on D.G. quote decorated good record brains character excellent war-work his application peacetime continuation seriously considered but refused owing rashness extravagance excessive independence conspicuous appearance"—

"Just what my chief grumbles at me for," commented Richard. "What else? 'But'—The Bloodhound never says that."

—"*but* valuable type in emergency unquote photo follows by post ports watched radio appeal today please report fuller."

Richard frowned, as one who toes, but does not kiss, the official line. But Kéhidiou looked pleased.

"That's really interesting," he said. "Dawson-Gower must be seriously in the army's bad books: they don't turn people of that caliber down in peacetime unless they have good reasons for it. And where did he get the money for expensive hobbies like car racing? And why did he tell those flimsy lies about his brother, if he really wanted to protect him? And how did he manage to disappear so easily, unless—— Ah! Dinner!"

The dinner was excellent, but Richard hardly tasted it. "Rashness, excessive independence?" Well, the haystack affair and the removal of Tim certainly showed that. And the murder of the old tramp? A quick, ruthless action. The commando, surprised in a house where he must not be found, rushes out, strips the old man, flings his body in the river, and lies down disguised in the tramp's clothes under the nose of the police. "Good type in emergency." If you could call it good.

"But why *should* Dawson-Gower be involved with the Despuys family?" he asked aloud. "He had a good war record."

Kéhidiou spoke his mind ruthlessly. "So had other people who were paid by both sides. Don't you see? Why was he sacked by your army? Why was he rich afterwards? Because he helped Blancbec to escape at the Liberation and got well paid for it. And Despuys found out and blackmailed him."

Richard's impulse was to reply, "A British officer of good family? Never!" But he restrained himself, and said, "Yes—but political treachery, killing old people—surely that's more in character for a timid, cautious type like Despuys?"

"A Sorbonne bursary-holder? Never!" exclaimed the Frenchman angrily. "Besides, Despuys is dead."

"We never properly identified the body," Richard argued. "I wonder. Suppose it was Blancbec in the haystack, and Despuys who killed him, and Dawson-Gower came in afterwards, just for the hell of it, and helped Despuys out? Humanly, it makes much better sense."

"Humanly! Are we policemen or novelists?" Kéhidiou exploded. "Ah! I see the fingerprints are being brought over at last. Let's consider some real evidence for a change."

The fingerprints averted a quarrel, but did not solve their problem. In Zézette's house, there were fingerprints of both the new prisoners—Big Drunk and Dress Trousers. Big Drunk's were on the outside of the front door, by the handle, and on the lavatory window, both inside and outside. Big Drunk explained this by saying that Zézette had got him in that morning to mend the catch on the window. No one could prove or disprove this statement.

The prints of Dress Trousers were all over the kitchen. Dress Trousers now confessed that he had slipped in by the open back door that morning in the hope of stealing a little food. No one could prove or disprove this statement.

There were no prints—other than Zézette's—in the upstairs rooms. On the "documents," however, a completely new print was found. As yet, they had not been able to identify it.

"Oh well!" Richard tried to comfort his colleague, "I expect that's the real clue. It'll be a forger's fingerprint, and your handwriting expert will prove it. By the way, are the prisoners going to be all right together? Won't eat each other in the night, or get out, or anything?"

"No one"—Kéhidiou's tone forbade levity—"could deplore the fact that our *violon* is so … picturesque, more than I do. The trouble is, there's never enough crime in Pontchâtelet to convince people it's worth paying, really *paying*, for a set of up-to-date cells. They exist on paper, I need hardly say. But—*enfin!* Our *violon* remains medieval. Still, there is no reason for alarm. The prisoners are now perfectly quiet; I have two men on duty outside the door all night; and the lock—well, our ancestors did take locks seriously. And the door is as thick as your arm. Nothing but dynamite could get them out of there." Then his eyes lightened. "Here's Jeannette arriving. Do you wish to be present at the identification?"

To his lasting regret, Richard declined. He said he wanted to work on his notes. Really, he was being tactful and leaving Kéhidiou to run his own show. So Kéhidiou ran downstairs, and Richard watched the scene from his bedroom window.

Jeannette was looking her best and basking in the adventure. The police on duty seemed unaccountably more numerous than usual, and stood admiring. Even Kéhidiou, hoisting her up to look through the crack in the top of the *violon* door, smiled as he sweated. Those inside the *violon* left no doubt of their feelings; there were whistles and smackings of lips. Jeannette slid down ruffled and trying to hide her laughter under affronted dignity. She could see nothing, she said. They must bring her a chair to stand upon and an electric torch to see the prisoners' faces. (Renewed cheering from the prisoners.)

"Shine it on your face, beautiful!"

"No, shine it on me, and watch the love light in my eyes!"

And so on. Jeannette, when the chair was brought, mounted it unsteadily in her high heels, begging Kéhidiou to hold her tight. Once up, she tried to cling to the top of the door, but she had bag and gloves in one hand and the torch in the other. She complained that she couldn't switch the torch on. Somebody switched it on for her and passed it back. The noise from inside swelled while the light in her hand wavered and came to rest; then she came down on top of Kéhidiou in a big silky heap, protesting against the ordeal. He set her on her feet and shouted,

"The next man who speaks will spend the night in chains!"

In the ensuing silence, Jeannette spoke with just her mother's quiet asperity.

"I congratulate you! Silence at last! I am now happy to tell you that the man Papa engaged to mend our boat is certainly in there. It's the tall one in the blue shirt. I saw him quite clearly and remember him. Oh dear! I've lost one of my gloves! Have you seen …?"

A small white glove came sailing through the crack from the prison and landed at her feet. She laughed nervously. Kéhidiou picked it up.

"Sure you didn't drop anything else? I can send a man in to look, if you like."

"Oh no! No! Wait, I'll make sure. Money, keys ... no, I've got everything. We'd better get away, hadn't we? Or you may lose control of your prisoners again."

And she sauntered towards the house. Kéhidiou, allowing himself an angry shrug and a laugh, followed.

Richard, alone at his bedroom table, thought and read and wrote, wrote and read and thought; and always ended by crossing out. Downstairs the conversation became louder and merrier as time went on, till at last Kéhidiou, almost rosy, almost boyish, burst in and said:

"I've been sent to fetch you! No refusal allowed! Jeannette wants to tell you—she's identified your Big Drunk."

"To the entertainment of all. I'm afraid I watched from here."

"What a temperament, *hein?* She expects admiration and is enraged to receive it. Ah, young girls! But, my dear man, you look dreadfully tired. I'm so sorry. Your immersion, your efforts ... Shall I send you up some remedies? Get in a doctor?"

"No! No! I'll come down! That girl's tonic enough for anybody."

"You are right," Kéhidiou replied seriously. "On every level, one may say, the feminine is an essential ingredient of happiness. Physically, morally, intellectually ..."

Oh Lord! Richard fidgeted. Not another disquisition on the fair sex!

"And come quickly—" Kéhidiou fidgeted—"or Jeannette will have to go."

The ladies were indeed deliciously lively; and champagne had been opened. True, the ladies dipped sponge-fingers into it, but bless them! Why shouldn't they, when they were competing to amuse? Richard found the ingredients of his happiness so well compounded that he was presently learning, and even attempting to sing, insulting French songs about policemen. The effects of champagne are rapid, though innocent and short-lived.

"You sing marvelously!" Sylvie exclaimed. "Just like a Frenchman."

"*Better* than a Frenchman," amended Jeannette, and looked at her watch. "Oh dear! Why have I got to be sent away to Angennes just when Pontchâtelet's waking up at last? Can't you all persuade Papa to let me stay? Monsieur, a little more wine? Don't move, Sylvie, it's my turn. And I ought to do it more professionally. We

Defays are all born with corks in our mouths."

No cork in *that* mouth, thought Richard, admiring her deftness and animation. She put down the glasses, powdered her nose, filled the glasses, tidied her hair, and carried them without a drop spilled, yet her talk and even her gestures were vivid as ever, the life and soul of the party.

"There! One for each of the great detectives, and good luck to them, because the bottle's empty! And I must fly, or Papa will beat me; he's a dreadful man. I think I'll get married, just to escape. Oh no! No! Don't see me home! Let me enjoy my freedom for once! But I'll tell you what you *can* do for me—if you want to make me happy?"

Who could wish otherwise?

"Take up your glasses, *un, deux!* Now drink a pledge to me! Say, 'We'll try to get you back before it's all over'."

"*Un, deux!*" cried Kéhidiou, beating time. "We'll try to get you back before it's all over."

They drank in high mock solemnity.

"Good night, my dear, kind friends. Mind you drink it before it goes flat. Papa says that drinking flat champagne is like kissing a girl in spectacles. We'll leave them to discuss it, Sylvie."

They whisked off, and the two men sat for a moment in reminiscent silence. Then Richard sneezed. "*Atishoo!*"

"Bless you!" cried his host. "I'm afraid you did catch cold after all. *Atchoum!* Now I've started. It's like yawning, one person starts, and then—*Atchoum!*" He laughed and wiped his eyes with his hand.

"*Atishoo*! We'd better separate. Or else—ha! ha!"

"In Brittany there's a proverb—*Atchoum!* Excuse me. Get a handkerchief. *Atchoum!*"

"Atishoo! Once a wish," counted Richard, sneezing by the book, "twice a kiss, three times a letter, four times—Heavens! *Come on, quick!* That was Jeannette screaming!"

A shot rang out, followed by another, louder scream. As Richard reached the courtyard, Kéhidiou came thundering downstairs and followed him out into the street. The screams came from round the corner of a side road. They turned into it, and found Jeannette ululating under a lamppost, while window-shutters opened and heads poked out all down the street. At first all she could say was "A man! A man!"

"What did he do? *Atchoum!*"

"Which way did he go? *Atishoo!*"

"Are you hurt? *Atchoum!*"

Lesser policemen, meanwhile, poured out into the street behind them. Jeannette suddenly pointed, screamed louder than
ever, and cried,

"There! There he is! In the doorway, right up there at the end! Oh
dear, I'm sure he's going to kill me! Don't go, he's got a gun. It's a
dangerous lunatic!" These were not remarks likely to deter gallant
men. Richard led the advance up the street. As he ran he reflected
that his constant sneezing made him an easy target, even in the dark.

But then a much louder bang sounded far behind him. "That's
not a shot," thought Richard, turning in his tracks. "That's blasting
of some sort. What on earth is happening?"

"Ah, Monsieur! Don't leave me!" Jeannette flung herself upon
him and fairly grappled him. He could hardly shake her off without
hurting her; for she was a strong girl. "Take care of me, Monsieur!
I'm frightened!"

Nevertheless, Richard struggled to get back to the police station,
half-carrying and half-dragging the sobbing girl.

"Oh, please stop, Monsieur! I feel so ill! Couldn't we take shelter—just for a moment?"

"I'll get an *agent* to look after you. Come here, *les pontchâtelétiens!*"

"No! No! Papa wouldn't like you to leave me with low-class
people!"

She was laughing and crying at once, leaning her whole weight
on him and beating with her heels against the pavement. At last he
managed to detach her, and two Pontchâtelet policemen, who had
been not quite silently condemning his brutality, received her with
enthusiasm. Richard ran full tilt for the prison. But as he approached, a man ran out and pelted down the street in the opposite direction. He went after him.

There were cries behind; Kéhidiou calling his name. He glanced
over his shoulder, and in that moment lost his quarry. The fugitive
was suddenly out of sight, and there was no sound of footsteps. This
old quarter of the town was a warren of little alleys and courts,
baffling to the stranger even in daylight. After a short, vain hunt,
Richard returned to headquarters.

He found Kéhidiou and his staff expressing deep emotion in the
typically French manner; that is, stony silence broken by an occa-
sional factual enquiry. This exceptional behavior was justified in
the circumstances. All three prisoners were gone. The door of the

violon was only held upright by its massive medieval lock; on the opposite side it gaped open, its hinges disrupted. Two *agents* lay on the ground, stunned though not seriously injured, and they, it turned out, were the only two who had remained at headquarters when Jeannette had screamed for help. They were in no state as yet to give information about the breakout.

"It was a high explosive by the looks of it," Kéhidiou said in a voice trembling with rage. "But why aren't the prisoners dead? They ought to be, there's no cover in there."

"Give me a torch, please," said Richard. "Ah! You see what they did. Wrenched up the leather bolster, turned the less worn side uppermost, and lay in the gap behind it against the wall. You can see where the bolster took the brunt of the explosion. They certainly planned well."

"Planned well! I tell you, it was impossible! Even given the fact that they were guarded by the silliest policemen in France. Where did they get the explosive? You saw them searched when you brought them in, didn't you? They weren't put in the lockup first, so that they could have hidden it then?"

"No. They were wet and we gave them a rubdown and first aid in the office before they were put in the *violon* at all." This had not been easy to arrange, and Richard was now glad he had insisted. "What type of explosive could they have used, do you think? Something small enough to hide actually on a naked body, or palm? It's amazing how they *can* hide things."

"I wonder." Kéhidiou mused. "We—I mean, they—had a thing we—they used in the Resistance for blowing up railway-points, and the effect was rather the same; great blasting power at the point of impact but not a widely diffused blast. It was about the size of a matchbox, in fact they gave us the things in real matchboxes for camouflage."

"Looks like something of the same sort. Well, there's only one thing—catch them. I'm convinced they haven't got far. That last man went to earth very near, I'd swear, for I heard his footsteps stop. You've already blocked the streets leading out of the quarter, you say? Well, let's start a house-to-house search. I'm sure we'll get them. Come on, let's begin."

"Useless. We can't do that till the morning."

"The morning? Don't be ridiculous, what's the good of that?" Richard cried, losing the last of his urbanity.

"It's the law. French law. No house may be entered by the police for search between dusk and dawn." Kéhidiou suddenly turned on his men venomously. "You idiots! It's all your fault. Why didn't you stay on duty? They'd never have got past the eight of you. And now look!"

"But Monsieur, when we heard the lady—*your* guest—calling ..."

"Well, don't stand there staring and arguing. Go and search the roads. Take the quarter street by street with a man each end on all the corners that lead anywhere. Get any citizens you can to help you. It's in their own interest—tell them that—but if they refuse, offer to pay them three hundred each. I'll get in touch with the railway station and the nearby villages. I'll telephone for reinforcements too. We need some keen, conscientious policemen on this job."

"How long before you officially forgive them?" asked Richard as the men went off dejected or angry.

"In official life," growled Kéhidiou, "one doesn't *forgive*. Sometimes one pretends to forget."

That, of course, was the whole trouble with French politics. Richard longed suddenly to hear an English voice uttering emollient clichés: "It'll all be the same in a hundred years," "Least said, soonest mended." All this tension and articulateness used up energy and he was tired to death.

"Jeannette next," he said. "Where is she?"

"Heavens, yes! You'll want to question her. It looks as if that attack on her was part of a plan. The fellow got right away. He seems to have shouted at her and then begun firing. She wasn't hit, luckily—or perhaps that was deliberate too, if he was merely creating a diversion. It looks as if we had a whole gang to deal with, doesn't it?"

"What did you do with Jeannette when you got her back here?"

"I sent her indoors to rest. She was very shaken."

"With free range of the house?"

"Naturally, after I'd made sure nobody was hiding there. She went straight in to Sylvie, who had rushed up to the baby."

Richard ran ahead, calling to Kéhidiou to leave him alone with Jeannette for a few minutes and to telephone Monsieur Defay.

In the drawing room sat Sylvie by herself, suckling her child. The sound of running water led Richard to the kitchen, where he found Jeannette washing up the champagne glasses under the tap at the sink. When he came in, she started and dropped the last glass. It broke, but she made a grab for it and cut her finger.

"Oh dear! No, it's nothing really. I'll just hold my finger under the cold tap a minute, may I? And I'd better rinse the little bit of glass down the hole too; they always tell you it's the small bits that are so dangerous. There, Monsieur. You wanted me?"

She turned at last, and he saw that she was very pale. He turned off the tap and handed her a large clean handkerchief to wrap round her finger.

"Why are you washing those up? Wouldn't it have been better to leave them?"

"Oh, no! When you're upset, it's always better to do something, I think. Sitting still only makes you worse."

"What else have you done since you came in, besides washing the glasses?"

"I just went upstairs. I felt rather sick."

"And were you?"

"Really!" She raised her eyebrows at this barbarity, and then shrugged her shoulders. "In fact, no, since you are so kind as to ask."

"And where's your handbag? I'm in the middle of a general search."

"It's on that chair. And by the way, if you aren't using the chair, perhaps I might sit down. If it doesn't inconvenience you."

Every word an icicle. She seemed much older than the delightful child who had been amusing them all before the trouble began. Now, she had a hard-edged look, like a statue carved out of some fine, pale wood; boxwood, perhaps; a shape that would not change except by breaking.

"But of course! I won't keep you in here a second. Perhaps you'd like to lie on a sofa while I question you. I'll just finish this small piece of routine."

He zipped open the bag, which was large but elegant. It contained two white gloves, one small snowy handkerchief, one notecase with a few hundred-franc notes in it, two keys on a ring, a comb, a lipstick, a powder compact, and piece of clean cotton wool in the inside pocket. She sat still, not watching him.

He opened the powder compact. Like most such things nowadays, it was made in two compartments or layers. The powder itself was in a bottom layer tightly closed by a spring lid, and above that was another space for a puff. Richard took a specimen of the powder in an envelope, and asked Jeannette,

"Where's the powder puff?"

"I don't use one. I prefer a clean bit of cotton wool each time."

"Yes, so does my wife. But where's the cotton wool? I saw a bit inside the lid when you opened it in the drawing room just before you left."

"You're very observant. I'd quite forgotten. I suppose I must have got rid of it since."

"Well, when? Try to remember."

"I—yes, I used it in the bathroom just now."

"And threw it down the pan? And pulled the plug?"

"Yes, Monsieur. And I assure you, it contained no dynamite."

Richard held open the door. "Let's move to the study to finish our talk, shall we? You'll be more comfortable. As a matter of fact—" he stood back at the door so that she must pass directly in front of him—"it's not dynamite I'm looking for just now. No, you first, please! What I'm looking for—is the light in your eyes?—I'm looking for a milder form of explosive at present."

"Ah?"

He looked at her very searchingly, and she met his eye, but blushed. The woodcarving turned back into childish, wavering curves of flesh and blood.

"The sort of thing they use at Carnival," he went on deliberately, "or on April Fools' Day."

She laughed irrepressibly, almost saucily. "They'd have needed an awful lot of fireworks to break down the door of the *violon*, wouldn't they?" Then she recovered herself. "No, I'm sorry. I see what you meant now. You're thinking that the horrid man in the street was just letting off things like that and not shooting at all. Yves said, I remember, that it was all part of a plan. I'm sorry. I wasn't very brave, I'm afraid."

"No, you weren't very," agreed Richard, watching how her eyes flashed at this and she bit her lip. "I say, that finger of yours is bleeding rather badly, isn't it?"

"Oh no! Just a scratch, that's all!" she replied, taking off the blood-soaked handkerchief and sucking at the cut. "Curious, how good one's own blood tastes, isn't it? Like the best beefsteak." Then she suddenly switched to pathos. "I expect you'll let me go home soon and have it seen to, won't you? I do feel rather funny, as a matter of fact, and also my parents must be wondering what's become of me. Papa gets worried if I'm late."

It was only the girls who could make one feel a hero, when they chose, who had the corresponding talent for making one feel a brute. Richard was not without experience of the treatment.

"We've already telephoned to your home to say that we'll be bringing you back. Would you like to put your feet up? Sure? Well, just try and tell me what happened."

"I said good night to Sylvie, on the stairs actually, because she was going up to the baby, and walked out through the courtyard. The street was empty. I turned the corner and walked on. Suddenly a man's voice said 'Stop!' I couldn't see him, but the voice seemed to come from one of those dark alleys, you know. I took no notice and walked on. He made an insulting remark."

"Oh, what?"

"Dirt." Jeannette dared him to ask more. "I still went on walking, but I did cross to the other side of the street. And then he said, 'Not so fast! Blancbec wants you.' I still went on walking and he—he fired a gun at me. I screamed."

"Did you see him?"

"Yes. He was medium height and had a hat pulled over his eyes and a scarf tied rather high around his chin."

"You saw all that, although he was standing in a dark alleyway?"

"Excuse me, Monsieur. When I screamed he ran down the street. That was when I saw him. Ah, what a feeling!"

"Just like a gangster film. Now, one more question and we'll send you home. I'll call Madame Kéhidiou; it concerns her too."

Sylvia came in and stood by her friend. They both looked absurdly juvenile.

"Which of you two played that trick with the sneezing powder?"

Four brown eyes grew round with innocent bewilderment; it was Sylvie who asked him to explain.

"Ever been to a Carnival supper? You can't make two men who haven't got colds both begin to sneeze at once, and sneeze hard for five minutes, and stop as suddenly as they began unless—*enfin*, one of you put sneezing powder in our drinks, surely?"

"Oh no! Not in good champagne!" Jeannette was shocked. "Did you, Sylvie?"

"Of course not! Yves can't bear practical jokes. Why do you ask? Have you found any traces of—er—sneezing powder?"

"I'm looking into it," he replied. "By the way, Jeannette, after this, we're certainly justified in asking your father to keep you here in Pontchâtelet under his care. So you'll get your wish."

"Oh … yes. But I'd really rather get away, *now*. I'm not so brave and adventurous as I thought I was. Papa's wise, it's better to be right out of Pontchâtelet."

"Right out? Angennes is only ten kilometers away."

"Oh, do let's stop arguing!" cried Jeannette, beginning to cry. "I can't take it any more! Please take me home, Monsieur."

CHAPTER 22

Although they were forbidden by law to enter houses before dawn, Kéhidiou and his men collected important evidence during the hours of darkness. Their first triumph was to find the gun that had frightened Jeannette. It was hidden behind a dustbin just inside a passage leading into the street where they had found her. And it was not even a real gun. It was a child's percussion pistol, quite free of fingerprints. When they opened it, they discovered a brand-new roll of caps inside, of which only two had been fired, the second very recently—probably when Jeannette screamed.

Kéhidiou made enquiries at the town cafés, which were open till quite late on summer evenings. The prisoners had not been seen in them, but the *Poisson Complaisant* reported Zézette's visit soon after six, recognizing her from the police description. She had met a man there—a man wearing a rather noticeable suit of diagonal black and white stripes. He sported sideburns, and his wavy black hair was worn long and brushed into two little duck's tails that crossed at the back of his neck. The waiters had noticed this man before, busy charming female tourists—there was no doubt of his occupation. What amused them was that this time his companion ...

"I will spare you the zoological comparisons," said Kéhidiou. "You know what waiters are. Anyhow, this same man was noticed hanging about the station an hour or so later. He fidgeted round for about an hour and then walked off towards the center of the town. It shouldn't be too difficult to pick him up tomorrow."

But the third piece of evidence that arrived seemed to Richard the most interesting of all. It was a report from the handwriting experts on the "documents" found on Zézette's dead body. They were forgeries. The forger was skilful; each letter was written in quick strokes of the pen, without any mark of hesitancy or retouching. But when they were compared with specimens of Despuys' and Blancbec's actual scripts, which had taken some time to obtain, differences could be seen. The microscope revealed certain habitual tremors of the hand, tricks not so much of forming the letters as of writing some more quickly or heavily than others, which reflected different physical rhythms. On the same principle of analysis, the experts said that the two forged documents had both been written by one person; there were the same marks of muscular and nervous variation in both. Richard was inclined to doubt the validity of the method, but Kéhidiou reminded him that during the war the Germans had learned to distinguish one Resistance Morse code operator from another on the same principle. Each had his own particular style of tapping, even when he was trying hard to do it regularly. Typists, too—each had a way of hitting some keys harder than others. In fact no one, even the most skilled craftsman, used his hands in a perfectly uniform way or produced a mechanically regular result; the only regular thing was that each individual had his own fairly constant pattern of irregularity. Nature, enunciated Kéhidiou, was never perfect.

"Not mass-produced, anyhow," said Richard. "It's a curious thing, but I've been working along the same lines, in a way. I've been trying to sort out this whole case on a basis of personal style—trying to see which of the actions fit which of the characters. I can't see Big Drunk throttling a sick woman; I can't see Dress Trousers jumping out of a high window. As for Jeannette—her behavior tonight gives the lie to every line of her face. She looks like Antigone and behaves like—"

"She's very young—and very feminine, as well."

"Feminine, yes. Also very proud, and no fool. She might enchant, be merry, or cry for help. But tonight she flirted, giggled, and shrieked. It was a sort of deliberate corruption of style."

"I understand you. She wasn't at her best tonight. But all the same, I'd stake my reputation on her essential decency. We *know* her. She can't have done what you think. The sneezing powder, yes; I'll grant you that. We'll never prove it, of course. She must have brought it on that piece of cotton wool she destroyed. There was none in the sample of face powder you gave me. Yes, she might have done that for a prank, and been ashamed to own up when she found the consequences had been so disastrous. She's half a child, after all. And in the abstract, I'd even agree that she might have tried, in some not entirely lawful way, to divert suspicion away from young Tim, of whom she's evidently very fond. Or even from the brother, for Tim's sake. But I'm sure she'd never do such a thing if it incriminated innocent people. And quite certainly, she'd never, never connive at murder. Put it right out of your head. We *know* her. I must say I'm more than ever glad that Monsieur Defay is sticking to his original plan and sending her off to the country tomorrow."

"I'm glad, too," said Richard, smiling sidelong. "Though not entirely for the same reasons as you. You know I told you young Tim was jealous and worried yesterday, because he thought Jeannette was slipping out to meet a ..."

"Yes, yes, yes, yes! You told me this morning. I'm sure you are wrong.

"*Yesterday* morning, don't you mean?" Richard was tired. "But listen! If she's been slipping out to meet somebody—and even you admit that her behavior today has been extremely odd—then that somebody must be a person unconnected with Tim. Otherwise the poor boy wouldn't be so obviously jealous, and in the dark. I don't ask you to accept my hypothesis. Only to check the reasoning."

Kéhidiou bowed. "All right. I grant, then, that *if* she's been meeting someone, it isn't Tim's brother. But who else could it be? Wait! I have an idea. Suppose that Despuys was *not* in fact the murdered man in the haystack. I never felt quite happy about that identification. Suppose, in fact, Despuys murdered the man in the haystack. In that case, the man in Zézette's house that first morning is explained. It was her brother. Naturally she'd hide him in her spare room. And when you came and he realized that the hunt was up, he ran out at the back, found the old tramp, killed him, and ... did he have time?"

"To change into his clothes? Perhaps, if he was very quick and ruthless. The buttons and things wouldn't matter. The grass was very long in the little hollow where he was lying. ..."

"So Despuys could have lain under our very noses, posing as the tramp asleep. And in that case—BON DIEU DE BON DIEU DE BON DIEU! Don't tell me that Despuys was Dress Trousers!" Kéhidiou shook his clenched fists in the air.

"I wouldn't venture to dogmatize. However——"

"Hence the fact that his fingerprints were all over the house, where it hadn't just been dusted. Hence the large sum of money found in his pockets. But, just a minute! You have the photograph of Despuys. Was Dress Trousers in fact at all like him?"

"Oh, my dear chap! The man I saw today was unshaven, had his nose bashed in, and was half-drowned into the bargain. And just between us two—don't spread it about, for God's sake—I've a rotten memory for faces. Facts I can remember, and words— my mind takes in like a recording-tape. But faces—I don't find it easy to compare my mental image of a small snapshot taken a couple of years ago of a smiling, up-and-coming young man putting all his goods in the shop window with the beaten-up drowned rat I saw yesterday. And alas! Our physical records of Despuys are far from detailed. It's just the usual passport catalogue of externals. Now if only there were one of your *fiches anthropométriques*...."

"Ah, yes! Then we could compare it with the one of Dress Trousers."

"You got one of him yesterday, then?"

"Certainly."

"And was there a medical examination too?"

"No. I'm sorry to say that the doctor wouldn't do anything about the tramp's postmortem till the next day. These Tourangeaux!"

"Never mind. You got the *fiche*. I do admire your system."

"Thank you. Well, I can easily ring up Lyons tomorrow and find out if Despuys *is* recorded there. It's not impossible. Lots of people are. And if they have a *fiche* for him, they can read out the measurements to me over the telephone. If they tally exactly with Dress Trousers—well, it will be a watertight, scientific solution." But then his face fell and he sighed.

"What's the use of talking? We absolutely must recapture the prisoners."

"Yes," said Richard. "And I hope Jeannette may lead us on our way. Did you notice how suddenly anxious she was to go to Angennes, as soon as I said she might not have to?"

"It was natural, after the fright she'd had."

"Also natural if she were planning to hide a man there. Yes, I know you hate the idea, but just consider her actions. She comes here in the morning—and promptly gets herself asked again this evening. It's her last night at home; she's got to pack; Tim is anxious for her company—but she comes here. Heavens! One doesn't generally visit the same house twice in making a round of good-byes! Well, she comes. She stands with her hands on the top edge of the prison door. She drops her glove—probably with the explosive tucked inside it——"

"Oh no, not that!"

"Then I'd like to know where the prisoners did get it from. She then waits, and incapacitates us with sneezing-powder just at the moment when a diversion is planned to cover the breakout ..."

"Monsieur!" Kéhidiou's voice was formidable. "You are making a somewhat serious accusation against the daughter of one of our leading citizens. Allow me to remind you that we are both tired, that the house-to-house search begins at dawn, and that you have certain pieces of evidence still to arrive from England by the morning post. Therefore...."

Richard sighed and murmured almost to himself, "I wonder if there will be any news of my wife."

Kéhidiou, in a quick return of sympathy, took him by the shoulders.

"*Courage, mon vieux!* Things will turn out all right."

As Richard went to his room, each tread of the stairs was a separate obstacle to be negotiated. Things will turn out all right. But nobody likes to think of his fate as some great inanimate blancmange that merely turns out.

At daylight they began to search the houses of Pontchâtelet's old quarter. Two hours later they were still working slowly and smoothly through them.

"In Brittany," said the Commissaire, "every citizen would have offered to help us so as to catch the criminal. In Paris, they'd have broken our cordon so as to get to work on time, and we'd have had street fighting. But these Tourangeaux! They just love any excuse to talk and sit still." The general reaction had indeed been good-humored curiosity and a second coffeepot on the stove.

Meanwhile the *Sûreté* at Paris had rung through warning Inspector Ringwood to stand by for a call from London at seven. A little before that time, the bell rang; an operator with a vile Parisian accent was persuaded to withdraw from the line, and the voice of the Bloodhound was heard in the hand.

"Ringwood there? Now listen and don't interrupt because it's expensive. Well, I reckon I've tied up your case for you. My radio appeal was answered at 11:30 yesterday evening by an ex-R.A.F. bomber pilot now flying for Royce-Bentley. He confesses that he dropped Nigel Dawson-Gower by parachute over your district at three twenty-two on Wednesday morning. Got that? This pilot has a good record and seemed O.K. to us, though of course we're keeping him taped. His story is that he thought Dawson-Gower was on a hush-hush job for the War Office and so he asked no questions. Bit shaken now. He pinpointed the position for us, so send for a map. No time to waste.

"I rang the brigadier I saw before. Got him up from his bed, in fact, and he wasn't too pleased. He said Dawson-Gower is not, re-peat, *not*, working for his department and hasn't done since the war. Of course he was still sticking up for him—a good type and cetera and so on. Well, p'raps I'd do the same for you if you got across the M.I. lot. But be that as it may, and mind you, I don't say it will be … Have you got a decent map there now?"

"Yes, I bought a Michelin road-map as soon as …"

"Michelin? But that's in kilometers. I'd have got you one of the army ones if—oh well, never mind. I'll describe the position. Got a pencil and paper?"

"Yes." Richard folded his hands. He could trust his verbal memory.

"The river Cher, C-H-E-R—that's the one the town's on—passes through the forest of Pont—wait, I'll spell it."

"Pontchâtelet. Only forest round here."

"Yes. A mile and a quarter west of the town. Up-river, that is."

"Yes. I know."

"In the middle of this forest, or large wood as we'd call it, the river takes a right-angle bend south, enclosing a low hill. O.K.? The top of this hill is clear of trees. Like a bald head, the pilot said it is, you can't miss it. Got that down? When I told the brigadier he ad-mitted there are caves there and Dawson-Gower used them in the war. Well, that's the place. I reckon you ought to find his parachute around somewhere. But find him first. You'll get his photo and dabs by airmail today first thing. Anything new to report your end?"

"New, yes, but probably irrelevant after what you say. I've been barking up the wrong tree. Oh, Mercury and the muses!" he ex-claimed softly.

"Well, least said, soonest mended. What? No, I haven't rung off; don't get excited. Something you want?"

"Yes. Yes, please, at once. Will you ask Oxford to put the best man they've got to search the hollow trees in Priory Road?"

"Search hollow trees in Priory Road, Oxford?"

"Minutely. Owls or no owls."

"No what? Spell it. Oh, *owls*! Why? What have they got to do with it?"

"Nothing, nothing. Don't ring off! Don't ring off, I beg you! Are you there? How's my wife?"

"Owls your life? Are you all right, Inspector? Been in a fight or something?"

"No, I mean yes, but never mind. How's my *wife*? Mrs. Ringwood? My MISSUS?"

"Oh, her! Don't you worry about the little woman. Everything's under control. Nothing you can do but put it out of your mind like I've learned to. It'll be all the same in a hundred years, eh?"

The Bloodhound rang off. Richard went to the Defays' house in the Rue Descartes.

"Well, I found Tim Dawson-Gower in bed asleep," Richard told Kéhidiou later, "and I scared him stiff. But he still stuck to his story. Big Brother had nothing to do with the haystack affair; no idea that he was in France; most unlikely; hadn't seen him. So I felt that the time had come to apply the policeman's war cry."

"Which is?"

"Jeopardy, captivity, brutality! I told him to dress, said I was arresting him as an accomplice. Heard a sound outside, opened the door, and found Jeannette in a white dressing gown with her hair down her back, looking about fifteen."

"Well!"

"She in turn swore she knew nothing about Nigel. Watched us handcuff young Tim with a kind of calm despair. Kissed him goodbye, asked if she could visit him. I said, no, we were taking him to a larger prison and she hadn't a hope. She stared me down.

"At this point the two Defay children joined the party and started asking questions, which was just what I wanted. I told them that Tim's brother was a bad man who ought to be arrested, and that he's been dropped into the forest by parachute. If they knew anything they ought to tell me. François immediately began to bargain with me—that child has brains—saying, if they found Nigel for me, would I let their friend Tim go free? I said, yes, very probably. Chantal, the girl, pointed out that foreigners who parachuted into French territory were invaders, like Julius Caesar, and it was up to the French, like Vercingetorix, to wipe them out. Finally they both asserted that they knew every single hiding-place in the forest, on account of playing Vercingetorix all over it. Jeannette was looking furious. So I've engaged them as temporary assistants, and we are starting for the forest at ten. Goodness knows what their mother will say, but I got their father's permission. Surprisingly, he didn't object."

"He wouldn't. Anything to show off the family talents. I don't like it, though. Suppose Dawson-Gower starts shooting?"

"First, I very much doubt that he's there still. Second, I'll see that the children have our bodies all round them. Really, if their father thinks it's all right …"

"He's the rashest man in Pontchâtelet. Why, they say that during the war he used to climb up his windmill at Angennes and fire at aircraft with a rook rifle. And he'd expect his children to do the same. Ah! There's the postman at last."

Ignoring the rest of the sheaf, Ringwood opened the airmail packet and propped Nigel's photograph on the table. It was a clever picture, by a young photographer who had since made a name in films, and it held the eye. Trick lighting exaggerated the gloss on every eyelash, the quilted solidity of each muscle in the neck, the heavy bones of brow and chin, as though displaying the points of a fighting animal in show condition.

"Yes," sighed Kéhidiou. "It's Big Drunk all right—if we only had him!"

Richard was still studying the face of his adversary.

"Typical fighter's eyes, aren't they? See how they're set—well away from a nose which is nevertheless massive enough to protect them. And yet not deep-set, although the heavy brow structure makes you think so. He must have twenty percent better peripheral vision than you or me—two-thirds of a circle, maybe. And notice the pupils. They aren't focused on a narrow point. They have that deceptively lazy look, like a wolf's. They're taking in the whole field of vision, not just one thing. They'd only focus on the object of immediate attack. And when they did—!"

"Yes, he's wicked, but still he's handsome. That sleek look just adds to his menace; he didn't look half so dangerous yesterday when he was rough with stubble and mud. Party, I suppose, one didn't see the lines of his mouth. Or rather, one saw the sensuality but missed the hardness. Do they tell us his coloring?"

"Black hair, ruddy tanned complexion, eyes with large reddish-brown iris ringed and rayed with black. Thorough, isn't it? That's my own pet reform."

"Yes, I read your article on identification by iris patterns when I was still at Paris. I remember my chief remarking that here our measuring system made it unnecessary, but that all the English criminals would have to spend a fortune on getting colored contact lenses. Did they?"

"Oh no! My work's far too obscure. Or rather," Richard added with unconscious vanity, "crime doesn't pay well enough. Only film stars and American senators can afford to change the color of their eyes. Well, now, how do we get hold of Dawson-Gower?"

"The house-to-house search may do it for us. But I'd better telephone at once to alert all the police stations within forty kilometers, in case he's slipped through. Or do you think a hundred?"

"My own guess is that he'll either stick about here, protected by his Resistance friends, or make a dash back to England. If he does that, we're ready for him."

"*Bon!* And the other prisoners? We're still interested in them?"

"Certainly. *And* the professional lady-killer who took Zézette into the Café Centrale yesterday. The more the better. We always said, didn't we, that Dawson-Gower could count on a large criminal acquaintance in this district?"

"Right! Well, I'll have some breakfast sent in to you while you finish your paperwork. Got a letter from your wife?"

"Heavens! I never looked."

Clare had sent a picture postcard of the dome of Saint Paul's with the sentence, "Still looking like this." It had been posted yesterday morning.

A letter with a Tours postmark was from Lévy, that schoolmaster of Despuys who had worked for the Resistance, and who had arranged for Francis Clandon to stay with the Defays. He explained that he was unable to come to Pontchâtelet in person at present, because there was a schoolmasters' strike going on. Term being over, the *professeurs de lycée* had refused to correct matriculation papers till the government raised their salaries. Unfortunately, the strike was due to end any day now and the arrears of work would be formidable. One must do one's possible to prevent the dislocation of the educational program. He trusted a letter would suffice.

"Jean Despuys," the letter continued, "was a good pupil, though not naturally gifted in philosophy, which is my own subject. He did indeed volunteer to work for the Resistance during the last six months of the Occupation, but was refused, against my advice. The reason given for refusal was that he had been a favorite with a former professor who had by then become a notorious traitor—I mean, Maxime Fleurat. Moreover Fleurat had taken as his mistress a married sister of Despuys and this fact also told against his application. I pointed out that the boy had been Fleurat's favorite merely because he was good at history, and Fleurat, despite his faults, was an excellent historian. I also argued that the boy had unusual opportunities of gaining information about Fleurat's plans, and if he was willing to exploit them for the sake of his country, he should be allowed to make the attempt. But even patriots had at that time forgotten the liberal tradition of our glorious republic. The boy was refused on family grounds.

"His subsequent career justified my belief in him. He left school with high honors, won a scholarship to the Sorbonne, got a good degree, and was *agrégé* at the first attempt."

Was he, though? The *agrégation* is a stiff competitive examination for the cream of all the universities.

"In writing to congratulate him, I told him that my support of his plans dated back to the time of his ostracism during the war, and he replied at once with touching and well-expressed gratitude. We have been friends ever since. And must I now, with how many others, mourn the untimely loss of so bright an example of our tradition of humane education? Liberal, intelligent …"

Richard skimmed the rest. It was not a bright example of their tradition of funeral rhetoric. French liberalism was fine if they let you off the speeches.

There was a second letter from the praefect of Pentecost, in a pointed, sloping hand that looked beautifully clear till you tried to read it.

"Being a little worried over the matter of keys—I am, after all, a curator—I thought it would look well, in case of trouble, that I should have made enquiries. I must confess that my own key is mislaid, but Miss Pinfold says I dropped it through that chink in the back stairs—I suppose we'll have to get a workman in to see, though just now there isn't an opportunity. However, I did call on Sansom and Upjohn. Sansom was out: I was told he was in town for a few days doing some research at Apsley House. But Upjohn was in, and told me he remembered seeing Sansom use his key last term. I'm afraid Upjohn couldn't find his *own* key at short notice. But in the course of our talk he told me a great deal about poor Despuys, which may be of use to you.

"I'm afraid Despuys was a thoroughly unconvincing man. He was accepted on the strength of his excellent French degrees, but Upjohn always thought there was something plausible about him, and in fact he showed up hardly any written work at all. Upjohn considered that he was battening on poor Mrs. Raymond Gyles, who is perhaps easily imposed upon, and described him as a caterpillar of the commonwealth. He inveighed bitterly against the practice of taking foreigners on mere paper qualifications, excluding such men as Sansom, who is, it seems, a far more competent historian although he has no paper qualifications except some flimsy transatlantic degree. He was of course one of Massé's much-abused "discoveries," and Upjohn was wishing we had more industrialists from the New World on our admissions boards. I cannot say I agree in principle.

"His view about Despuys is that either his was a precocious mind that burned itself out early, or that some other ambition caused him to abandon academic work. He thought it was social; my own view is that no one without money of his own could have social ambition *per se*. His first concern would be hard cash; Despuys was surely after money and had some hope of getting it. I have not yet discovered from whom. I hope not the Dawson-Gowers, for they have had quite a struggle to pay Tim's bills—their income is just above the level for government grants, and they have that expensive journey to Ceylon twice a year. I shall continue to make enquiries.

"Francis tells me your bloodhound is well but missing you. He took three nights off to console her. I squared the dean.

"P.S. Do try the Montlouis '47 while you are in the district."

Kéhidiou looked in, gray and stringy after his night's work.

"Still no luck, but they're just closing in on the worst quarter, the Sainte Radegonde. I came in to say that Dawson-Gower was seen in the post office yesterday shortly before you caught him. He bought a fifteen-franc stamp and wrote a letter at the common table which he posted at once. So we can't trace it, but we know at least by the stamp that it wasn't for overseas. Dress Trousers was in too, a bit earlier, posting a parcel to some Paris post office to await collection. They don't remember the name of the addressee, and it went off by the evening mail. I don't think they'd have remembered anything if he hadn't made them change a thousand-franc note."

"Probably getting some change for Dawson-Gower. Can I come and help you in Sainte-Radegonde?"

"Well—thank you, but I don't think, unless one knows it already—"

"Right! Well then, I'll get off to the forest. May I take a car and Painlevé?"

"Toussaint Painlevé? He's a bad driver and not very clever."

"I'll drive. Painlevé's zealous, good with children, and fat enough to provide excellent cover for them. I suppose he can at least hold a gun?"

"Better. He's a great hunter—gets a bunch of blackbirds for the pot most weeks, they say."

A truly Republican huntin' type.

CHAPTER 23

Madame Defay exacted promises and reassurances. Jeannette, meanwhile, was crossly disarming the children of daggers, penknives, and bits of rope, which bulged under their light summer clothes.

"Keep still, stupid! You're just showing off as usual. Do you want everybody to laugh at you? Now, for goodness' sake, try to behave properly! And above all, François—" she whipped out a handkerchief—"don't cry. Do you hear me?"

The child had, it seemed, lost his "new gun."

They started rather subdued, but recovered when Richard talked to them like reasonable creatures. He asked them how they came to know the forest so well.

"Oh, Jeannette used to take us there often," François said. "But she's grown up now and won't play with us any more."

His sister disagreed.

"Silly! Really grown-up people don't mind children. Jeannette's half and half. She has to do what Papa says, so she takes it out on us. And I think she's jealous of Tim liking us best. He's much jollier with us, you know, poor thing."

"We'll save him, won't we?" François cocked his head like a robin. "And then he can come to Angennes and see me steering the *Truc*. Yes, I *can* steer, Chantal, so shut up!"

"The *Truc*—is that your sailing boat? But I thought it needed mending?"

"Well, it does let in a lot of water, but once we're there I'm sure Jeannette will get it done. We'll have to, or we can't go to the island and we always do that."

"But I thought you'd got another boat too. Weren't you all on the river that first day I came?"

"That was just the rowboat. That lives at Pontchâtelet, not Angennes. Turn left here. Oh! You know the way!"

"Listen. I want to get to the place where there's a hill without trees on the top, and the river bends round. Do you know it?"

"It's the best part for hiding," replied Chantal. "Furthest from the paths. Better leave the car here."

"Oh, super! Oh, that's smashing! Let's go!" cried François, leaping at the car door. Richard caught him.

"Just a minute! We're going to make an advance in echelon. I go first, you two keep close behind me, Painlevé brings up the rear. I expect you both know what to avoid when in echelon formation."

"Certainly. Just remind us, please," said Chantal, almost humbly.

"The object is to keep a lookout all round—back, front, and sides. So what might happen if someone went dashing off on his own?"

"He'd get killed," François' voice was small as his eyes were big with apprehension.

"No, I'd shoot the enemy first. I always do. What would happen is this. One direction wouldn't have anyone to watch it, and we might miss something very important. So keep in formation, shoulder to shoulder. Better take hands. Report anything that seems funny as soon as you see it, but otherwise we won't talk, and we'll try to walk very quietly."

Painlevé, in the rear, allowed himself one wink over the children's heads, and they set off.

It is said that between infancy and maturity man goes through every stage of civilization. Children between seven and twelve are certainly natural forest dwellers if you give them half a chance. No one could have moved more neatly or kept a sharper lookout than François. When they reached the hill, he noticed at once the new "landslide" engineered by Nigel. Both children agreed that the fallen earth ought to have stayed in position until some rain had loosened it further. A little digging soon uncovered the parachute. The cave was not so easy to find, for the ledge on which it opened fell sheer for five and a half feet, just too high for a child's reach. Chantal spotted scratches where Auguste had scrabbled for a foothold. Richard decided to go up alone.

He made the children stand against the rock, with Painlevé in front of them, under promise not to move till he gave the word. Up on the shelf, Richard still could not see the cave till he had moved the hanging plants away from the dark hole of the mouth. It was a low, narrow passage, and a man with a gun might be inside. Richard needed one hand for his torch and the other for crawling; he would make an excellent target. Having realized this, he stopped planning and went in on hands and knees. It seemed a long way.

He was glad when he saw the roof of the cave lift in the torch-light, and the space widen into a natural chamber, smooth-walled and quite empty. Closer search revealed traces of recent occupation.

The children were allowed in; and when at last they left the forest, Chantal carried a bully-beef tin and François a whisky bottle, both with English labels, both well hidden in holes, and both discovered by themselves: spoils of the campaign.

"I've thought of another couplet," said Chantal after a long silence, "for Vercingetorix.

> "My chief, let's cross these woods so dense
> We'll move with care; that's our defense."

"Ah!" commented her coauthor, "that's nice. Us or Vercingetorix, it's just the same, eh?"

At the police station, meanwhile, a less pleasing scene had taken place. The searchers in Sainte-Radegonde had recaptured Titi, who had found his mother beginning a heart attack and stayed at home with her. They also discovered Auguste having himself polished up in a barber's shop. Titi still had nothing to say. Auguste broke down under bullying and told them a lot.

He confessed that he had forged the documents found in Zézette's house, on Nigel Dawson-Gower's instructions; also that he had made an assignation with Zézette herself in order to keep her out of the house while Nigel planted them. He denied all knowledge of her death or that of the old tramp. His only part in the affair was the forgery and the undertaking to keep Zézette away from her house between six and a quarter to seven. He admitted that he had visited Nigel in the forest cave, but said he had gone there alone. It was a former Resistance rendezvous, and old loyalties had made him respond to Nigel's appeal and try to save him from a false murder charge—as he then thought. No money had passed between them. Under more pressure, he admitted that he *had* expected to be paid, and would not perhaps have told the police so much if Nigel had forked out—but he hadn't. No, he didn't know where Nigel was hiding now. That was all he knew.

Kéhidiou, seeing the man sweat and babble in his fear, thought that it was, indeed, all he knew. Titi, it seemed, was not an accomplice; and Kéhidiou decided to let him go back and nurse his mother under police supervision; for Kéhidiou was a just and merciful man. Only, as Richard remarked long afterwards, you can't expect these black-and-white moralists to guess that even rogues are sometimes capable of showing gratitude to comrades who have not betrayed them. The Breton despised Auguste too much to imagine that he would stick at incriminating Titi; and when Auguste denied all knowledge of him, he was believed.

"Did this Titi throw any light on the prison-breaking?" asked Richard.

"Not really. He's pretty dumb, doesn't get much beyond yes and no." Kéhidiou consulted his notes. "Had he seen the young lady drop her glove? Yes. Did he see who threw it back? No. Did he see one of the prisoners working on the hinge? No. Why, was he asleep? Yes. On the bolster? Yes. Did he wake when they started pulling it loose? Yes. Did they warn him to take cover? No. Did they tell him to expect an explosion? No. Did he guess? No. But he took cover behind the bolster with the other two? Yes. Why? Shrug, silence. Did he just copy their actions like a sheep? Yes."

"Heavens! He said that?"

"Sure. He's one of those witnesses that you can't either sting or frighten into putting on a show—too stupid. You know how difficult that sort is."

"Indeed I do. The technique was discovered by the early Christian martyrs, and embodied in due course in the War Office manual on how to behave if captured. I respect this man. Are you sure he can't escape again?"

"Oh no! He's well guarded. And what's more, he does seem to be genuinely concerned about his mother. In fact, if it wasn't for his record I'd—Oh, well! Would you like to see him? Or will you take this Auguste Bruco first?"

"Neither, thank you. I'm going straight back to the Rue Descartes. Jeannette Defay is the most important subject for questioning—and this time I'm not letting her get away with anything."

"No! You're wrong. As I said before, Jeannette …"

"You forbid me?" Richard's eyebrows and tone conveyed a courteous recognition of outrage. "Well, of course: I've no *right* at all. I'm afraid all your kindness has made me forget that I'm here on sufferance. Forgive me. I'm in your hands."

"Oh, my dear colleague, please! It's not that."

"What then? You're afraid I'll browbeat her? Frighten her into saying more than she means? Well, come too and see fair play!"

"No, no, no, no, no! Of course I trust you. But partly, I don't believe Jeannette can tell you anything, and partly her father—Pontchâtelet's a small town, and if it should turn out—"

"I understand. But that's just why I proposed going on my own. I could tell her father that I've disregarded your advice. I could channel off all his resentment on myself. Not that I really expect him to be difficult. I've noticed that if you tell people you're waiting for them to bite you, they seldom do."

"And," said the other with a wintry twinkle, "you tried your theory out on me to make sure! Good, good, good! Take my car."

He arrived too late. Madame Defay was apologetic.

"I'm sorry, but Jeannette's at Angennes already—a change of plan. Should I have warned you? You see, they *were* all going there this afternoon in my sister-in-law's car; in fact, the children still are. But when Jeannette heard that my husband was sending a van with the stores and a little maid for cleaning this morning, she offered to go too and get the house really nice for her aunt. And I must say I was delighted to see her taking an interest."

"Why? Doesn't she help in the house as a rule?"

"She's very sweet, but she doesn't really give her mind to it. Though lately she's shown a rather sudden curiosity about cooking. I actually found a recipe-book I'd missed in her bedroom! So when she offered, I said to myself, 'So much the better! She's growing up!' "

"I think she is." Something of gravity in his voice made the mother say,

"Do you think she's in danger? Should I go to her? Surely at Angennes …? It's such a quiet place."

"I was thinking of going there myself," he said, "to ask her these really rather important questions about last night. But I don't know—perhaps you'd object? Monsieur Kéhidiou as good as told me that you'd never forgive him for letting me call here, though he did do his best to dissuade me. He said I ought to be ashamed, and any decent man would spare a girl's nerves."

Madame Defay's eyebrows went up, and the temperature went down.

"I think her mother is the judge of that. In any case, Monsieur Kéhidiou need not torment himself on the subject of my daughter's nerves; there is nothing at all the matter with them. And—" she passed in a flash from asperity to charm—"I'd really be so grateful if you'd go. I'm tied here waiting for my sister-in-law, and somehow, unreasonable though it is, I've been uneasy about the girl ever since she left. Won't you bring her back here to lunch? There's nothing fit to offer you at Angennes."

"Oh, *lunch*! What does lunch matter?" Madame Defay had never heard a man say such a thing before. "Please tell me, what time is her aunt arriving there with the children? Half-past two? Good. I'll see she's looked after till then. Is there a telephone? Good. And another, in case it's out of order? The farm. Excellent! Goodbye!"

CHAPTER 24

He drove down a main road shaded by plane trees, turned at a village (one church, two shops, six cafés) and continued along a narrow track that dazzled dusty white in the heat, between unfenced fields, striped with plantations and loud with cicadas; until the land fell gently towards the river, and he saw a cluster of buildings half-hidden by trees behind a high wall. Passing between the tall gateposts, each crowned with a stone ball, he followed a sandy drive that gave glimpses between trees of the garden—brilliant flowers, and a lawn of unmowed grass-heads, tall, dry, and hardly stirring. The drive ended in a courtyard with a well in one corner, a stone-built shed in the other, and the long, unpretentious house, half-buried in wistaria, lounging along the side. All the windows were open, and rugs, cushions, and bedclothes were airing at every one. The maid—a thickset, incurious country girl—was standing on a step-ladder cleaning the fanlight over the front door. She clambered down hastily to fetch "Mademoiselle," and did not protest when Richard followed her.

Jeannette was in the larder checking stores. It was dark there, and slate shelves gave the air coolness. Jeannette, cooler still, looked up from the packing case she sat on and asked why he had not been shown into the drawing room. *That* at least was in a state to receive visitors. She had exactly her mother's voice.

"Yes, I know I'm trespassing," said Richard, not at all out of countenance, "but I've never seen a French country larder before. What's in those big stone jars?"

"Green beans in salt for the winter. But really …"

"And what are those things in glass jars? Shellfish?"

"No. Preserved mushrooms."

"Are you sure? I can see something alive moving about in this one. Something large and wriggly."

"No!" She jumped up and ran to look. Richard could now see into the packing case. It was open, and full of fresh stores—cheese, sausages, fruit, wine, bread—curious things to sit on, even if exactly similar stores had not been already set out on the larder shelves.

"*I* can't see anything moving," she said, turning with a swirl of her white skirts. She followed his eye.

"No," he replied. It was enough. "Shall we be overheard in the drawing room?"

She hesitated. "Perhaps. Let's go out in the garden."

She led him over the hayfield lawn and gave him an iron chair under a great walnut tree. She herself sat in the child's swing that hung from a high bough and swayed there, her hands on the ropes—an attitude that became her well; and perhaps the inconstant motion of the swing helped to disguise her own trepidation.

"What a silence!" she laughed, after a moment. "An angel passing, as we say."

"In England, we say it's a goose walking over your grave."

"*Oh la la*! That's not very cheerful." She pushed with one red-sandaled foot, and swung up away from him like a bird taking flight. Then, settling to earth again, "I hope the children behaved themselves. They can be so silly."

"They can, of course. Though not so silly as a goose walking over a grave and pretending it's just a new kind of flower bed. Jeannette, may I tell you a story?"

"Delighted. If it isn't wasting your time."

"I hope not. Once upon a time there was an English soldier who was sent on a wartime mission of great trust to fight secretly in an occupied country. He was brave and clever, but his generals at home gradually began to discover that he wasn't quite as trustworthy as they'd thought. He didn't obey orders, he quarreled with his comrades-in-arms, and worse still, they suspected that he was spending the money they sent him for the war on his own pleasures. But, as I said, he was brave and clever. They didn't recall him.

"At last the war in that country was won. But in the part of it where this soldier was in charge, a bad taste was left behind. The chief enemy—or rather, the chief traitor, for he was a French citizen originally—was never caught and brought to justice. He'd tortured hundreds of people, including children—hundreds, all of them his fellow-countrymen. Some died. Some he released to drag out their time as living wrecks, cripples or madmen. Everyone hated this public enemy; everyone was waiting and watching to bring him to justice at last. But in the very hour of victory, he disappeared. Here's a picture of him. It isn't a face you'd fail to spot, is it? Not a face that could slip unnoticed through crowds of injured people who were watching for it? Do you know who it is?"

"I—I think it's Fleurat, isn't it? The man they called Blancbec. Ugh! Those light eyes! The color of skim milk, people say. But— Papa always told me he'd been killed."

"People thought so, because his escape seemed so impossible. But consider the sequel. The English soldier returned home and asked his generals to keep him in the army, although the war was over. Fighting was the thing he liked doing, the thing he was really good at. But they refused to have him. Why? The soldier wasn't rich at the time, but people noticed he was spending money as freely as ever—cars, flying, rowdy parties. And yet he never seemed to be out of funds. No one, *then*, connected the escape of the war criminal with the soldier's wealth. The generals may have suspected; but the soldier had served them well in his way, they'd since washed their hands of him, and there was no proof. So it went on for nearly ten years. Did you say something?"

"No, Monsieur. I'm listening."

"So it went on, till a French boy, Jean Despuys, the brother of Blancbec's wartime mistress, came to England, and quite by chance met and recognized the soldier. Now, remember, this boy's whole life had been overshadowed by Fleurat. He'd been ostracized at school. His sister had been made into something worse than an outcast—something worse than the worst of Fleurat's other victims. She wasn't only physically broken; she was morally poisoned. And she'd been a gentle, beautiful creature once, just as her brother had been a promising and devoted scholar. Can you wonder, then, that when Despuys came to England and recognized the soldier, the man he'd seen arranging Fleurat's escape, he wanted revenge? The soldier, too, had a face it wasn't easy to forget. Look!"

He put Nigel's photograph into her hands, and the swing ropes, which had hung motionless for some minutes, shook and creaked.

She sat with her head bent down over the picture; her pale lips moved.

"Who is it, Jeannette? What's the soldier's name?"

She uttered a soft plaining sound like a bird. Richard realized that she was trying to free her voice for speech.

"Sorry, Monsieur! I'm thirsty. No, I don't know the face. I've never seen it, I believe."

"Well, give me back the picture." He waited. "The picture, please! I want all your attention. Shall I tell the servant to bring you some water?"

She jumped up. "I'll go."

"I'm sorry. You must stay and listen. As I was saying, Despuys threatened to unmask Nigel Dawson-Gower" (she did not start at the name) "unless he'd share the spoils. It was reasonable, in a way. Money could repair some of their injuries. With money, Despuys could have in England the social pleasures he'd been refused in France. With money, his sister Zézette could at least start life in a new place and regain her physical health. But Nigel Dawson-Gower liked money, too. And *he* was a trained fighter, remember, which Despuys wasn't.

"So he killed Despuys under some trees near his Oxford lodgings. He'd been taught many ways of killing even a strong man with his bare hands, and I don't think Despuys was strong. He killed him, I say, and left him there in the road for a car to run over, so that the whole thing would look like a motor accident. Unfortunately, the car that *did* run him over was his own brother's, for that road is lonelier than you'd think. Still, Nigel was a fighter. He rather enjoyed a crisis. Perhaps he also liked playing the hero to his brother Tim, whom he somehow convinced that the police would blame him for the death if he reported it. So Nigel lugged the body into the car, took it to a haystack in the country outside Oxford, and burned it. Luckily for us, the wind changed before the body was completely burnt. We found the feet. One could see they'd been a poor boy's feet, Jeannette. The toes were cramped by the cheap shoes he'd had to go on wearing when he'd outgrown them; the insteps were sagging, the stumps …"

"No!" she cried sharply, her hands over her eyes. Then, composing herself a little, "Please give me the photograph again. The—soldier's."

He let her have it. She could be trusted to listen now.

"When Jean Despuys was in his grave—what was left of him—Nigel found that so far from being clear of his past, he was in greater danger than ever. First, because we'd identified the feet and discovered that Tim's car was used to move the body. Second, Tim had taken alarm and run away to Pontchâtelet. Why was that a danger? you'll say. Nothing could be proved. Why didn't Nigel have a little patience and nerve, and play a waiting game? I thought that too, at first; he isn't the panicky kind, is he? There's only one answer. I guess that Zézette Despuys possessed written or photographic proof of Nigel's treachery; and that once the police made enquiries in Pontchâtelet, they'd very soon find out what a strong motive for murder Nigel had. So he needed to come here and destroy the evidence."

"You *guess*, Monsieur." He had forgotten that she could smile.

"Yes, for he did destroy it. But now for some plain facts. I know he dropped by parachute over the forest early on Wednesday morning. I know there was a man in Zézette's house when I arrived there on Wednesday at half-past nine. I could see that the woman had been up for hours, and was in a pitiable state of terror. He must have had to work on her for a long time before she gave him the papers— I suppose that's why he didn't get away earlier—and probably he pretended to be acting for her brother. The news of his death was certainly a shock when we told her. Jean was perhaps the only living person Zézette cared about.

"As we talked, I became aware that there was someone else in the house. And he, somehow realizing his danger, escaped just before I went to look. He escaped—at the cost of a second murder. Are you going to walk over this grave, too, Jeannette?"

"I—I'm listening, Monsieur. How did he escape?"

"He slipped out of the back, towards the river. It was only a minute or two before I followed him. There was absolutely no cover. Or rather—there was only cover for a very ruthless, very experienced fighter, who had been taught not to be captured at any price. There was an old half-witted tramp asleep in the long grass of a little hollow beside the towing path. Nigel killed him, put on his clothes, and lay down in his place. I *hope*—but we can't be sure—I hope the old man wasn't still conscious when his clothes were stripped off him. Before he was pitched into the river. The current is swift there, and he was carried off quickly. You read in the papers where we found him—and in what state?"

Jeannette did not reply. He went on,

"I was completely taken in. When I saw a familiar, ragged figure, half-hidden in the tufts of grass, with the battered old hat over his face, and one broken boot sticking up, I thought, 'Poor old man! Let him have his sleep out!' Wouldn't you have felt the same?"

"Why are you telling me this? I'm not a judge." She paused, and added on a sharp breath, "Thank God!"

"A judge is only acting for the whole body of citizens. Don't deceive yourself. You can't shuffle off morals and patriotism on to priests and legislators. They're *you* … Shall I go on? You don't look well. Rest a bit, if you like."

"Give me a minute, please. Then I'll listen. I—I ought to!"

Her knuckles, gripping on the ropes of the swing, were no whiter than her face. She shut her eyes. Her lips moved a little. She gazed at the photograph again, and then said, with a strangely childlike formality,

"Would you please go on now, Monsieur?"

"With—*not* with pleasure. Nigel got away in the tramp's clothes, but quickly sold them to another tramp, who was at once suspected of the murder. Meanwhile, Nigel thought that, now, it wasn't enough to have destroyed the written evidence against himself. Other things had piled up; he was a suspect anyhow. He decided to fake a case against somebody else, to divert suspicion. So he got some false papers forged for him, by a very crooked friend that he'd picked up here in the war, making out that Fleurat was back and had done the murders. He arranged to plant them in the woman's house while the crooked friend kept her in play in a café.

"The friend has since confessed all this. Nigel was also seen actually leaving the house, and we found prints to corroborate the witness. We also found the false documents, and proved them a forgery. But the worst thing we found was the woman—Zézette—dead just inside her own house, with the marks of a man's fingers on her neck. I suppose she got home a moment too soon, or perhaps she'd realized the truth and was trying to do her duty. Anyhow—there's the third grave. Are you going to take that in your stride too? I could go on, but—is it necessary?"

She looked up at him, or tried to; he doubted if she could see much through the tears that filled her eyes and ran down her cheeks.

"No, don't go on, Monsieur. You have—you are—"

The first sob came rending through her lungs, and then another and another; the swing ropes shook, the bough above rustled. Then she was on her feet, crying fiercely.

"No, go on! Go on! But don't tell me! Ask me! Put me in prison like Tim! Question me! Trap me if you can! Do you think I'm de-

ceived by your—your delicacy? I'm not! I'm not! If I seemed weak
to you just now, it's only because I didn't expect to be treated as if,
as if—"

"As if you were on my side?" Richard moved towards her, but
she turned away, her forehead against the tree trunk. "But you are,
aren't you? Love and honor, love and duty—it's only in the theater
that they conflict. They're never really on opposite sides. If you
really love a man, you love his honor. I don't mean what people
think of him—that'll only last for fifty years or so at most. I mean
… You and I really believe the same things, don't we?"

Her sobs had ceased; she was listening intently.

"I know people say, 'I'll go to hell with you, darling, if need be.'
Mostly they don't mean it. But if they did, it isn't *love* that makes
them say it—there's no love in hell, anyway—it's just greed and
stupidity. It's saying, 'Be in misery for ever, darling, so long as you
don't give me the slip.' "

He saw her back quiver. People don't flinch from the truth unless
they recognize it. But she said nothing. Richard forced himself to
press the point home.

"Jeannette, in my job I've seen a lot of unrepentant murderers.
And I tell you, week by week, even day by day, they become less—
less human. Their faces move, but you can't call it expression. Their
eyes function, but they don't really see. They aren't mad, they aren't
dead. They're just—infinitely separated. It's an awful thing to
watch."

"But the few who confess or repent—they're—how can I describe them? Brave, yes, often; resigned, considerate. But it's more
than that, more positive. It's as if they suddenly found themselves,
suddenly begun to live. A kind of joy and splendor that makes nothing
of prison or …"

He could not speak the word, execution, nor did he think she
could hear it. But when she turned, white against the tree that rose
like a martyr's stake behind her, only her voice faltered.

"I—I do believe as you do. I—will help you. In the way—you do
it, if necessary. But it may not … I hope … perhaps … Will you give
me an hour? One hour alone? I might be able to think of a—better
way."

"Will you promise not to—hurt yourself?"

She stared. "Not hurt …?" Then she almost laughed. "I understand. You're afraid I'll kill myself? Or cut out my tongue? I promise I won't. No, no! You'll give me this hour? For I warn you—" her

old mettle flashed for a second—"if you don't, I may change my mind."

"You won't," he said heavily. "Take your hour, though. And I should warn *you* that the approaches to the house are blocked. I'll be going the rounds presently. Can I use your telephone, please? *Monsieur le Commissaire* will wonder what's keeping me."

"Please do, Monsieur. I'll show you where it is."

She walked quickly towards the house, as though there were no time to waste. He followed, longing to offer her comfort, and knowing that of all men he had least right to do so.

"The telephone's here. Are you hungry? Well ... in an hour, then. And, Monsieur!" She paused at the door.

"What is it?"

"Don't worry! It's bad for you too, I know."

"*Monsieur le Commissaire*? Ringwood speaking, from Angennes. Jeannette is willing to make a statement to us at one o'clock. She needs an hour to rest and think things over; she's had about as much as she can take. No. Yes, of course I will. Is she what? Yes, in a way she is; but *you* were right about her too. Listen. I've had to warn her that there's a police cordon of thirty men, including aquatic reinforcements, guarding the estate, so that no one can get in or out unobserved. Yes. Yes, that's it. Urgently. The farm. Till then."

Once out of the house, he unconsciously made for the water, like any West Countryman in trouble. The river was some distance away. He followed a pleached alley of fruit trees through the kitchen garden, and then had to thread through the low copper-green stocks of a vineyard. He had expected a narrow river, but the Cher was wide here—wide and winding and still, reflecting the purple valerian flowers that grew up the opposite bank. Bank? No. It was the shore of an island. François had spoken of it, of course. It was so near the other bank, which rose to a woody hill, that it seemed part of it, especially as the trees began on the island and continued on the far side.

And there was the boat. *Le Truc*—the *Thingummy.* A family joke, probably become habit while they were arguing about the name. She lay hauled up on the mud, an old boat, broad-beamed, not easily capsizable by children. He went down to see where she needed repairs. Had he not gone down on to the mud, he would never have seen the freshly scored mark there, where another, smaller boat had recently been pulled up and launched again. It was unmistakable—

and appalling. There was the print of a man's foot.

He forced himself to loiter back to the house as though nothing was wrong, though every second seemed an age. He started the car (Jeannette was nowhere in sight) and drove off through the trees and between the gateposts, not stopping till the farm buildings hid him from view. The farmer's family, eight of them, were eating and drinking stolidly, under a cloud of flies, in the huge hot kitchen. He burst in.

"Mademoiselle Defay is in danger. I'm with the police. Can I use your telephone?"

When at last they agreed, he telephoned very briefly. Then he raced back on foot to the river, not by the road, but along a line of willows that ran right to the verge. He left his clothes there and took to the water.

CHAPTER 25

He had planned to swim along the bank, under cover of reedbeds and willows, but the shallows made it impracticable. He dived and swam into midstream. The water was cooler and deeper here, and carried him fast towards the island. He only had to surface twice, and he did it as quietly as an otter, his face turned aside so that nothing would be visible to the enemy but a wet black head. The third time he emerged was under the lee of the island; not the shore directly opposite the house, but behind a spit of land that just hid it from view. A lucky guess. He listened, crouched on the sandy bottom with only his head out of water, and heard voices in the distance. One was a woman's.

In great fear—for her, not himself—Richard began swimming alongshore towards the sound, using a noiseless sidestroke. He knew that if he showed himself prematurely, he would do more harm than good. Fortunately the bank was steep enough here to hide him, and fringed with bushes and tall flowering weeds.

The voices were near now, and, as he dreaded, one was Jeannette's. He could distinguish almost every word. He crept out of the water inch by inch, so that not a drop splashed back to betray him—Auguste had told them why Nigel was nicknamed Radar—and peered between the valerian and willow-herb.

Jeannette and—yes, it was Nigel—were facing each other behind an elder bush which partly hid them from view, but he could
see that she was wearing a bathing dress. So she must have swum
out of her own will, not been taken in his boat. She had only waited
till he was out of sight, then, before running off to warn her lover!
And yet, he'd have sworn ... Perhaps it was trying her too high, to
trust her as he had. She was only eighteen, after all.

The man's voice was deep, not loud, and yet strangely disturb-
ing. The volcanic quality of the overtones came out more strongly,
in the correct French it was speaking now, than in the broad local
accent Richard had heard before, from Big Drunk.

"Well, suppose I did? Suppose he *can* prove it? You wouldn't
believe him, would you, Jeannette?"

"If he really proved it, logically, I couldn't *not,* could I? Unless I
was mad."

Her voice did not tremble now. But it sounded terribly like a
child's, and his low laugh that answered her, terribly unchildlike.

"You know everything and nothing, don't you? And yet you came
over here to warn me! Listen, Jeannette. You must go back at once
before you're spotted. Did the maid see you? Can you hide your wet
bathing dress? Go along! Don't worry, *mon lapin,* they won't get
me this time. Come here, though ... Why, what ...?"

"No, Nigel. Can't you understand? I didn't come to warn you. I
came to beg you to.... No! Don't touch me! ... to say that if you
don't give yourself up, I shall—oh, Nigel, don't make me! Don't
make me have to betray you!"

"Jeannette?" There was a new note in his voice, baffling to the
listener. "You'd do that? You, to me?" Richard lost sight of Jeannette behind Nigel's bulk, and there was silence. Then he said,

"So you do love me. You do. Why, you'd even let me ..."

"Oh, my dear! My dear!"

"And yet you'd have me hanged as a murderer?" It was a long
moment before she answered.

"I'd—have to. I couldn't—let you go on like this. Just *because* I
love you."

"You've got a nerve, haven't you?" There was something besides irony in the question—a tone Richard had not heard before.
"Do you really think a murderer will let you go on like *t*his? Stand
back while you go and ...?' Look at your little neck in my hands!
Aren't you afraid I'll kill you?"

Richard gathered himself for a charge; but something in the ring of her reply made him wait. Even its sadness held authority.

"Afraid? For myself? My poor Nigel, can't you see that I've hated being alive ever since … I knew you were … How shall I be able to bear it when …? But you mustn't kill me, darling. I can't give you another sin to—to answer for. It wouldn't be—" she paused—"fair of me. Nigel, come to the police. We'll go together. I'll say I made you do the—the ones here. Perhaps they won't …"

She stopped with a smothered sound, and Richard sprang up. But the bush, and Nigel's sharp ears, prevented him from being quite quick enough. Nigel moved round the bush, the girl still in his arms, looked between the branches, and—grinned.

"Come to move us along, copper?" He spoke in English. "My God! Might as well be in Hyde Park. No privacy left anywhere."

"Nigel Dawson-Gower, I …"

He got no further; Jeannette was round the bush and at him like a fury, scratching his face, kicking and shouting,

"Cheat! Cheat! You said an hour! Filthy beast!" She became aware of Nigel beside her. "Run, darling, run! Go!" And she set upon Richard afresh. But Nigel had both her wrists in one hand now, and his other arm was across her body, pressing it back against his.

"You were saying, copper?" He was laughing—even more than he had laughed fighting Richard in the café—with his cheek against Jeannette's hair; while she struggled and called him imbecile and worse. Yet she looked more angry than stricken now, more Amazon than martyr.

"You can skip the first bit, copper. We heard that. Go on from 'I arrest you.' I've never had it said to me in English before."

"What's he going to do, Nigel? What are you saying? Speak French!"

"He's going to say he arrests me, and what for, and so on. They have to say that. Then I think he just leads me off in chains. Is there a pair of handcuffs in those natty little white Aertex pants? I think not. Anyone got a piece of string? I'm sure Jeannette hasn't. Look in my right-hand pocket."

"Shut up, you bloody fool!" said Richard roughly. The heavy lids flew up; the bright eyes focused. "And stop hiding behind that girl. Are you coming quietly? Don't you want to say anything?"

"Wait and see, copper, wait and see. You haven't said *your* piece yet. And if you don't make it snappy … Correct me if I'm wrong, but I make it four cars stopping at the farm and two motorboats coming up the river. Nice work. The boats will be here first. We'd better stand where they can see us. Save them time."

He moved off with his arm round Jeannette.

"Four cars and two motorboats, darling! Hear them now? Also one copper on our right, imported, but a very useful fighter. Running, swimming, elementary judo … wonderful what they can learn if you start 'em young. Some of them even learn to think."

Richard's temper was up. He had lost the initiative, and things were not going as he had foreseen. By the time they reached the grassy point of the spit and the boats were in sight, his fists were clenching.

"Well, come on, copper! Or do I have to hit you first?" Nigel faced round, pushing Jeannette behind him. Richard suddenly saw that the man was as angry and anxious as himself.

"Don't fight him, Monsieur! They'll shoot from the boats and you'll both be killed. And you, you idiot, that's enough!"

"She's good, isn't she?" Nigel said, and suddenly sat down. Jeannette placed herself between him and the boats.

Kéhidiou was first ashore, pistol in hand, smart but flustered. He spoke hastily.

"Congratulations, my dear colleague. And you, assassin, I've got you covered, and I'll shoot you if you move. Is Jeannette …? Have we got to …? That is …"

Richard saw the second boat, and who was in it.

"Give me that pistol," he said. "I can see you're going to have your hands full. And listen! Any shooting to be done, I'll do. Tell them no one's to fire without orders. All the same! Why on earth?"

"Monsieur Defay insisted. They all did. I couldn't help it."

"Papa!" cried Jeannette, on a high note of appeal. "Papa, come here! I'm here."

The wide mustache lifted visibly, even twenty yards away.

"So I see, you bit of filth! Not even properly dressed. Don't you dare to speak to me, you piece of garbage! I'm ashamed to look at you. Come away! Come away from him, I say, you—you bitch! My God, I'd rather see you dead!"

He leaped out of the boat and waded the last few yards through the mud, in his fresh cream-colored trousers, gesticulating and shouting. Kéhidiou met him and waved him back.

"No, and no, and no! Let me pass! Have you no respect for paternal love?" He dropped to a tense, businesslike whisper. "But first, tell me frankly. Did he rape you?"

Richard and Jeannette did not hear, but Nigel shouted,

"Of course I didn't, you insolent old dung-eater! Stop calling her names and find her some lunch. She's starving. Go on, Jeannette. Everything's under control."

The girl shook her head. The father floundered for a minute and then, magnificently, recovered his initiative by a simple change of victim. He glared at Kéhidiou.

"Then why did you waste time disquieting me with your filthy innuendoes ..."

"But, Monsieur, on the contrary."

"... when, meanwhile some fool," continued Monsieur Defay, "has started a fire in the wood? Look behind you! It's like tinder. You'll have the whole island on fire if you aren't quick!"

They all turned and stared at the smoke. All, that is, except Nigel and Richard. Nigel acted like lightning, knocking the pistol from Richard's hand even as he began to run. Richard did not waste a movement, either; he fielded the pistol on his toe, grasped it, and set off in pursuit, shouting,

"Don't shoot! Don't let them shoot!"

Fugitive and pursuer disappeared into the wood; a hail of bullets and conflicting orders flew after them. So did Jeannette, crying,

"Help them! Oh, quick, quick!"

They streamed after her and soon outstripped her; indeed, she would have fallen but for the solid, unexpected support of her father's arm.

"Oh, I feel terrible, papa!"

"Armagnac," he said, pulling a small bottle out of his pocket. "A traveler's sample. Gently, little beast! Don't choke yourself! There was some bread too, but I've eaten it."

"Ah, that's better; Papa, dear darling papa, I'd have told you, only ... Listen! What's that?"

"Hmm! Different voices! Is it possible that ...?"

"Come on, papa. I'm all right now."

Hand-in-hand they resumed the path, their bright brown eyes raking the wood, their ears alert.

"They're by your 'house willow'?"

She nodded. They turned like one person into what seemed impenetrable thicket.

Richard Ringwood soon realized, with grim satisfaction, that even if his judo was elementary and his feet bare, he was a better runner than Dawson-Gower and was gaining on him fast. But the other merely looked over his shoulder and grunted.

"Go on, pass me! Bear left at the fork. There's two of them."

"Oh, you unspeakable fool!" Richard said, and shot ahead.

He came out into a clearing of dry grass round a gnarled silvery old willow tree. The grass was burning in front of the tree, and a man lay there motionless. Richard stamped a way across the little flames with his bare feet, got the man under the armpits, and dragged him clear. At least he was still breathing, but his lips were blue; and he was unconscious. The face was new to Richard—one would not forget scars like those.

Nigel had caught up and fallen on his knees beside him.

"Is he alive?" he asked urgently. "I shouldn't have left them together. Is he alive?"

"Yes. Looks like a heart attack. Start stamping the fire out. You've got shoes. I'll get a branch."

Together they fought the fire, choking and red-eyed. Then Richard became suddenly aware of a different cough—neither Nigel's nor his own.

"Who's that?"

"Why, him. You said he was alive, didn't you look? In the hollow tree. Wait, though!" He took Richard in a hard grip. "Just notice this cigarette, will you? Dropped out of my chum's hand when he got his fit. You see? It's still alight and not half-smoked. So don't go saying Jeannot started the fire on purpose. Mind you, I wouldn't blame him. But he didn't. He was just guarding the prisoner. Shall I get the bastard out for you? It's warm over there."

When the French police arrived, they saw a man, coughing, sagging, and bound hand and foot, being hauled out of the cavernous tree-trunk.

"Dress Trousers!" exclaimed Kéhidiou.

The glazed hazel eyes stared, pale-lidded, above the broken, purple nose.

"Alias Mathieu Sansom," said Richard. "Alias Maxime Fleurat. Alias Blancbec."

(Cries, exclamations by local police.)

"But this man isn't Fleurat," Kéhidiou protested. "Why, his eyes alone …"

"Precisely—his eyes. You'll notice that the rims aren't at all reddened by the smoke, though he's been in it longer than we have, and look at ours! Yesterday, when we'd all been under water, it was just the same. He's wearing colored contact lenses. Hold the head while

I show you." He pulled down the man's lower eyelid. "I don't know how you take these things off without injury."

"I do," said Nigel, and quickly gripped the head between his knees. The man cried out twice under Nigel's fingers, and fell back with closed eyes when Nigel released him. "But I didn't recognize him. It was Jeannot's cop, not mine. That's why I tried to make you waste time quarreling with me, Ringwood. I wanted to keep Blancbec till the French police turned up. I'd promised that Jeannot should give him up to them, and get the reward—only fair. You won't refuse it just because he can't speak for himself at the moment?"

"Nonsense!" said Kéhidiou coldly. "It was Monsieur Ringwood who denounced him. In any case, I'm not convinced."

Richard interposed. "But *they* caught him. If it hadn't been for Dawson-Gower and his, er, friends, he'd be miles away by now. How did this Jeannot know? And can he prove it?"

"How did you, for that matter?" Nigel was aggressive. "And can you?"

"*They sometimes*—" with a crooked smile Richard spoke in exactly Nigel's intonation—"*They sometimes even teach us to think.* Yes, I can. Up to the hilt."

Nigel dropped his eyes. "I'm sorry. I knew you were damn good, but I didn't—" he looked up again. Heavens! He was blushing!— "Anyhow, I'll shut up from now on. Oh, you'll want these."

He dropped the pair of hazel-tinted contact lenses into Richard's hand and turned away. The two nearest *agents* seized him.

"Let go! He's innocent!" Jeannette sprang out from the bushes, ready to fight anybody.

"Yes," said Richard. "Let him go! But, Jeannette, how did *you* know? And when?"

"He told me. It was when you—disturbed us. Spy!"

"He's damn good, Jeannette. Even *I* didn't hear him coming. You jolly well apologize. I have."

"Look," said Richard, embarrassed, "Your friend Jeannot's coming round a bit, I believe. Do tell him everything's all right."

"Wait a minute!" Kéhidiou interrupted. "Nothing whatever is clear. I must insist that they all remain under arrest until we've thrashed it out."

Monsieur Defay, releasing his daughter's arm, went to the man in dress trousers and opened with two fingers one of his closed eyes. It was the color of skim milk.

"Look, *les Pontchâtelétiens!*" he began—but then exclaimed and drew back his hand. He was only just in time; the snapping teeth met on air. The man fell back with closed eyes, and neither moved nor uttered when Defay kicked at him and a low growl went up from the rest. Richard pulled him away, and turned again to the Commissaire.

"Some of the actual proofs are at the police station, and others abroad. But I'm ready to explain to you all the steps of my reasoning."

"But not here! Not now! We haven't eaten!" A great sigh of agreement went up from Defay's fellow-countrymen. "Come over to my house! There's *paté*, at least, and bread, and a good sparkling wine of Saumur ..."

"Your rowboat's over there, sir," said Nigel. "Shall I take Jeannette on ahead and ..."

Defay snapped his fingers. Nigel subsided.

"I'll go in my own boat with my daughter." He moved off, attended by a policeman. His voice boomed in the thicket,

"And first of all, Jeannette, get dressed! Something pretty but, above all, discreet ... There are impressions to be effaced. What stores have you?"

"For thirty? Papa dear, you're mad! Why, the bread alone won't ..."

Nigel grinned. "It will if they say so." He picked up Jeannot and began carrying him to the boats. "Come on, chum! I'll see you're O.K."

CHAPTER 26

Richard collected his clothes, and dried and dressed at the farm. Kéhidiou supervised fire precautions and first aid on the island, and ferried the prisoners across under guard. By the time they all converged at Angennes, the Defays, father and daughter, were ready for them. Jeannette, in dark linen with a snowy muslin collar, hardly raised her smooth head from the trestle table where she was arranging an *al fresco* meal. Her father bustled and bawled at the helpers he had raised from nowhere.

Kéhidiou allowed Nigel a seat at table, provided his feet were tied together, and Jeannot, now sufficiently recovered to lie in a *chaise longue*, reclined at his side. The man in dress trousers, however, would neither move nor open his eyes, so they tied him to his stretcher and laid him on the ground beside the well. Then all the Pontchâtelet men crowded around the table, thirsting for wine and information. Their host supplied the first, while the Commissaire addressed them:

"Before I ask Monsieur Ringwood to explain matters, I must pay a tribute to your fellow citizen here—" he indicated Jeannot. "We have now been given full proof that he is that famous Jeannot who was tortured by Maxime Fleurat for twenty-four hours on end and refused to betray his fellow patriots. He says that the prisoner there is Fleurat, he recognized him by his hands. Monsieur Ringwood believes he is right. If so, I am sure we honor him and will do our best to see that he receives the most ample recognition."

There were cheers and demonstrations.

"Easy!" said Nigel. "Old Jeannot's shy. Never been kissed before—not by a policeman. Let's hear all about it."

Richard stood up. It was awful having to make speeches in French and he decided just to talk.

"It does seem rather fantastic to identify Sansom, the Oxford don, with Fleurat, the vanished war criminal, I know. Specially when he looks so different. I'll explain about his looks in a minute. Well, actually, it was the mental correspondence that struck me first. Fleurat specialized on Napoleon; Sansom, I discovered today, on Wellington. Fleurat disappeared from France; shortly afterwards, Sansom's academic career began in Canada. Imagine! A fullblown *savant* just 'discovered' by Massé in his late forties. No published work, no previous reputation. That set me thinking.

"And then I remembered his looks. Sansom's face was most unnatural for a man of his age—not a wrinkle in it. Actually, that smoothness is the result of plastic surgery. I found the operation scars under those sideburns he wears. His coloring, too, was peculiar. That dead-white nose—"

Several men gasped. Monsieur Defay hit the table.

"Of course!" he said. "That's how he got nicknamed Blancbec."

"Well, I wish somebody had thought to tell me so. The usual meaning of *blancbec* isn't the literal whitebeak: it's just stupid. Or as we say, greenhorn. It wasn't till I got hold of Fleurat's dossier last night that I discovered his nose really *was* white—and remembered Sansom's. Well, then, you ask, why didn't I recognize Sansom yesterday when he was taken prisoner? Why! Because his characteristic feature was spoilt. I think I'd have penetrated the rest of his disguise, if Dawson-Gower here hadn't just punched that white nose into a bleeding ruin. Never mind, Nigel; I expect it'll go white again. If a clever plastic surgeon couldn't get rid of the color, I doubt if an amateur bruiser can."

Nigel opened his mouth. "Shut up!" said Defay. Nigel obeyed.

"Face, nose, and lastly of course eyes," Richard went on. "That was the real giveaway, discovering that he was wearing contact lenses. I expect you know how they work. They're glasses which fit right over the eyeball, under the lids, and they're practically undetectable. Some actors use them. And of course, they can have a colored iris put in. So long as the pupil is clear the colored iris won't impair vision. Blancbec has very light blue eyes—the color of skim milk. The contact lenses made them hazel."

"But how did you realize?" insisted Kéhidiou.

"A chance remark of yours, first. You said, did English criminals wear colored contact lenses. Then I remembered that when Blancbec had been under water yesterday, his eyes weren't red-rimmed like Nigel's and mine. And again today in the smoke. Not red, not watering. The lenses protected his eyes, you see, from what irritated our naked eyeballs. Also—remember that little bottle of salt water—the gargle? Well, I recollected that saline's the stuff one uses to soak contact lenses in when one takes them off—they can't be worn continuously—and so naturally Blancbec couldn't be without it, even in disguise.

"As for proving his identity—that's easy, thanks to the French system of Bertillon measurements, the *fiches anthropométriques*. You possess Blancbec's original record, all but the fingerprints, and we took another of Dress Trousers' yesterday. We shall find that the big toe joint, the middle finger, the earlobe, and so on are identical in both records. No two men have the same Bertillon measurements, as you know."

At this, Kéhidiou jumped up and embraced him. Richard took a swig of the wine and was about to continue, when a voice addressed him in English. Blancbec, trussed on his stretcher, had stopped shamming dead, and spoke in the dry, precise English of Sansom.

"I congratulate you, Ringwood. I admire intelligence, even in an enemy. I will see that you get credit for it in court. Meanwhile—" the voice cracked—"I am ill and very thirsty. I never refused a prisoner wine. Give me some, please."

Richard translated. The Frenchmen replied with curses; they knew when and why Blancbec had given his prisoners wine. Jeannot's teeth began to chatter. Richard pleaded, and at last—

"Well, give him a glass of water!" said Kéhidiou. "You, Painlevé!"

Painlevé began feeding sips of water to the prisoner. But it was a slow, awkward task, and Painlevé wanted to hear the rest of the Englishman's story.

"Listen, pig!" he whispered. "I won't untie your hands. But I'll wedge the glass in between them; you can just reach it if you're careful. And if it spills, too bad! You'll get no more."

Afterwards, Painlevé said that he'd been too soft-hearted. Richard proceeded.

"Now about the murders. Blancbec was of course recognized and blackmailed in Oxford by his old pupil, Despuys, the brother of his former mistress; and Blancbec murdered Despuys in Priory Road, leaving his body in a position that suggested it had been run over. Two and a half hours later, Tim Dawson-Gower actually did run it over. His elder brother, although he has since admitted that he realized Despuys had been dead some time, took the body off and burned it in a haystack. An act of pure anarchy. Nigel, why did you do it? If it hadn't been for my bloodhound …"

Nigel replied, almost abstractedly, "I'm afraid I lost my temper with Tim arguing. You see, I was bored—then. Whereas now … Listen! There *is* a bloodhound. D'you hear? Just arrived at the farm. On a trail, too, it seems."

It *was* a bloodhound; no other sound was like it. At first high notes of excitement and pleasure. Then a solemn, deeper baying betokening a scent found and followed: a thrilling tone, and rarely uttered. So thought Richard, by habit, the scent is good, good and recent; the hound's running fast; lovely throat, it'd almost match Ranter's … But why a bloodhound *here?* Coming this way—baying again—Oh, surely, surely…

He was whistling and shouting.

"Ranter! Here, girl, here! Ranter, my beauty!"

And before he had stopped, a smother of loose, furry silkiness, a weight of bone, a resilience of muscle, was on top of him, and he was mingling his joyful tears with Ranter's slobber. It was home. It was Eden. He hadn't realized how much she'd meant to him. She was in good condition. She was pouring tears and dribble down his neck, and he loved it. He was just in time to prevent an *agent* aiming a pistol and killing them both. And Francis Clandon—but this must be delirium—was standing over him and panting:

"Sorry, sir! She picked up your scent at the farm, and when you called, the lead broke. We flew to Poitiers in my uncle's plane and got a car on to here. Chief Inspector Bludden arranged it, after they'd found the weapon in that hollow tree in Priory Road, with Sansom's prints on it—he's disappeared, sir, did you know? So Chief Inspector Bludden thought—he's fixed it all up about quarantine for Ranter, by the way ... I must say, at least he's efficient, that chap. My goodness! He turned the praefect inside out! Well! Jeannette, my dear! You're looking absolutely ... Hullo, sorry, Nigel. Didn't expect to see *you* here. Where's Tim? Oh, how do you do, Monsieur Defay? Nice to see you again! And Madame? Yes, my uncle had us flown out, and Nigel's firm laid a car on to meet us. Sorry I couldn't let you know instead of barging in, but we *have* had lunch, so ... I say, do tell me what's been happening!"

Most of those present told him; *cet honorable* Clandon somehow encouraged eloquence. A minority gathered in alarm or fascination round the famous bloodhound. Kéhidiou pressed Richard for the rest of his explanation. Richard tried to satisfy him, control Ranter's excitement, and reassure or restrain her admirers. It was Jeannot, raising himself and twisting painfully to look behind him, who brought them all to their senses by crying out that the prisoner had gone.

"It was the glass of water!" cried Kéhidiou, after a quick inspection. "See! He broke it here against the well and used it to saw through the rope. Why was it left near him? Painlevé, you, you animal! Your fault! Magny, Gomard, stay on guard here. The rest—hurry up, imbeciles! Before he reaches the forest, or pinches a car ... if it isn't already too late!"

They began to scatter like quicksilver.

"Wait!" shouted Richard. They stopped. "Francis, is Ranter all right after all? In working form?"

"Right as rain." Francis looked puzzled, then blushed. "Good Lord! Didn't you get my ...?"

But Richard had Ranter over by the stretcher, smelling at the blanket. She found Blancbec's line eagerly, began to run, and then stopped and looked back at her master, quivering with the effort to stand still. He hadn't put her on the lead, as he always did for work, and always against her inclination; now, she was waiting for it. Richard understood, and marveled.

"Go on, Ranter! I'm coming!" He began to run.

She started forward, and passed him, dealing a glancing bump with her shoulder that showed the bruise a week later. Then, nose down, tail high, throat pealing, tan-brown flanks springing and flexing, eating up distance, she was away down the drive. When Richard reached the gateposts, she was out of sight, but by her voice he knew that she had doubled back outside the garden wall, towards the valley and the forest edge. There he presently saw her, black and tawny among the gray tree trunks; she was turning sharply to the right again, and making straight for the river.

So Blancbec thought he could shake her off by taking to the water, did he? He didn't know that bloodhounds can keep the scent even through snow. Well, he would learn.

Richard took a short cut and reached the river in time to see her swimming away round a bend and out of sight. Kéhidiou and his men were catching up along the bank when Ranter's voice pealed, and they knew she had found her quarry. They all ran to see.

Ranter was standing on a sandbank in midstream, a shallow perhaps four inches deep, and Blancbec lay between her front paws with his face in the water and the back of his head sticking out.

"He'll drown if he doesn't turn over!" exclaimed Richard. "Here, Ranter! Here! He's probably afraid to move."

Ranter seemed puzzled what to do. She paused a long time, wrinkling her forehead. Then she decided on her duty. She opened her jaws, took a careful grip on Blancbec's jacket, braced her legs, and—lifted him into the water. Lifted him, and swam across the deep water, and delivered him into her master's hands. Then she lay down, wagging her tail, and Kéhidiou and Richard got to work on Blancbec.

"It's no good," said Kéhidiou after five minutes' artificial respiration. "He's dead. But there isn't a mark on him. He's drowned. Is your dog trained to drown people?"

"Of course she isn't. She probably thought she was saving him. Only when she got him to the sandbank she put him down the wrong way up, with his face in a few inches of water. Five minutes of that probably finished him. My guess is that he fainted, or half-drowned himself, in sheer panic when he was swimming and suddenly saw Ranter in the water beside him—he was very frightened of her from the first. I expect he was unconscious when she tenderly laid him down the wrong way up. I must teach her not to do that again."

"But how on earth did she manage the weight? First she got him on to the sandbank, and then again across to us. And not a scratch on him."

"Bloodhounds *are* remarkable at lifting. Shall I finish telling you the clues?"

"I say, sir!" Francis Clandon came up.

"In ten minutes, Francis. Could you find Ranter a biscuit or something for her reward?" And he walked off with Kéhidiou.

"The extraordinary thing is that Sansom, I mean Fleurat, gave himself away twice during that interview at Oxford. Only I didn't realize it till I'd got to France, and begun poring over my notes. When I told him Despuys was dead, he said, 'Ah! A motor accident?' He shouldn't have had any reason to suppose it was a motor accident. Only, as we found out later, he'd originally staged the murder to look *look* like a motor accident."

"Before the Dawson-Gowers took the body off. Yes, I see."

"Again, he was obviously terrified of Ranter, but he couldn't resist coming right across the park with her—always trying to head her off the right line. Finally, he fainted, you remember. And came round muttering, '*Qu'il me laisse tranquille, cette sale bête!*' That gender—you see?—*Il* was Despuys. Ranter was correctly spoken of as *elle* both before and after he fainted.

"Then again, the time. Sansom (Blancbec) got home at ten. Nigel found the body at midnight, and by his description it had been dead about two hours. That fits: Sansom will have taken Despuys across the parks, using his private key. I expect he took good care to lose it afterwards. From the way my hound behaved, I think that Blancbec knocked Despuys out by the pillar box, dragged him across the road, and finished him off under the trees. That's where they found the blood and the weapon."

"Exactly! But what about the events in Pontchâtelet this week?"

"There again, words were the first clue. Zézette, on the morning I called, made an unconsciously revealing remark. 'Don't tell him you know I'm his sister! He'd kill me!' Well, clearly, that 'he' was not her '*petit Jean.*' *He* wouldn't kill her. Nor could it have been Nigel; he wasn't living in her house and having her buy and cook him food, for we know he was elsewhere; we found his cave. It was Blancbec in the house, Blancbec who searched Jean's papers just before we got at them. Silly, that—in the excitement of proving the forged papers forgeries, we forgot that there might previously have been real ones! Worth a fortune, Despuys had said to his sister. So it was Blancbec who hid in the house, Blancbec who killed the tramp for his clothes, Blancbec who posted his own clothes and passport in a parcel to a Paris post-office, as we'll find …"

They were at the house now, where Kéhidiou's men still stood over Nigel with drawn pistols. Kéhidiou was unwilling to dismiss them.

"How can you be sure Dawson-Gower didn't kill the tramp?"

Richard laughed. "Haven't you noticed? He's much too big to get the tramp's clothes on.

'That heart and eyes, that weight and size,
Won't touch and turn to living air.' "

"What?" said Nigel, "Sshh!" whispered Jeannette. "It's from Tennyson."

Richard sat down at the table. "Tell me, Nigel. What was that letter you sent off from the post office yesterday?"

"Money for Jeannette to buy us food. I'd left my—er, luggage with Jeannot."

"Good. Someone's been teaching you to think. Still, you *did* make it pretty obvious yesterday that you wanted us to arrest you; and when you broke jail, with Jeannette's assistance, I realized why. You planned it all so as to rescue Titi. But where did you get that very effective and portable explosive?"

"Just had it by me. Useful, if you lose your latchkey …" At a look from Jeannette, Nigel abandoned his flippant tone. "When we bust the door, Blancbec would have got away, if Jeannot hadn't been waiting outside and told us who he was. So we knocked him out and brought him here in the rowboat which Jeannette had left ready for us. What's the matter, Francis? Can't you let my chum the copper alone?"

"But Ranter …"

A car came up the drive and disgorged Madame Defay, the children, and a plump, smart woman of forty-five who rushed straight to Nigel and hugged him.

"Radar! Ah, when I rang up London for my naughty Jeannette, my heart told me—that voice! My old Radar!"

"Alex!" Nigel patted her on the back. "Be an angel and untie my legs. It's not the first time."

Meanwhile Monsieur Defay was booming. "My children!" This included his wife and sister. "Imagine! This man, Tim's brother, invents a false criminal, false papers, false motives, to put the police off his own track. Monsieur Ringwood here saw through the trick, naturally—but the truth is the same as the deception! The false criminal is real. IT WAS BLANCBEC ALL THE TIME!"

"Nigel," said Richard softly in English, "you're lucky. You seem to have a trick of doing the wrong thing and getting the right result. But just one more question—How did you come by so much spending money the year after you were demobbed? From Blancbec?"

Nigel replied very audibly, and in French.

"Where did I get my money? Well, I just *do* make money, somehow. Lucky over deals and investments and what not. I made quite a packet even that first year—no hanky-panky, you can check my records. Actually that's why they put me on the executive at—" he named a firm of which everyone present had heard—"but now I've got some capital, I'm thinking of changing over to the wine trade. Always wanted to live in France."

"Hold on!" exclaimed the Defay parents in concert. Then Madame Defay remembered her errand, and said,

"Ah! I forget everything! Monsieur, I have brought you telegrams from Pontchâtelet. And since Madame your wife entertains intimate hopes, evidently you may wish ..."

Richard fumbled at the flap, his fingers trembling.

"TWO OF EACH ALL FIVE DOING WELL."

"Father of quads?" Nigel read over his shoulder. "Not a bad start, copper. So she lives at Wycombe, does she? In—kennels?"

"This is awful!" Francis Clandon was scarlet. "I—I *think* I sent it off the same day. I seem to remember the postmistress looked a bit dopy ... She pupped on the Monday night."

"Ranter did—" Nigel kindly explained. "Francis left the pups at the farm. Thought I heard them. Take the bitch along, Francis. My chum the copper—What is it? Oh Lord, I'm sorry! What's wrong?"

Richard had opened the second telegram, dropped it, and buried his face in his hands. Nigel read the telegram.

"Nothing wrong," he said. "And it's a boy."

THE END

If you enjoyed *Gownsman's Gallows* ask your bookseller for the other two Inspector Ringwood mysteries, *The Missing Link* (0-915230-72-0) and *The Cretan Countefeit* (0-915230-73-9), $14.95 each, also published by The Rue Morgue Press.

About the Rue Morgue Press

"Rue Morgue Press is the old-mystery lover's best friend, reprinting high quality books from the 1930s and '40s."
—*Ellery Queen's Mystery Magazine*

Since 1997, the Rue Morgue Press has reprinted scores of traditional mysteries, the kind of books that were the hallmark of the Golden Age of detective fiction. Authors reprinted or to be reprinted by the Rue Morgue include Dorothy Bowers, Joanna Cannan, Glyn Carr, Torrey Chanslor, Clyde B. Clason, Joan Coggin, Manning Coles, Lucy Cores, Frances Crane, Norbert Davis, Elizabeth Dean, Constance & Gwenyth Little, Marlys Millhiser, James Norman, Stuart Palmer, Craig Rice, Kelley Roos, Charlotte Murray Russell, Maureen Sarsfield, and Juanita Sheridan.

To suggest titles or to receive a catalog of Rue Morgue Press books write P.O. Box 4119, Boulder, CO 80306, telephone 800-699-6214, or see our website, www.ruemorguepress.com, which lists complete descriptions of all of our titles, along with lengthy biographies of our writers.